continued . . .

The Diva Steals
a Chocolate Kiss

KRISTA DAVIS

BERKLEY PRIME CRIME, NEW YORK

BERKLEY
PRIME
CRIME

An imprint of Penguin Random House LLC
375 Hudson Street, New York, New York 10014

THE DIVA STEALS A CHOCOLATE KISS

A Berkley Prime Crime Book / published by arrangement with the author

BERKLEY® PRIME CRIME and the PRIME CRIME design are trademarks
of Penguin Random House LLC.
For more information, visit penguin.com.

· ISBN: 978-0-425-25815-6

PUBLISHING HISTORY
Berkley Prime Crime mass-market edition / June 2015

PRINTED IN THE UNITED STATES OF AMERICA

10 9 8 7 6 5 4 3 2

Cover illustration by Teresa Fasolino.
Cover design by Diana Kolsky.
Interior text design by Laura K. Corless.

Penguin
Random
House

To Elizabeth Nina Strickland

ACKNOWLEDGMENTS

As always, there are many people to thank for their assistance in writing this book. Cheryl Maiorca and Lori Speer were most generous and such great sports about having their names used for characters. Naturally, the characters, their behavior, and their relationships to others in the story are pure fiction. The characters do not reflect in any way on their true personalities, but I can say that they were both lovely to work with and very daring to allow me to make them suspects—and perhaps the killer!

My good friends, Susan Smith Erba and Betsy Strickland, were kind enough to suffer through a weekend of nonstop taste testing for this book. I have a feeling neither of them wants to see chocolate anytime soon. Thanks also to Janet Bolin, Daryl Wood Gerber, Peg Cochran, Kaye George, Marilyn Levinson, and Laurie Cass, for their suggestions and for always being at the water cooler when I need to talk. I cannot omit my thanks to my mother, Marianne, and my dear friend Amy Wheeler for being so supportive and encouraging.

Huge thanks are due my editor, Sandra Harding, who has the remarkable ability to make every book better. And I would be lost without my agent, Jessica Faust, who makes me laugh (often at myself) and keeps me straight about this crazy business.

Accents and English learned on the fly vary considerably and can be tricky. Some readers may feel I have erred with Nonni's English. I hope you'll indulge me because this darling little character showed up in my head and this is how I heard her speak.

Most of all, I thank my readers. I hope you'll enjoy this book and have fun visiting with Sophie and her friends again. May you always have plenty of chocolate.

Sophie's Friends and Old Town Residents

Nina Reid Norwood–Sophie's best friend.

Natasha Earlene Smith–Desperate domestic diva.

Mars Winston–Sophie's ex-husband.

Bernie Frei–Best man at Sophie's wedding.

Humphrey Brown–Sophie's childhood friend.

Alex German–Sophie's new beau.

Francie Vanderhoosen–Sophie's next-door neighbor.

Wolf Fleishman–Homicide investigator whom Sophie once dated.

Arnaud Turnèbe–Chocolatier, new to town.

The Amore Chocolates Family and Employees

Joe Merano–CEO of Amore Chocolates.

Nonni Merano–Joe's mom. Co-founder of Amore.

Coco Ross–Joe's daughter. Vice President of Marketing at Amore.

Mitch Ross–Coco's husband. Vice president at Amore.

Dan Merano–Joe's son. Head chocolatier at Amore.

Stella Simpson–Dan's girlfriend. Manages an Amore store.

Vince Wilson–Amore employee.
Randy Hicks–Amore employee.
Marla Eldridge–Joe's assistant.

Recipe Winners

Cheryl Maiorca–Queen of the chocolate
cake.
Lori Speer–Queen of the chocolate truffle.

CHAPTER ONE

Dear Sophie,

My mother-in-law gave me a box of chocolates that she made herself. They've turned gray! I think she's trying to poison me. My husband insists they're fine but I don't believe him. What if they're in cahoots? Is it normal for chocolate to turn gray?

—Suspicious in Graysville, Tennessee

Dear Suspicious,

It's so common that it has a name. The powdery gray on your chocolates is called a bloom. It's caused by moisture and often happens when chocolates are stored in the refrigerator. Chocolates with a bloom are perfectly fine to eat but not very attractive.

—Sophie

The first box of chocolates arrived on a Monday. I assumed they were a gift from Joe Merano, the chairman of Amore Chocolates, because I was working on events for the sixtieth anniversary of his company. But the bold red box wasn't embossed with the Amore logo of entwined gold hearts. Nor was there a card. It had simply been left at my front door.

A second box arrived on Tuesday and another on Wednesday.

On Thursday morning, Nina Reid Norwood, my across-the-street neighbor and best friend, discovered another box at my front door. She now stared at the four open boxes on my kitchen table. "They're like perfect little brown gems. Handmade, don't you think?"

"Definitely." In each box, six chocolates nestled on crimped white papers. No two chocolates were alike.

Nina's fingers hovered, rotating in the air above them. "You haven't eaten any."

"Get your greedy little hand away. I don't know who or where they came from."

"But they're so beautiful. You have to try one! They're probably filled with something rich and creamy."

"You are *not* eating any until we know who left them at my door."

Nina signed with exasperation. "I'm sure they're from Alex."

I had been dating Alex German for a while. When he was in town, anyway. "I phoned Alex to thank him. He didn't know a thing about them."

"Mars, then."

I shook my head. They weren't from my ex-husband, either.

A grin spread across Nina's face. "You have an admirer!"

"Don't be silly." The notion *had* crossed my mind, though. Chocolates hinted at romance, didn't they? But if nothing else, I was a realist. "More likely they're some kind of promotional effort in connection with the opening of

Célébration de Chocolat." Arnaud Turnèbe, the famous Belgian chocolatier, had chosen Old Town as the location for his first American shop. Until now, his exquisite chocolates had been available only by special order, flown in fresh from Belgium at considerable cost. I was looking forward to actually trying one of them.

Nina frowned and picked up a lid to examine it. "What kind of promotion doesn't mention the name of the business?"

The doorknocker sounded. I headed to the foyer and opened the front door.

Coco Ross rushed inside, breathless. "I hope you don't mind my stopping by." A well-known socialite, Coco had been my contact at the company for the anniversary events. I guessed her to be about fifty but she had the energy of a much younger woman. Coco laughed easily, and her expressive, dark brown eyes didn't hide her emotions. "This is Nonni."

A tiny woman dressed all in blue followed Coco at a slower pace, aided by a cane. Her white hair was pinned up in a tidy bun. Not a speck of makeup touched her face. She couldn't have weighed more than ninety pounds.

I shook Nonni's frail hand. "It's a pleasure to meet you, Nonni. Won't you come in and have a seat?"

They followed me into my kitchen, where Coco greeted Nina and introduced Nonni.

"I am going to strangle Natasha," announced Coco.

Leaning against the center island, Nina said, "Get in line."

"No, seriously. I'm beginning to worry about myself." Coco flapped the neckline of her pink and green Lilly Pulitzer dress as though she thought the air would cool her. "Really. I lie in bed at night, thinking of ways to knock her off."

"Could I offer you iced tea or lemonade?" I asked.

Coco responded, "Iced tea, please. It's hotter than blazes

outside." She lifted the back of her neatly bobbed hair off her neck and fanned herself.

Nonni sat down in an armchair by the fireplace.

"Natasha entered ten recipes in our contest. We rejected them all. Correction. *I* rejected them all." Coco pressed the heel of her hand against her forehead briefly. "I didn't *know* they were from her. They were atrocious. Who wants to eat a chocolate dill cream roll? Now she's offended and seeking revenge by bad-mouthing Amore."

I filled tall glasses with ice cubes and poured the iced tea.

Happily, I spotted a leftover strawberry tart hiding behind the red peppers. Chocolate coated the bottom, and I had drizzled more chocolate on top of the strawberries, as well. The chocolate ought to please Coco and Nonni.

I placed slices on four square white plates and added a generous dollop of whipped cream to each.

Nonni sat in a chair by the fireplace watching me. My Ocicat, Mochie, nestled on her lap. I delivered a drink and slice of the tart to the table for her.

Nonni smiled at me. "I like you kitchen."

She spoke with a thick Italian accent and pronounced *kitchen* as *keetchen*.

"Thank you."

She waggled a gnarled forefinger at me. "I know everything about you when I see you keetchen. Is clean, is warm. You like you keetchen, too."

I couldn't help smiling. Judging a person by her kitchen was a new one to me. "Yes, I do like it."

"Sofia is good Italian name. You are Italian?"

I hedged. We definitely weren't Italian. "My family came from Europe."

That seemed to satisfy her. "We have problem in family. You will help us." With the aid of her walking stick, she rose to her feet and tottered to my kitchen table, where she took a seat.

I brought drinks and slices of the tart for the rest of us

and set them on the cool fern green tablecloth, along with forks and rose-colored napkins.

"All is settled," said Nonni. "Sofia will help us."

"At the risk of upsetting everyone, I haven't agreed to anything."

"Yes, yes," insisted Nonni. "You help. Now I eat."

Coco licked her lips nervously. She appeared too agitated to sit down. Coco and her brother, Dan, were the heirs to Amore Chocolates. The sixtieth anniversary events weren't the biggest projects I had ever put together, but they had certainly been different. Amore Chocolates was best known for delicious boxed chocolates, but they also made fabulous, yet lesser-known, cooking chocolate, both powdered and in squares. They had sponsored a contest for home cooks and were bringing the creators of the winning recipes to Old Town for a huge tasting in the gorgeous garden of Joe's home. The recipes had been included in a new Amore Chocolates cookbook.

Coco handled marketing for Amore. Gregarious and outgoing, she was the perfect person to represent the company. In fact, she had told me she would be taking over most of the outings planned for the winners. I suspected she wanted to be along to schmooze when they were on TV and participated in various contests and demonstrations around metropolitan Washington, DC. It was fine with me. I arranged the tasting, the farewell dinner, lodging, and transportation. The rest was up to her.

Coco chugged her iced tea and refilled her glass. "I don't understand Natasha. She's so lovely and perfect on her TV show that I thought she was a smart businesswoman." She gazed at the tart for a moment. "I had no idea that she's an egocentric, bullheaded—"

"—nincompoop." Nonni ended the sentence for her.

Nina slid into the banquette and listened while she sampled the tart.

I placed the pitcher of iced tea on the table, and Coco finally settled into a chair.

I joined them.

Lowering her voice, Coco continued, "There's really not much that doesn't work with chocolate. Nuts, spices, fruit, even chicken. But who wants to eat brownies made with bleu cheese? Now she's offended and seeking revenge. She's making it sound like we're snobs because the Amore tasting is by ticket only."

"I thought that was because your dad's garden will only hold so many people," said Nina.

"Well, *of course* that's the reason. We're not turning away the public. We've been giving away tickets in contests, through radio stations, at our stores—just everywhere! It was that or sell them but we didn't want to charge for our tasting celebration." Coco placed her forearms on the table, leaned on them, and looked at me. "What now? She's making us look terrible! It's a public relations nightmare."

I had known Natasha since childhood. We grew up in the same small town and competed at everything in school. Everything except the beauty pageants she had enjoyed so much. Sometimes I was reluctant to admit it, but Natasha was a part of my life, especially since she had set up housekeeping with my ex-husband after our divorce. As though that wasn't bad enough, they moved into a house on my street, just a few doors down. In the divorce, neither my ex, Mars, short for Marshall, nor I had the heart to give up Daisy, our mixed-breed hound, so we split custody, and she went back and forth between us. I had to admit that living close to Mars had made that easier for us. Because the Amore events would keep me very busy, she was spending the week with Mars.

I looked into Coco's eyes. "I'll have a word with Natasha but I'm afraid the damage might already have been done."

Coco rolled her sweating iced tea glass across her forehead. "How can it be this hot? We have to find a new venue, make more food"—she spoke with her hands in true Italian fashion, raising them over her head and swinging them down in a huge circle—"and invite the general public, no tickets necessary."

The words "find a new venue" chilled me more than any iced tea could have. I spoke gently, calmly, trying not to give away my panic. "But the tasting is this Saturday." To make my point abundantly clear, I added, "Less than three days away."

"Everyone says you can work magic. Surely you can find another venue."

"For the last Saturday in June?" Was she kidding? "Brides booked Saturdays in Old Town over a year ago. And I should point out that tastings always require tickets. You have to know how many people you're going to serve."

"Could you move it out of Old Town?" asked Nina.

Coco gasped as though Nina had said something unimaginable. "That's not an option. What about the Torpedo Factory?"

She was delusional if she thought one of the best venues in town wasn't booked. Once a real torpedo factory, the fabulous building now housed art galleries and artists' studios. The atrium, main hall, and patio could be rented for private functions, but there wasn't a chance they would be available. "I can make some calls." I said it more to soothe her than anything else. I knew I wouldn't find a venue in Old Town. We had hired a caterer to make the winning recipes for the party, but he would probably go ballistic if he had to produce ten times the quantity on such short notice. As gently as I could, I added, "But don't hold your breath. You realize we're talking about moving from four hundred people to . . . gosh, I don't know how many. Four thousand?"

Coco leaned back in her chair. "See what you can do."

I was shaking my head and thinking it might be easier to bring Natasha on board in some way when Coco cried out. "Nonni! I'm so sorry, Sophie, she's used to tasting chocolates from the store."

Nonni held one of the mystery chocolates in her hand. Half of it was missing. "*Bellissimo!*"

I jumped to my feet, "Oh, honey, don't eat the rest of that. I'm sorry, I don't mean to be rude, but I don't know where they came from."

Nonni paid no attention whatsoever and ate the other half. "Belgian or Swiss? Is familiar."

Coco stood up to take them from Nonni. But when she saw them, her eyes widened. She selected one without care, bit in, and savored it. "Oh no," she moaned. But she consumed the rest of it anyway. And then she keeled over and hit the floor with a thud.

CHAPTER TWO

Dear Sophie,

My neighbor asked me if I was going to temper my chocolate. I looked it up but it sounds incredibly complicated. Will my cake be ruined if I don't temper the chocolate first?

—Mr. Mom in Temperance, Georgia

Dear Mr. Mom,

You don't need to temper chocolate when you bake with it. Tempering is generally only necessary for chocolates used to make candies. The tempering process allows them to be boxed and displayed at room temperature.

—Sophie

"Coco!" I thrust her chair aside and knelt by her. "Nina, call 911!"

I tapped Coco's tanned cheeks, which were rapidly losing their color. "Coco! Coco!" She was still breathing.

Nonni calmly poured the remainder of her iced tea over Coco's face. Ice cubes skittered across the floor. For a second I worried that Coco might inhale the liquid and choke.

Coco opened her eyes and blinked. She focused on my face.

"Coco, how do you feel?" I asked gently.

She moaned and blinked repeatedly as though she wasn't quite right yet.

Outside, the siren of an ambulance drew closer.

I dabbed her wet face to dry it off. Coco tried to lift her head but the effort appeared to wear her out.

Nina opened the front door for the rescue squad.

I backed away from Coco to make room for them. Nonni seized my hand, and I gently squeezed hers in silent solidarity. One of the emergency medical technicians asked us what had happened.

Nina handed her all four of the boxes of chocolates while I explained that they had been found on my doorstep.

"Nonni!" I turned to her. "Nonni ate the chocolate, too. How are you feeling?"

Nonni patted my arm with a delicate hand. "I am quite fine."

"I am, too," Coco muttered. "I don't need an ambulance. I just had a light-headed moment and felt dizzy."

"Coco! You pregnant?" asked Nonni.

Coco snorted. "More likely having a hot flash."

The EMTs encouraged her to go to the emergency room to be checked out. They got their way when Coco tried to sit up and passed out again.

"You'd better take Nonni, too," I suggested. "I'd hate to have her collapse the moment you pulled away."

Nina and I followed them outside. We watched the EMTs load Coco and Nonni into the ambulance. Nonni smiled and waved at us before they closed the door.

When the ambulance started down the street, Nina turned to me. "Have you aggravated anyone lately?"

"What? No! Why would you ask a thing like that?"

The corners of her mouth twitched down. "Those chocolates were obviously meant for you."

"But . . . that's . . . ridiculous," I sputtered.

"No events that went badly? No irate neighbors? No jealous wives? Have you been poking your nose into a murder again?"

"No!" I had been busy with work these last few months, but nothing had ended in a disaster. And I certainly wasn't having a fling with a married man!

Nina nodded. "If I were you, I wouldn't eat anything I didn't cook myself."

"You're making a big deal out of nothing."

"Of all people, you should know better than that, Sophie. And it started out as such a nice day," said Nina. "Thank goodness you wouldn't let me eat a chocolate! I'm going home. I think I have some chocolate bars stashed in the fridge."

"You know you shouldn't keep them there, right?"

But Nina was already halfway to her house, evidently in dire need of a chocolate fix.

Back in my kitchen, I phoned Joe Merano at Amore Chocolates and explained what had happened. He was surprisingly kind given the circumstances, but we kept our conversation brief so he and Coco's husband could rush to the hospital.

Guilt hammered at me while I mopped up the melting ice cubes on the floor. I should have tucked those chocolates away where no one could eat them. It was my fault that Coco and Nonni were in the emergency room. I had to go there. It was the least I could do.

I dashed upstairs to change clothes and was just slipping a dress off the hanger when the phone rang. Joe's assistant, Marla, asked me to come to his office that afternoon at two. She didn't have any updates on the condition of Nonni or Coco.

I hung up thinking, *Uh-oh. A command performance.* I checked the time. One and a half hours. I'd better have some solutions for the Natasha situation at the meeting. As much as I wanted to go to the hospital, I knew they were relying on me to take care of other matters.

I nixed the hospital, pulled my skort and sleeveless top back on, and hurried to my tiny home office to make some phone calls to see if there was any possibility of moving the event. The Torpedo Factory was booked. No surprise there. I worked the phone for the next hour without any luck.

In the middle of my quest, Alex called. "Have you received any more chocolates?"

"Every day this week."

"Should I be worried?"

"Because they're poisoned?"

"You're joking, right?"

I filled him in on what had happened to Coco.

"What did you do to make someone mad at you?"

"Why do people keep asking me that? I didn't do anything."

There was silence on the other end of the phone. "Alex? You still there?"

"When I called, I was upset because some anonymous admirer was sending you chocolates, but now I'm worried that someone is out to get you."

I listened to his lecture about being careful for a full minute before cutting him off. I had work to do and not much time.

I had exactly one idea that might solve the Natasha problem. If Amore nixed that, I had nothing else.

Amore's recipe winners would be arriving at the hotel anytime now. Anticipating a long day, I dressed in a slenderizing navy blue sheath, a simple pearl necklace, and matching earrings that would be appropriate for the meeting and take me through dinner. I shot a glance at the cute thong sandals that were so comfortable, but slid my feet into open-toed navy sling backs with white bows on the rear straps.

I filled Mochie's bowl with his favorite tuna and explained

that I would be out late. He took it like a cat, opening one eye and purring his acceptance of the situation. I left a light on in the kitchen and made sure the lights by the front door were on, too, since it would be dark when I came home. Carrying my briefcase, I walked five blocks toward the river and strode into the amazingly elegant offices of Amore Chocolates.

A chubby guy with round wire-rimmed glasses was just leaving. He ate a chocolate and was so intent on another one in his hand that he nearly ran into me.

The receptionist called out, "Randy! You forgot your package."

Randy stuffed the second chocolate in his mouth and ran back to her desk to collect a box.

The receptionist nodded at me. "They're waiting for you upstairs in the boardroom."

As I walked up the stairs, I wondered why I felt like I was heading into doom. I hadn't poisoned Coco or Nonni. I hadn't wanted them to eat the chocolates at all! But they *had* been on the table, and I felt guilty for leaving them out. Natasha's shenanigans weren't my fault, either. Still, a heavy weight pressed on me as though I had done something wrong and now had to face the people I had disappointed.

I could see them through the glass doors that led to the boardroom. Joe Merano, the patriarch and chairman, and Mitch Ross, vice president of Amore and husband of Coco, awaited me. I opened the door and walked in.

They shook my hand in a very cordial businesslike manner. I asked about Coco and Nonni immediately.

"Coco's official diagnosis is heat exhaustion," said Joe. "She's resting at my house now. And my mom is perfectly fine."

"No poisoning?"

"Nothing was detected. According to the doctor, there is no general test for known poisons. They're analyzing the chocolates and if they find something there, then they'll check Coco and Nonni for it. Coco is recovering well, so the doctors don't think she was poisoned."

"That's a relief!" I didn't want to belabor the subject but I breathed a little bit easier.

Mitch smiled at me graciously. He slid his palms against each other in a slow methodical motion. "The reason we called you here is this business with Natasha."

Joe rose and walked to the window, his back to us.

"While it may seem somewhat minor and inconsequential to you," said Mitch, "Amore Chocolates takes great pride in our exemplary community relations. To have a recognized local celebrity putting us down and claiming that we are in some way elitist is a major blow, especially at this time of our sixtieth anniversary."

I nodded but I was watching Joe. He wore a well-tailored dark gray business suit with a red tie. The horseshoe of hair remaining from male-pattern baldness showed considerable silver. He wore none of the trappings of wealth. Had I seen him on the street, he would have meshed with the throngs of other gray-suited businessmen.

The boardroom of Amore Chocolates revealed the success of the company in a way that its plain CEO did not. On the second floor of a huge three-story house, it featured a marble fireplace and dark hardwood floors that looked to be original or at least reclaimed wood. French doors flanked by additional windows of the same size led to a balcony. Plush red and gold oriental rugs defined the areas of the room with the biggest one in the center, where I sat at a large round table. The shape of the table told me a lot about Joe's management style. He brought everyone in as equals. No one sat in the head chair looking down a row of peons here. I recognized a young Nonni in the oil portrait over the fireplace. She and her husband had founded the company.

"We really can't tolerate this kind of slander," said Mitch. "With Célébration de Chocolat opening, we're going to feel the pinch while our local customers sample their goods. We cannot afford to lose customers because some woman paints us with a dirty brush. Especially a lie! I've been in touch with a leading crisis management company. They've seen this kind of thing before, and said it can spiral out of control." Mitch smoothed back graying hair, and I realized that he was speaking to Joe, not to me.

He and Coco made a striking couple. A large man with broad shoulders and an ample physique, he sported a tan that rivaled Coco's. He was still attractive by anyone's standards, and I could imagine that his amiable face had been adorably boyish in his youth.

In the hallway outside the glass, Randy, the handyman, peered in.

Mitch glanced up at him. Raising his voice, he called, "Need something, Randy?"

Randy pushed open the door. "Sorry to interrupt. I'll catch you later."

Mitch consulted his notes. "They recommend a three-pronged approach. First, a Twitter campaign. We find unfortunate misstatements that Natasha has made on her show, and we send them into the Twittersphere to discredit her. Apparently, that's a very powerful tool, and if we do it right, it won't reflect on us. Second, the night of our tasting, we make and serve some of her terrible recipes to the press, making clear that they are hers. That's supposed to be a passive way to handle it. You know, it looks like we're honoring her, but the tasters get to come to their own conclusions, which makes her look bad and discredits her as an authority. Third, we hire a private detective to dig up dirt on this woman . . ."

CHAPTER THREE

Dear Natasha,

My son-in-law gave me chocolate nibs as a present. They're funny little things and very bitter. What are they, and what am I supposed to do with them?

—Sweet Tooth Irishwoman in Sweets Corner, Massachusetts

Dear Sweet Tooth,

The nib is the center of the cocoa bean, the part from which chocolate is made. It's chocolate in its purest form, before sugar is added, which is why it tastes bitter. Some people consider it health food because it's pure dark chocolate and full of antioxidants. You might find them more palatable if you mix them with some dried cherries or apricots like a trail mix to sweeten them up.

—Natasha

I was appalled. Natasha might not be my favorite person, but she wasn't *all* bad, and I would never agree to destroying her or anyone else for that matter. I could feel my face heating up. Even the tops of my ears burned.

"No." Joe swung around to face us. "We are not in the business of ruining people. Amore Chocolates does not lash out and stoop to the lowest, basest behavior. Sophie, did you have any luck finding another venue?"

"I'm afraid not. But I did come up with one idea." I was afraid to pitch it to them. It wasn't nearly as aggressive as the ideas of the experts.

"Let's hear it, then," said Joe.

Mitch watched me with eager eyes and leaned forward.

"We invite Natasha to the tasting as a special guest. We give her some kind of made-up title like 'Local Chocolate Expert' and act as though she's someone special in the community. She'll have to change her own tune if she's part of the celebration."

"What if she doesn't go along with it?" asked Mitch.

Natasha could never turn down an honor. If they pretended she was an expert, she would think she *was* an expert. "I can't make promises, but I would bet that she'll jump at any opportunity to be an honored guest. Maybe make some kind of plaque to give her?"

Joe smiled. "A simple and elegant solution, my dear. The best kind. Mitch, get on that within the hour. The sooner Natasha feels included, the sooner she'll stop this badmouthing nonsense. Maybe call her Amore's finest taster. Give her roses, champagne, and of course, Amore chocolates. Dan can create a small chocolate sculpture of some kind to give to her."

Joe shook my hand and strode out of the room, thus ending the meeting and leaving me with Mitch.

He smiled at me. "I'm kind of relieved. Those other recommendations sounded below the belt to me." He shrugged. "Besides, I've never even heard of this Natasha woman before. How big a star can she be? It's not like she's Martha Stewart or anything. I'll see you at the dinner tonight, Sophie."

He waved and returned to his own office, while I took the stairs. I released a sigh of relief, shifted gears, and headed for the hotel where Amore was putting up the people who had submitted winning recipes. They would be checking in soon.

The hotel was on the small side but very gracious and personal with exquisite service. Colonial from top to bottom, it featured elegant rooms and a piano for singing along in the foyer. A favorite for weddings because of the romantic atmosphere, I knew it would be booked solid, and I didn't want any problems.

Happily, the hotel was on top of things. They had the registration packets with maps and schedules that I had prepared according to Coco's instructions. The welcome baskets, chock-full of Amore chocolates and copies of the new cookbook, were already in the guest rooms, and the private dining room was being set up for their welcome dinner.

The hotel had arranged a wine and appetizer bar at my request so the winners could mingle after checking in, and it wasn't long before the first of the sixty winners began arriving. Some were excited, some exhausted. They had come from all over the United States, by car, plane, and train. They fit every imaginable description, male and female, young and old. As they mingled with glasses of wine, talk soon turned to the one thing they all shared—a love of chocolate.

※

At ten o'clock that night, the recipe winners had been wined and dined by the Amore family—Joe, Nonni, Coco, Mitch, and Dan. Nonni looked like her usual self in a summery lavender dress, but Coco appeared tired and drawn. Not that it dampened her enthusiasm for a moment. She flitted between the guests like a social butterfly, clearly in her element. Mitch glad-handed their guests, slapping men on the back and air-kissing women. It was Dan who seemed the least comfortable in the social milieu, often standing by himself, nursing a glass of wine.

By eleven, the Amore family had gone home and most of their guests had retired for the night. A handful remained in the lobby, singing show tunes.

A portly gentleman, wearing a suit with his tie untied and hanging loosely on his shirt, approached me. He was about fifty, I guessed, with shoulders that rolled forward a bit. His thin, dark hair had become disheveled. "*Ma chérie*," he murmured, picking up my hand and kissing it. "No wedding ring?"

The accent was French. I didn't recall that he was one of the winners but I probably hadn't met all of them. Not daring to be rude, I withdrew my hand and asked, "Are you enjoying yourself?"

"Now I am. How can such a beautiful woman be without a husband?"

I recoiled from the gin on his breath. His blue eyes stood out in a round face the color and, oddly enough, the shape of a ripe red tomato. He teetered uncertainly and regained his balance.

"Do you like *chocolat*?" he asked, pronouncing the word as the French do. A narrow strand of hair fell into his fleshy face. "I'm sick of *chocolat*. I would"—he tucked his chin in and struggled to continue speaking—"be happiest if I never saw another *chocolat* in my life."

I strained to maintain a smile. Hoping he would take the hint, I said, "Well, it's been a lovely evening. It looks like most people are going to bed."

He swayed sideways. I reached out to steady him.

"Will you come with me?" he asked.

Ugh! Ugh, ugh, ugh. Shivers crawled up my arms. I tried not to squirm in disgust. What a slimy creep. It wasn't the first time I had encountered a lecherous drunk, though. It came with the territory of being an event planner. I used my standard line. "Not tonight. My boyfriend is waiting for me."

Those who weren't too intoxicated to think straight usually laughed or apologized and left me alone. Those who were so loaded they wouldn't remember anything in the morning often suggested I ditch the boyfriend.

"Get rid of him. Room 210." He pushed a room card at me.

I winked at him and lied in an exaggerated whisper. "You go ahead so my boyfriend won't see us leaving together."

He nodded with his entire upper body, nearly falling over. His hand twisting, he lifted a finger to his lips in a sign that he wouldn't say a word, and he weaved toward the elevators.

I strode over to the handful of winners who were relaxing in the cushy sofas, chatting. "If no one needs anything, then I'll say good night and see you in the morning."

"Good night," they chorused, and I took my leave.

I stepped out of the hotel into a warm summer night—the kind of night meant for sitting on porches or at outdoor cafes. The sidewalks of Old Town still teemed with people. Lights glowed inside the historic houses and on front stoops. I strolled along the brick sidewalks, enjoying the casual summertime ambiance.

The moon garden at the Honeysuckle Bed-and-Breakfast across the street caught my eye. I slowed to take it in. White roses climbed up trellises that marked the garden entrance to the B and B. At their feet, Shasta daisies and snow-in-summer seemed to glow in the light of the moon. It was a charming and clever idea to plant white flowers there. They were very welcoming for guests coming back to the B and B in the dark.

At that moment, Coco Ross hurried along the sidewalk and took a sharp right into the B and B property. I had seen her just over an hour ago. She had changed into pedal pushers and a top in the interim.

It was none of my business what she was doing there, but that didn't stop me from dashing across the street for a better view. I arrived just in time to see Coco step inside the house.

That was odd. After the day she'd had, I would have expected her to go home to bed. Maybe she was a night owl and the owner was a friend.

I went on my way, too dog-tired to contemplate Coco's behavior.

A large basket awaited me at the front door. Wrapped in cellophane and tied with a red bow, it was huge. I unlocked the door and carried it inside.

As though he had a mysterious cat radar and knew I was on my way home, Mochie waited for me in the foyer. He wound around my ankles until I picked him up. "Did you miss me or is your food bowl empty?" He purred a response, which I took to mean he was lonely—until I walked into the kitchen with him on my shoulder and realized that his cute little bowl was indeed empty.

He waited patiently next to it while I opened a can of minced turkey and spooned it into the bowl. He sniffed the food first, as though he wasn't sure I had correctly interpreted his menu request. But it must have passed muster, because he settled in to eat.

I carried the giant basket into the kitchen and opened the wrapping. Inside, five boxes of Amore chocolates in graduating sizes formed a pyramid. The enclosed card read *For my sweet, safe to eat, love from Pete (because Alex doesn't rhyme with anything)*.

It made me laugh. I checked the clock. Too late to call to thank him.

I made sure the doors were locked, poured myself a glass of sparkling water, and headed upstairs to bed. The next few days would be hectic. After changing clothes, I opened the curtains and the windows in the bedroom to let the gentle night air waft into the house. I crawled under a light blanket, and the last thing I saw before closing my eyes was Mochie's silhouette in the window.

⋙⋘

Before I started working in the morning, I phoned Alex to thank him for his lovely gift. I had no time to get together with him, but he promised to come to the chocolate tasting.

Between wrangling the winners and preparing for the tasting, Friday flew by. I'd had the good sense to hire a tour company to take the winners on a daylong tour of the Smithsonian, the White House, the Capitol, and the monuments.

The bad news was that another box of chocolates showed up at my front door. I hid it in a desk drawer, safely away from anyone who might be tempted to taste one.

On Saturday morning, I was mixing batter for blueberry muffins when Nina burst into my kitchen, still wearing a lavender bathrobe, which added a little bulk to her figure. I had never understood how she could eat constantly but not find her clothes were too tight like I did. I had an ongoing battle with my weight.

Nina's hair usually varied between a short cut and shoulder length. At the moment, it was short for summer. She needed only to run her fingers through her thick hair, and it fell into place.

"Are you watching Natasha's show?" She turned the small TV in the kitchen to *Natasha Live!* on a local channel.

We watched as Natasha received two dozen red roses on air from Amore Chocolates and bragged about being their special guest of honor because of her refined taste and superior palate.

Nina and I high-fived in my kitchen, and she switched it off.

"You've been so busy. I feel like I've hardly seen you for the past couple of days," Nina complained.

"I'm making blueberry muffins and ham and cheese omelets for breakfast. Want some?"

She nodded and poured coffee for both of us.

"The busiest part will be over tonight. The winners have a free day tomorrow. I'm on call in case they run into problems, but I don't anticipate any. How about brunch in my garden tomorrow morning? I can whip up a quiche."

"Sounds wonderful. I know it's a lot of work for you, but I'm looking forward to the tasting tonight. Word around town is that there will be five different chocolate cakes."

"For once the gossip is correct. You wouldn't believe how many variations there can be on something as basic as chocolate cake." For just a second, I thought Nina might start drooling.

The timer on my oven dinged. I pulled out the muffins.

"Gosh, but those smell good. They should bottle scents like that," exclaimed Nina.

I poured her a cup of coffee and set the muffins on the table.

My kitchen door opened again and Daisy ran to me, wagging her tail as though she had missed seeing me. I hugged my sweet dog and gushed over her.

"You know we're in the room, too," said Mars.

"Good morning, Mars. Good morning, Bernie," I said with mock formality. "Could I interest you in omelets?"

Mars slid onto the banquette next to Nina and picked up a muffin. "These are still warm!" A political advisor, Mars had the good fortune to possess wholesome looks that encouraged people to confide in him. He still had a full head of dark chocolate hair, though a glimmer of gray had moved in just around his ears. I had fallen in love with him because of his humor, which showed in his eyes and the little crinkles on their outer edges.

Bernie, who had been the best man at our wedding and always sounded clever with his British accent, said, "If it's not too much trouble." Bernie and Mars couldn't have been more opposite in appearance. Bernie's sandy hair was always unruly, as though he had just rolled out of bed. His nose had been broken at least once and sported a very slight kink. He shared Mars's sense of humor, though, and had astonished all of us by running the most popular restaurant in Old Town.

I cracked more eggs into a bowl and chopped additional peppered ham while Bernie poured coffee for everyone, and Nina set the table with summery Marlborough Sprays dishes and pink napkins.

We sat down to eat, and I relaxed with my friends, knowing full well that once I dressed and left for Joe's house, I would be putting out fires until night fell.

"You know Natasha has been a real pill about Amore's tasting," said Nina, selecting a muffin. "Why did she have to bad-mouth them? Doesn't she understand that it makes her look bad?"

Mars sucked in air. "When isn't she a pill?"

Bernie's fork fell out of his hand and clattered to his plate. Nina choked on a muffin.

I stared at Mars in shock. He always defended Natasha! "What's going on?" I asked.

Mars studied his plate. "Life shouldn't have to be so hard. Everything is going well. I should be the happiest guy on the planet. But with Nat there's always a drama, always a crisis, always a new plan to break out of the local market and finally become a nationally recognized name in every household."

"Like Martha Stewart?" asked Nina.

"Just like that. I'm tired of it."

"Did something happen?" Bernie ate a bite of his muffin but kept his eyes on Mars.

"She wants to become a chocolatier. She even ordered chocolate beans, a roaster, and some kind of special grinder."

Nina guffawed. "Natasha and The Chocolate Factory?"

I had no idea what to say, and from the startled look on his face, neither did Bernie.

Nina, however, reached over and slapped Mars on the

back. "Well, maybe it's time you left her to her craziness. I can't imagine what you were thinking to stay with her this long. Let me know if you need help packing." And then she smiled at me. "Sophie has an extra room."

Bernie quickly shifted the conversation back to the chocolate tasting, but the spectre of a major change hung over us. Poor Mars.

While my friends cleaned up the kitchen, Daisy and Mochie bounded up the stairs with me. Experience had taught me to wear clothes that would allow me to handle any catastrophes that came along. I could come home midafternoon to change into clothes more suited to the tasting. I pulled on cotton crop pants in periwinkle blue that, thanks to my short legs, actually came to my ankles. A sleeveless white top looked cool and tidy. A pair of simple silver hoops were all the jewelry I needed. I slid my feet into ultra-comfy white thong sandals with glittering sparkles on top.

When I returned to the kitchen, my three friends had loaded the dishwasher and tidied up. After leaving a bowl of salmon for Mochie to nosh on during my absence, we left the house and went our separate ways.

Coco answered the door at Joe's mansion and showed me to the guesthouse where the goodie bags had been stashed. Before I started on them, I checked out the path that our guests would use when they arrived. Instead of knocking on the front door, they would step to the side and come through the garden gate. I pounded a sign into the dirt near the front door. It read *Chocolate Tasting,* with an arrow pointing to the right. The garden gate would be open.

The first thing they would see was a group of tall, flowering bushes in front of a huge old tree. The perfect backdrop for the centerpiece table.

That settled, I made quick work of loading each gift bag with a copy of the Amore recipe book. Just as I finished, an older man with a long gray ponytail and a full white beard

arrived with four hundred boxes of Amore chocolates. He
wore an Amore baseball cap and an Amore sixtieth anniversary T-shirt and introduced himself as Vince Wilson. He
spoke with a very slight speech impediment, as though his
dentures didn't fit quite right.

I thanked him.

"There's more," he promised.

I had only stuffed a few of the bags with chocolates when
he returned with packages of baking chocolate, hot chocolate mix, and cocoa powder. He retrieved load after load of
T-shirts, caps, chocolates in the shape of the Capitol building, boxed truffles, pink chocolate roses on sticks, chocolate-
dipped pretzels, and adorable chocolate bumble bees
wrapped in gold and black foil with transparent paper wings.

Overload time. I needed help, and I knew just who to
call. I heard someone shout my name and headed for the
main house while I phoned Nina for reinforcement. She
promised to come ASAP.

I strolled into the magnificent kitchen of the main house.
I loved my kitchen, but Joe's was a true dream kitchen,
featuring a six-burner Viking stove with a grill, and a
walk-in pantry that was half the size of my kitchen. Unlike
some mansion kitchens, this one was built to be used by
home cooks, not just teams of caterers.

Dan Merano, Joe's son and head chocolatier of Amore
Chocolates, had delivered an unbelievably detailed four-
foot-high chocolate sculpture. Three cherubs, one white
chocolate, one milk chocolate, and one dark chocolate, held
hands and looked so real that I expected them to frolic right
off the kitchen counter. Tiny bits of edible gold accented
their wings and the wrap around their torsos. They were
stunningly beautiful, from the tips of their curls right down
to their teeny-tiny toenails.

Nonni beamed with pride. She rattled off something in
Italian but I didn't need a translation. Her face radiated joy,
and she hugged her grandson who towered over her.

Dan looked like he could be an outdoorsy type. He wore his beard in the current fashion of two days' growth. A loose cotton shirt hung over his Amore T-shirt and cargo pants. In his late forties, I guessed.

I gushed over his work. "Clearly this is the centerpiece. I'll have them place it where it's the first thing everyone sees when they walk in. It's fantastic!"

Dan blushed, and Nonni stretched up to kiss his cheek.

I returned to the guesthouse to continue packing the bags. Hearing voices, I stepped outside and had a quick chat with the table rental guy about where to set up. Everything was coming together. As long as it didn't rain, the chocolate tasting ought to come off perfectly. I was checking out the dark clouds in the sky at the exact moment that I heard a crash.

CHAPTER FOUR

Dear Natasha,

Why do recipes always say to melt chocolate in a double boiler? I never use my double boiler for anything and can't even find the silly thing. Why can't I just melt chocolate in a pot?

—At My Melting Point in Meltzer, Indiana

Dear At My Melting Point,

Dark chocolate begins to melt at 95 degrees and burns at 120 degrees. Milk chocolate burns at 110 degrees. That's a very small window. A double boiler allows the chocolate time to melt without raising the temperature so high that it burns.

—Natasha

I ran back to the kitchen, arriving at the same time as Dan and Nonni. The beautiful cherubs lay in shards on the hardwood floor.

The three of us gazed in pained silence for a long moment.

Dan fell to his knees and tenderly picked up one of the heads. He held it, seemingly in shock.

Behind him, Nonni said, "How can this happen?"

Coco rushed in, breathless. "What was that?"

She took in the scene and pressed her hands against her perfectly coiffed bob. Unlike her slender brother, Coco had the generous curves of a woman who liked to eat. "This is a nightmare! What happened?"

Nonni held up her hand with her forefinger and little finger raised. "It's the curse."

The curse? I knew nothing about a curse.

Coco *tsk*ed at Nonni. "If only that would really ward off evil. Dan, can you make another one in"— Coco checked her watch—"seven hours?"

Dan rose to his feet and heaved a great sigh. "Sure. It only takes a few minutes."

Coco glared at him much like I would have looked at *my* brother had he said something sarcastic.

Nonni smiled. "Wonderful. You better hurry back and get started on it. I take care of everything here."

Evidently Dan's sarcasm was lost on Nonni.

He kissed her gently on the forehead and winked at her. "Just for you, Nonni. I'll make something else just for you."

He beat a hasty exit, leaving the mess on the floor.

Coco fanned herself with both hands. "Ohhh. That's just like Dan. Who does he think is going to clean this up? Nonni?"

Coco hurried to a closet and returned with a broom and dustpan.

She would never be able to clean in that pencil skirt. It fit her perfectly but it wasn't wide enough around the hips for Coco to kneel on the floor.

I dropped to my knees and collected the larger pieces of chocolate. The fabulous scent wafted up to me.

Nonni held open a garbage bag, which I promptly filled. Between the three of us, it didn't take long to clean up the mess. I rose and washed my hands, glad that was behind us, but I harbored serious doubts that Dan could create another centerpiece in time for the tasting.

I turned around just in time to see a paper towel catch fire on the stove. I seized a pot lid and plunked it down over top of the little blaze.

Coco had missed the whole thing. She looked out the window at the garden.

Nonni shook her head. "Coco! What is the matter with you?"

"Hmm?" Coco faced us, chewing on her bottom lip. "I need espresso"—she glanced at the stove—"is something burning?" She wrinkled her nose. With trembling hands she poured bottled water into an aluminum macchinetta.

"Give to me," said Nonni. "You will burn it."

If you asked me, the last thing Coco needed was a dose of caffeine. Something was troubling her. I babbled in an effort to provide reassurance. "Coco, don't worry, we'll have a beautiful centerpiece. The clouds might be dark but they seem to be passing."

Coco had insisted that she did not want a tent. She envisioned an upscale casual tasting with people milling through the garden and on the patio. "A garden party that doesn't look like a wedding," she had said. I agreed that a tent would change the atmosphere but I had one on standby, just in case she had a last-minute change of heart.

Coco smiled at me kindly. "I guess I should relax and trust you to pull this off."

Coco didn't fool me for a minute. She was active in the Old Town social scene and had hosted plenty of parties. A little tasting like this shouldn't be making a wreck out of her. She twisted a chunky bangle on her wrist with restless fingers.

I could solve problem number one—the centerpiece—by calling in a favor from a florist. No one had to know that a fabulous chocolate centerpiece had been planned. But I had

about as much control over Coco as I did the clouds. Maybe
if I left Coco alone with Nonni, she would confide her problems to her grandmother.

I excused myself and headed outdoors to call the florist.
Seated on a garden bench, I gazed at the house.

Joe Merano's property was one of the biggest in Old
Town. The home of everyone's dreams. Originally built in
the 1700s, it had been added to in each succeeding century.
The rooms were massive, the furniture classic, the chande-
liers and heavy moldings like pieces of fine jewelry accent-
ing the décor. Everything was top of the line.

Most people only saw the property from the outside. The
beautiful white brick home had a walled garden seen only
by invitation. Inside, where I sat, an impeccable green lawn
sprawled with manicured boxwoods, an arcade of arches,
charming arbors, and patios with benches. Two stone lions
perched on pillars on either side of the gate leading into the
yard.

Shrub roses, rose of Sharon, butterfly bushes, and annu-
als burst with the colors of summer and gave the space a
sense of seclusion.

While I talked, my gaze drifted to French doors that
opened to a Juliet balcony on the second floor. Someone
closed the doors with a snap and drew the curtains. It was
probably Joe. I hadn't seen him since I arrived.

Nina trailed in behind men who were carrying tables into
the yard. I finished my call, satisfied that we would have a
spectacular centerpiece no matter what happened.

I showed her into the guesthouse. "Thank you so much
for coming to help."

Nina gazed around. "Are you kidding? I've always
wanted to see this house. It's beautiful. Are you sure this is
the guesthouse? It's gorgeous."

I showed her what to do, and we got to work. The tasting
was scheduled to begin at six in the evening to take advantage of the cooler temperatures. By one in the afternoon,

the basics were in place. Coco's adamant instruction that it not look like a wedding had posed challenges. I had debated colors for the tablecloths and finally chose peach verging on pink. Definitely wedding colors, but these days, with brides choosing browns and grays, what wasn't a wedding color? The round tables and summery white chairs were clustered on the brick patio just outside the kitchen and dining room. They could have gone a little weddinglike but I had kept them plain, avoiding ribbons and other dressy, decorative items. While we expected most people to mingle and eat the tiny tasting portions while standing, we had brought in ample seating around the tables and in the grassy yard as well. To keep people moving, the beverage tables were set up on the patio, near the set of three arched French doors leading to the main house.

When guests arrived, the pastry tasting table with the centerpiece was the first thing they would see in the garden. The rest of the tasting tables were set up around the lawn a decent distance from each other to help spread out the crowd.

Nina hung around with me, pitching in and begging for an excuse to see the main house.

Satisfied that we had done everything we could at that point, Nina and I walked home to change clothes and grab a bite of lunch.

I shared a quick turkey sandwich with Mochie, then dashed upstairs to shower and change. I stepped into a floral dress of cool polished cotton. The fit-and-flare style suited me because the big skirt made my waist appear smaller. The skirt came just below my knees, which meant I could clean up messes on the ground if necessary without worrying about bending over. My two rose-colored bangles and matching earrings were encrusted with a smattering of rhinestones for bling. I slid my feet into flat, strappy white sandals with rubber bottoms that wouldn't slide on the grass, and I was ready to go.

Nina met me at the front of her house. Her sleeveless turquoise and white color-blocked dress looked cool and summery. She fell in step with me. "I'm glad that I get to eat tonight instead of just admiring how pretty the food is." She shot me a wicked glance. "And I still want to peek inside the main house!"

When we reached the guesthouse, I pulled signs out of my briefcase and handed them to her. "Don't go upstairs, okay?"

The signs read *Family Only. Please use restrooms in the guesthouse.* "Post these on the outside doors—"

"Aww, I want to see the kitchen!"

"Let me finish. And attach one to the newel posts on each of the staircases."

She wiggled her eyebrows and grinned. I couldn't help laughing. I understood her curiosity. Joe's house was very special. I would have wanted to sneak inside for a peek, too.

Before long the caterer arrived. As his people set up, I inserted little cards into tall name holders. Each card identified the recipe and stated the name of the person who had submitted it. I divided the tables according to category—cakes, cookies, brownies, savory dishes, ice cream, pastries, candy, desserts, and snacks. The pastries and candies were arranged in beautiful rows on massive platters on the centerpiece table.

The florist delivered gerbera daises in vases for the tables on the patio. His emergency centerpiece turned out to be a huge extravaganza of pink and blush peonies, green hydrangea, purple lilacs, and roses and tulips in colors from blush to magenta and from pink to peach. The mound of flowers arched over the lip of a huge, classic weathered bowl on a wide-fluted foot. I asked him to set it on the cake table. If we needed it as the main centerpiece, we could move it to the pastry table and rearrange the cakes. If not, it would draw the eye and the tasters along to the cake table.

Thanks to the blooming garden, we hadn't needed much

in the way of flowers, but I'd ordered additional medium-sized vases of gerbera daisies for the three bathrooms in the guesthouse, as well as a larger bowl of flowers for the living room of the guest quarters. Triple ball topiaries already stood on either side of the entrance door to the guesthouse. I had debated dressing them up, but bows smacked too much of a wedding.

Nina rushed toward me. "Did you know they have an elevator? And that kitchen is just to die for. Can you even imagine living in a place like that?" She gasped. "It's gorgeous out here. The sun is making a reappearance! Hurrah! No rain."

Everything was on track. I heaved a sigh of relief. Food: check. Favor bags: check. Flowers: check. Beverages . . . ? I looked at the rustic table on the patio. A waiter arranged champagne glasses, tall iced tea glasses, and an ice bucket. Small white dishes held a selection of savory treats for those suffering from chocolate overload—the ingredients of an Italian antipasto platter. Green and black olives, cherry tomatoes on the vine, round slices of bruschetta, smoked mozzarella, salami, prosciutto, marinated mushrooms, artichokes, and zesty pickled peppers. Coffee and tea urns: check.

"Seems like something is missing," I said.

"I know just the thing. I saw it in the house." Nina dashed into the kitchen before I could stop her. A moment later, she placed a crystal candelabra on the end of the rough table. "Coco said we could use this."

"It's perfect. Thanks, Nina. How was Coco?" I asked.

Her mouth pulled back in concern. "I'm beginning to wonder if there was poison in that chocolate after all. She looks terrible. Pale and shaking like a leaf."

Oh no! I took off for the kitchen at a fast trot, with Nina right behind me. I knocked as a courtesy but opened the door and hurried inside. I could hear a man say in a kind tone, "Aww, Coco, I'm upset, too, but we have to pull ourselves together."

I stopped short, and Nina bumped into me. "Who is that?" I whispered.

"Must be Mitch. He came in when I asked about the candelabra."

Something tickled my ankle, and I almost swatted it before I realized a cat was sniffing me. A large Maine coon cat with a white bib under his face looked up at me before jumping on the counter. A door slammed upstairs.

"Maybe this isn't a good time," I whispered to Nina. We hustled out in a hurry. But the view from the patio forced me to stop and admire the tasting setup. Everything was in place.

Dan strolled through the garden gate next to the guesthouse. We walked toward him.

Gazing at the massive flower arrangement on the cake table, he said, "I see you're more sensible than Nonni and my sister. Didn't think I'd come through with another centerpiece, did you?"

I didn't want to insult him! I chose my words carefully. "I always like to have a backup plan. Just in case."

A thin young woman in a black dress stumbled through the lawn, yanking her long spiky heels out of the grass with each step. Straight, highlighted hair tumbled in her face. She brushed it back, mumbling, "I hate these garden events."

Dan grinned. "Stella, what's the problem now?"

"Why must your family always party outside? What's wrong with a nice restaurant or a hotel? Someplace with a floor and a roof?"

Dan introduced Stella as his girlfriend.

I wasn't always right about ages, but it appeared to me that she was a good twenty years younger than Dan.

She whisked her long hair back with both hands. "Wait until you see what he brought!"

Vince, the Amore delivery man, and Randy, the guy who nearly ran into me at the Amore offices, carried a five-foot-tall chocolate sculpture of *The Birth of Venus* into the garden.

Dan had re-created the goddess Venus rising from the sea in a scallop shell with amazing accuracy. He might be a chocolatier but he was also an incredible artist.

Coco and Mitch emerged from the house to watch. Joe's assistant, Marla, was with them. An attractive woman, Marla's petite figure seemed dwarfed by Coco and Mitch. Heavy streaks of blond shot through her short haircut.

I held my breath, hoping neither Vince nor Randy would stumble. They made it to the pastry table and slid the sculpture onto it intact. We broke into applause.

Dan stuck two fingers in his mouth and whistled. "Great job, guys!"

Coco slapped her brother on the back in a congratulatory way. "Your talent always amazes me, Dan. How could you possibly have created that huge sculpture so fast?"

"I was working on it as a gift for Dad and Nonni, so it was almost done. I *thought* this would be as good a time as any to give it to them."

Coco inhaled sharply.

Mitch wrapped his arm around her in a comforting way and shot Dan a look that could have melted a chocolate bar.

Coco sucked in a deep breath. "Sophie, this is Marla Eldridge, Daddy's administrative assistant."

"We've met at Amore."

"Of course you have. How silly of me." Coco raised her voice. "Gather round, everyone. I had these adorable lapel pins made for us in honor of the anniversary. This way, the guests will know who we are."

Coco handed them out to her family members and employees. She'd even had one created for me. Formed in the shape of a miniature Amore chocolate bar, the name Amore was incorporated in a gold script, with the person's name right beneath it

She crooked a finger at Mitch. "Come here, Mitch. Let me help you."

Mitch grumbled, "Do I have to wear it? It will make a hole in the fabric of my suit."

"Nonsense. They're magnetic. See?" She showed him how the magnet in back pulled away from the pin.

He grudgingly allowed her to affix it to his lapel.

I was about to ask where Joe was, but we were all distracted when recipe winners began to walk through the gate into the yard. As soon as they realized their recipes were marked with their names, they acted like kids at an Easter egg hunt, spreading out in search of their names and chattering excitedly.

"Still want me to collect tickets?" asked Randy.

"Seems so formal," said Coco. "Let's dispense with that. You can remove anyone who causes trouble."

"Try to smile, Coco, sweetheart," muttered Mitch. "It's showtime." He strode out to the winners, congratulating them and admiring the caterer's creativity with their recipes.

Marla followed him.

I turned to Coco. "Is Joe feeling all right? I haven't seen him all day."

Her eyes grew wide. "Yes. He's fine. Thank you for asking." She delivered the sentence like a preprogrammed robot.

I grabbed Coco by the arm and propelled her away from the others. In a whisper, I said, "I think you'd better tell me what's going on."

Dan overheard and joined us. "Tell her, Coco."

She burst into tears. "Daddy's missing."

CHAPTER FIVE

Dear Sophie,

My husband and I are inviting friends for a chocolate party. Dear hubby insists that one serves red wine with chocolate. I think a dry white wine would be better. We don't want to be gauche! What does one serve with chocolate desserts?

—Chocolate Hostess in Partee, Arkansas

Dear Chocolate Hostess,

How about champagne? Happily, chocolate lends itself to both white and red wines. There are even some chocolate red wines. But offer your guests hot tea and coffee, too. They're classic matches for chocolate cakes and pastries.

—Sophie

That simple sentence struck fear into my heart. "What do you mean Joe is missing?"

"No one has seen him since Thursday."

"He was at the welcome dinner for the recipe winners."

Coco nodded. "That was the last time any of us saw him. He came back here with Nonni, and"—she gulped and dabbed her eyes with a tissue—"Friday morning no one could find him. I'm just sick over it. I . . . I don't know what to do. What could have happened to him?"

No wonder Coco was so distracted and emotional. I would be, too, if my father had disappeared. I had some ideas but none of them were of a happy nature. "Did you report it to the police?"

Her lips bunched up as though she would cry if she said another word. Suddenly her shoulders hunched.

Mitch joined us and slung an arm around his wife's waist. "One . . . two . . . three. Everyone laugh." He threw back his head and laughed aloud. "Quick, into the house."

We obeyed like children.

When we reached the kitchen, Mitch said, "I thought we all agreed that this was not to go beyond family members."

Coco winced. "She had to know, Mitch. She was asking about Daddy."

"Joe's not here to tell us what to do, but you know he would want us to entertain our guests and be gracious. If we try, no one will even notice his absence. Coco, sugar, fix your makeup, put on a happy face, and come on out to mingle with our guests."

Coco ran up the stairs, no doubt to fix her face.

"Sophie"—he turned to me, wiping his brow—"we're trying to keep this quiet for the time being. I can't emphasize enough the importance of not leaking a word of this. For Joe's safety, it's vital that this be completely hush-hush."

"Have you notified the police?"

"We have. I hope we can count on your cooperation?"

I nodded. "Yes, of course."

"Thanks." Mitch walked out of the room.

I took a minute to compose myself. I hadn't expected anything like this. What could have happened to Joe? This event had been planned for over a year. I thought he was looking forward to it. Surely he wouldn't have left with so much going on. He was supposed to make a little speech tonight. I had so many questions. Where was Coco?

She probably needed a moment alone. I returned to the patio and mingled with the crowd, trying my best to smile. It wasn't easy. I couldn't help thinking that something terrible had happened to Joe. I spotted my ex-husband, Mars, and felt comforted by his presence. I flung my arms around him and planted a kiss on his cheek. Just my luck, that was the exact moment that Alex arrived.

He looked dashing in a dark gray suit, white shirt, and burgundy tie. I had never seen his cocoa brown hair even half an inch too long. I attributed his precision about his appearance to his days in the military. He would always walk with his chin held high and his back erect.

But his expression showed his displeasure at my friendliness toward my former husband. He turned and walked toward the gate like he was leaving.

I dodged through the crowd after him, "Alex! Alex!"

He paused for a moment and gazed at me.

"Alex, it's not what it looked like. You see—"

"That's the problem. I *do* see. I wish Mars would just marry Natasha and move on." Alex strode out of the garden.

I watched him go. This wasn't the place or the time for a fuss. I would have to explain to him later when he cooled off. My spirits dragging a little bit, I returned to Mars.

"Wow, what did I do to deserve that?" Mars acted surprised.

"I was just happy to see you." I changed the subject in a hurry. "Have you tasted anything yet?"

"Only every single chocolate cake. I'm in heaven here."

I giggled at him. Across the way, Dan was tasting chocolates. He nodded vigorously and fed one to Stella, looking far more comfortable than he had at dinner the night before. I wondered if he was simply more at ease in the garden of his childhood home or if he found Stella's presence reassuring.

Humphrey, whom I had known since childhood, joined us with a tiny piece of cake to taste. So blond that his hair was almost white, Humphrey had the physique of the classic ninety-pound weakling. Pale and thin, he had most surely taken a lot of teasing as a child. Humphrey had had a crush on me when we were in grade school. I had been involved with my own childhood obsessions and had never noticed. In recent years, he'd become a good and trusted friend. Who would have ever thought it would work out that way?

"How is everything?" I asked.

"I think I'm in love with Cheryl Maiorca. Have you tasted her cake? Do you know if she's married?" He peered over my head in her direction.

"Happily married. But I suppose that proves the old adage that the way to a man's heart is through his stomach."

"So which of them isn't married?" asked Humphrey.

"Stop that. This isn't a dating game."

"I do love women who can bake."

He did. I wondered what happened to the cupcake baker he liked so much.

Bernie ambled toward us and offered me a miniature éclair. "I have to buy this cookbook. Some of these recipes are fantastic."

"Not to worry. You'll receive one in your favor bag when you leave. Think you might serve some of them at The Laughing Hound?"

"Most definitely. Cheryl Maiorca's chocolate cake has to be the best I've ever tasted."

"Um, I hate to burst your bubble but if everyone has the recipe, why would they order it at The Laughing Hound?" asked Mars.

"Right. Exactly when were *you* planning to bake it?" Bernie grinned at his friend.

The intoxicated Frenchman who had tried to coax me to his room two nights before leaned toward us. Once again, he wore his shirt unbuttoned with his tie, this time a cream-colored silk with a collage of truffles and chocolates on it, hanging open. He waved an empty champagne glass. "Did I hear an expat speaking over here?"

He didn't seem to recognize me, and I thought it better not to remind him of his embarrassing behavior. Besides, I saw Natasha holding up a champagne glass with a fork positioned as though she planned to clink it and make a speech. I excused myself and hurried toward her.

As always, Natasha looked gorgeous. No amount of time in a gym would make clothes hang on me like they did on her. She wore a strapless dress in a bluish silver. The skirt crossed over the front in graceful folds, showing off her long, slender legs.

"Natasha!" I called. "I haven't seen you all night."

She kissed the air over each of my shoulders. "I'm sorry I can't chat right now. I have to make a speech. I'm the official taster, you know."

"I heard about that. I, uh, didn't know it involved a speech, though."

"Oh my, yes. You're so funny, Sophie. What else would an official taster do?"

Aha. If I knew Natasha, she hadn't eaten a bite. "So you tried all the dishes?"

The smile left her face. "Not *all* of them."

It was mean of me, but I just couldn't help myself. I bet she hadn't tried a single one. "Isn't that what a taster does? I thought you were supposed to give Amore an official report."

Natasha swallowed hard. She leaned toward me. "Do you know how many calories that would be? All the butter and eggs and chocolate and cream?"

"I think they would be disappointed if you didn't try *some* of the dishes."

She looked slightly sick at the thought.

"Here comes Mitch. I'll cover for you while you start tasting."

I released a breath of relief when Natasha scuttled away. All I needed was for Natasha to make a speech. The Meranos would be furious with me if she made the event about herself.

Mitch did exactly what I had feared Natasha would do. A good thing she hadn't upstaged him. I sucked in a deep breath and forced a smile. Something had to be very wrong. It wasn't as though I knew Joe like a best friend, but he didn't strike me as the kind of guy who missed a major event for his company.

Mitch clinked a fork against a champagne glass to get everyone's attention. "I'm Mitch Ross. I think most of you know me by now. We are honored to have you as our guests in celebrating the sixtieth anniversary of Amore Chocolates. This is a very special year for us. It's hard to imagine that we have been in business for six decades. We're looking forward to our next sixty years. We thank our very special guests—the winners of our recipe contest—for coming to join in our celebration. Are you having fun?"

The crowd sang, "Yes!"

"Have you had enough chocolate?"

I heard a few yeses, but the majority shouted, "No!"

"Then party on!"

As they applauded, Mitch walked past me and whispered, "I think it's going well. No one is thinking about Joe."

My gaze drifted over to Coco and Nonni. That wasn't totally accurate. Somebody was thinking about Joe all right.

Randy, the Amore employee, lingered near the champagne with Dan and Stella, while Vince, with the long ponytail, joined the lines of people tasting the food.

I headed for Nina who, unlike Natasha, truly was trying to sample everything. I wasn't sure it was possible, but each tasting item was only a bite or two. She pointed out her favorites, propelling me to the cake table where Cheryl

Maiorca was the star of the hour, talking about her chocolate cake and how she lost one hundred pounds. Red highlights gleamed in her shoulder-length dark brown hair. She wore a short cotton sweater over a summer dress that nipped in at the waist, showing off her new figure. When we heard her say that she worked out at the gym three days a week, Nina choked and had a little coughing fit.

When she recuperated, Nina steered me to Lori Speer's hand-dipped chocolates. I popped a creamy Kahlúa truffle in my mouth and almost swooned. She had made Irish cream, hazelnut, blackberry, and tiramisu truffles. I dared to eat another while Lori regaled the crowd with stories of her days as a police officer. It was hard to imagine the laughing woman with wild blond hair being a tough cop. How could she keep a trim figure with such fabulous chocolates around all the time?

I forced myself away from the chocolates and moseyed up to the drinks. Except for Joe's absence, I thought the tasting was going well.

Natasha offered me half a cookie. "Ugh. I never want to see chocolate again."

"Didn't you like any of them?"

"None of them are anywhere near the caliber of the recipes I submitted. I see that they were in search of mundane, ordinary recipes. They should have said so." Natasha turned her gaze to the house. "I always wanted your house, but this one is much more my style. Can you imagine living here? It's so elegant. I would take out all those Palladian arches. They're so passé. And have you been in the guesthouse? My word. That place needs to be ripped down. It's so old. That dreadful stone fireplace and the beams in the ceilings. Some nice stainless steel and gray paint would spruce it up."

"I think it's beautiful just the way it is."

"The main house would be like living in a palace. You just know the residents have a perfect life." Natasha sighed.

"Not like me, struggling for every little thing, working my fingers to the bone."

"I don't know about that. I suspect Joe and his family worked hard for what they have."

"Do you think I'll ever be a success, Sophie?"

"I think you already are." Whew. Dodged that one!

"Thank you. There's a reason you're my best friend. I wish Mars would see me the same way you do. Honestly, I'm beginning to wonder if he's jealous of me. He tries to discourage all of my clever ideas. I'm really a business genius, like Martha."

She didn't have to tell me which Martha.

A couple of hours later, Nonni, Coco, and I took turns standing by the garden entrance to hand out favor bags as guests departed. Vince and Randy fetched the bags and brought them to us, a few at a time. By twilight, the favor bags were gone, and we were packing up.

As I headed for the patio, Mitch approached me. "Thank you for cooperating. We'd appreciate it if you kept the news about Joe to yourself. His life could depend on it."

His last sentence hung in the air, frightening me. It wouldn't have been right to ask questions. The family was clearly distraught by whatever had happened.

I assured him I would honor their request and keep Joe's disappearance to myself. People would probably speculate about his absence tonight, though. It wouldn't be long before it was the talk of the town.

Tables collapsed as the legs slammed down. Between the caterers and equipment supplier, the garden swarmed with people engaged in noisy activities.

I whisked the crystal candelabra away so it wouldn't be a casualty as the tables were folded and removed. I carried it into the house, once again knocking on the door out of politeness even though I opened it and went inside.

Coco, Nonni, Stella, and Dan sat around the kitchen table

in such a deep discussion that I wasn't sure they'd heard me.
A tray of leftovers occupied the middle of the table.

Coco picked at the contents. "There's not a doubt in my
mind that they were his. Nonni agrees with me. But why
come back now? Why come back at all?"

"For love, Coco. True love never dies," said Nonni.

Dan spoke softly. "How can you say that, Nonni? That
man has brought nothing but heartache to this family."

"Excuse me," I said. "Sorry to interrupt. Thanks for letting us use the candelabra. It made all the difference. I'll
just put it up here." I placed it on the kitchen counter.

"Thank you, Sophie. I'm sorry I've been such a basket
case, but I'm sick over Daddy. You know, deep inside I hoped
he might walk in tonight, all smiles, and surprise us. Now
I'm devastated."

Nonni patted Coco's arm. "Joe will come home. You
will see."

Coco smiled at her grandmother but raised her eyebrows
at me in a way that said she thought her grandmother was
out of it.

"I hope he comes back soon." What else could I say?
"They're almost done packing up. I'll do a quick swing
through the yard and the guesthouse when they're finished,
and then I'll be taking off, too. Um, for what it's worth,
under the circumstances, I thought it went very well."

They thanked me again. I said *good night* and walked
out onto the patio. All of the outdoor lights shone. Spotlights
mounted on the ground highlighted the lions on the garden
gate pillars, and accented the branches of select trees. It was
both lovely and a little spooky at the same time. The rush
and calamitous sounds of breaking down the event were
over. I was the only one left.

I collected my flashlight and a trash bag. It was such a
small gesture but I knew my clients appreciated it. No one,
not a homeowner or hotel employees, wanted to find the
property trashed after a party. I had never understood why

someone would toss garbage on someone's deck or pour out a drink on a hotel carpet. I bet they didn't act that way at home.

I walked the perimeter of the garden, shining my light toward the grassy middle and then flicking it at the bushes and flowers that lined the yard. Sure enough, I found plenty of little wrappers and paper dishes that had been used to serve food. One champagne glass, intact, thank heaven. A matchbook with a phone number written on it. That one cracked me up. I wondered if the recipient ditched it on purpose or would be sad when he or she realized it had been lost.

Something moved in the dark just ahead of me. I raised my light and shone it on Cheryl Maiorca.

She shielded her face with her hand. "Hi, Sophie."

I strode toward her. "I thought everyone had left."

She cocked her head and made a funny face. "I walked all the way back to the hotel before I realized that I left my purse here. Have you seen it?"

"Sorry, but I haven't. Where do you think you left it?"

"Right about there."

I aimed my flashlight at the bushes and caught a glimmer of something. Crouching, I saw the handbag tucked under a butterfly bush. I grabbed the strap and pulled out a white purse.

"There it is! Thank you, Sophie. I was beginning to panic because it has my wallet in it!"

"No problem. Should I call a taxi for you?"

"I'll walk with you!" A woman's voice shouted in the dark.

I scanned the garden with the flashlight. It landed on Lori Speer, who hurried toward us. "Let's not take a cab. It's so pretty here at night. I love peeking in all the windows. The houses are so close to the street that I just can't help looking inside."

"I'm sorry, I didn't notice you in the dark. Have you been here the whole time?" I asked.

"No. I . . . I was hoping I could find the little card with my name and recipe on it. As a keepsake."

"Too bad I didn't think of that." It dawned on me that the caterer must have left my cardholders. "Maybe it's not too late. Follow me."

We quickly located the box where the caterer had stashed everything that wasn't his. All the name cards were intact. "Do you want to take them to the hotel and pass them out?"

"Can we?" Lori asked. "I know everyone would love it."

"Bet that'll buy us free drinks all night," laughed Cheryl.

The two of them gabbed like old friends. Even when they were out of sight, I could hear them carrying on about something.

I went back to work collecting garbage. The far end of the garden contained no litter at all. Clearly not many people had wandered back that far. They all stayed close to the food, not that I blamed them.

I turned to make my way back on the other side of the garden, when my light caught two glowing orbs. Certain that I must be mistaken, I repeated my turn but slowly. And there they were—two cat eyes staring at me from deep in the bushes. Probably Joe's cat spying on his personal jungle now that it was quiet again.

Collecting bits of garbage, I made my way up the other side of the garden, and then proceeded to the guesthouse.

I straightened up a little. Evidently some people had made themselves comfortable in the small living room. The guest-house had been updated but they had wisely left what looked to be original beams in the ceiling. The stone fireplace bore signs of age, too. The guesthouse was quaint and charming, no matter what Natasha thought.

I threw away napkins and forks that had been left in the downstairs bathrooms and collected champagne glasses. In the little kitchen, I poured out leftover champagne and stored the empty glasses in a box to return to the caterer–until I found one flute with tablets dissolving in it.

I held the glass up to the light. Medicine? Antacids? Who took meds with champagne? Shaking my head, I was about to pour out the tablets, when I thought better of it. No one was sick. I hadn't heard any complaints. Still, I had been involved in enough odd situations to make me wary. I stashed the glass, complete with tablets and remaining champagne, in the box. It was silly of me, but maybe it would be best to take precautions and preserve it in case one of the guests complained of being sickened.

Leaving the box in the kitchen, I headed for the stairs. Long and narrow, they were typical of historic homes in the area and were probably part of the original structure. But the door at the bottom of the stairs was locked. Who would have done that?

For just a moment, I wondered if someone was staying in the guesthouse. But I had placed flowers upstairs in the morning and hadn't noticed any personal belongings.

I should probably ask Coco. Maybe someone was staying over. But it was late, and I was tired, and as soon as I checked the upstairs I could go home. I knocked on the door. "Hello?" I studied the doorknob. Nothing vintage about it. It was the kind my parents had in their house. It could probably be unlocked with a straightened paper clip.

Sighing, I gazed around. A small writing desk! In the top drawer I found pens, paper, and one paper clip. That was all I needed. I unbent one end of it and slid it into the hole in the doorknob. I felt it hit the tumbler inside and pushed gently. It made a little popping sound. I turned the knob and the door swung open.

CHAPTER SIX

Dear Sophie,

I'm so upset. I was melting chocolate to bake brownies and suddenly it turned into an impossible clump. I had to throw it out and start over. What went wrong? Did I buy bad chocolate?

—Baking Mom in Lumptown, North Carolina

Dear Baking Mom,

Your chocolate was fine. It just seized, a very common occurrence when water, or even steam, comes into contact with melted chocolate. Next time, don't throw it out right away. You might be able to rescue it by stirring in a little bit of cream, milk, or vegetable shortening. It will be thinner than plain melted chocolate, so you may wish to reduce a liquid ingredient in the recipe slightly.

—Sophie

I flicked on the lights and walked up the old stairs. The bedroom looked fine. Someone probably hit the lock by accident. I hustled into the small bathroom.

In the dim light that floated in from the bedroom, I could make out a man collapsed over a tall claw-foot tub. I drew in a sharp breath in surprise. His head and shoulders weren't visible, only his backside. Was he sick? "Hello?" I choked out. "Do you need help?"

When there was no response, I pushed through my instinct to bolt, and walked toward him. Gently prodding his back, I said, "Hello? Are you all right?"

He was bent at the waist over the high side of the old-fashioned bathtub. His legs didn't look right to me. He wasn't kneeling. They were at an odd angle. I dashed out of the room and down the stairs as fast as I could go.

My heart racing, I sprinted to the house and burst into Joe's kitchen. "There's someone in the guesthouse."

The Merano family looked at me with unconcerned faces. Why weren't they understanding me? "In the tub. With the lights off."

Okay, I wasn't making sense, no wonder they regarded me so strangely. I took a deep breath. "There's a man collapsed over the bathtub upstairs in the guesthouse."

Coco breathed, "Daddy!"

Dan jumped to his feet and ran out, with me right behind him.

We dashed up the stairs. I felt much braver in Dan's company. He barged into the bathroom while I turned on the lights.

Dan gasped and stepped back, right into me.

I was reeling myself. "Do you think he's alive?"

"Hey! Buddy!" Dan touched the guy's back. "Hey! Are you okay?"

Still no response. I edged next to Dan, relieved to see there was no water in the tub. I dared to reach down to shake the man's shoulder. Nothing. One thing was for sure—it wasn't Joe. The man was too large.

"There's a phone by the bed," said Dan. "Call 911."

I dodged Coco and Mitch as the rest of the family arrived, grabbed the phone and dialed.

They had just answered when Dan called out, "Don't just stand there, I need some help."

"Coco! Here." I handed her the phone. "Give them the address and tell them we need an ambulance." I circled around Nonni and Stella.

Mitch blocked my way into the bathroom. "What are you trying to do?" he asked Dan.

I could see exactly what Dan intended. He needed to lift the guy's shoulders out of the bathtub. I pushed past Mitch and jumped into the end of the tub to grab one of his arms. "Did you find a pulse?" I asked.

"No, but he's doubled over so I'm not sure. Mitch! Get out of the way already," Dan shouted.

Mitch moved as though he was in slow motion—as though he couldn't quite cope with the situation.

Dan and I heaved the man up. I hated to think it but the words drifted through my thoughts—*dead weight*.

"Step aside!" Dan barked at Mitch.

He squeezed against the wall so that Dan and I could shuffle out of the bathroom and lay the man on the floor. No small feat given his size.

Coco leaned over him. "His neck! Do you see that?"

I did. A straight, dark bruise ran around the front of his throat.

Stella shrieked and clasped a hand over her mouth.

"Who is he?" asked Mitch.

"He was a guest here tonight," said Dan. "I recall talking to him." He felt the man's neck. "I'm not getting a pulse. I'll start CPR."

I knew who he was. None other than the Frenchman who had tried to pick me up at the hotel on Thursday night. "I think he's one of your recipe winners."

"No!" breathed Mitch. "No, no, no."

"The poor man." Coco looked at me. "Do you know his name?"

"I haven't a clue. All I know is that he spoke with a French accent."

It was Nonni who finally stated the obvious. "Somebody kill him."

Through clenched teeth, Mitch muttered, "Thank you, Nonni. He must have some identification on him." Mitch bent over and felt the man's pockets. "Here we go." He flipped open the wallet. "Oh no! This just went from nightmare to catastrophe. It's Arnaud Turnèbe, the Belgian chocolatier."

"You mean the guy who is opening Celebration of Chocolate?" asked Dan, not bothering to try pronouncing the name of the store in French.

"The very same," Mitch groaned. "It's going to look like we tried to kill the competition."

"How can you say that?" Coco cried. "Have you no heart? This man had a life and people who loved him."

"Fine. It's *your* family's business. So what if it goes down the tubes? Excuse me while I go call an attorney."

"He look familiar," said Nonni.

Coco cocked her head like a puppy. "He does." I could have sworn she stifled a little cry.

I was glad to hear the siren of the approaching ambulance. I had a hunch that poor Arnaud could not be resuscitated, but I hoped that the trained responders could work some kind of magic.

I left the family and ran to the garden gate to show them the way. Three uniformed Emergency Medical Technicians followed me upstairs. One took over CPR immediately.

A male voice behind me asked, "Anyone know who he is?"

Unfortunately, I knew that voice. Wolf Fleishman, my old boyfriend, the homicide investigator. Why, oh why, did he have to be the one to respond to the call tonight?

"Hi, Wolf."

He nodded at me. "Sophie."

"Apparently it's Arnaud Turnèbe who is . . . was supposed to open a new chocolate shop. Give him the wallet, Coco."

She handed it over to Wolf. "How could this possibly have happened?" asked Coco. "There were hundreds of people here. Someone must have noticed something."

"He was lying here on the floor? Who found him?" asked Wolf.

I raised my hand and wiggled my fingers.

"I should have known."

I explained that I had been gathering trash when I spotted Arnaud doubled over the side of the bathtub.

Wolf sighed. He kept his calm, though. Typical Wolf. "If you wouldn't mind, everyone, except Sophie, please return to the main house. I'll come and speak to each of you."

He watched as they walked away. "This crime scene is a mess. Pulling him out of the tub? You know better than that."

"You're kidding, right? We weren't even sure he was dead. What would you have done?"

One corner of Wolf's mouth turned up in a suppressed grin. "The same thing, I guess."

"Wolf?" called one of the EMTs. "We've got petechiae."

I frowned at Wolf. "What's that?"

"Spots of blood in the eyes. Usually means strangulation."

I sucked in a noisy breath of air. I'd known he was probably dead but somehow that made it so much worse!

"Who was here tonight?" asked Wolf.

"All kinds of people. I can print off a list for you."

"That would be very helpful, thanks."

"Somebody must have done it fast is all I can say. I saw Arnaud during the tasting, so we know he was alive then."

"What do you know about these folks?"

"They're the Amore Chocolates family—"

"This is Joe Merano's place?"

"Yes. Do you know him?"

"He's a great guy. A big supporter of our youth league. You know, the program that gives kids something to do to keep them out of trouble."

"He went missing sometime Thursday night," I said, thinking about how outraged Mitch would be that I spilled the beans.

Wolf nodded. "Yeah, I heard about that."

Wolf always had a poker face. I guessed that was good for a cop, but he seemed too calm. "Don't you think there could be a connection? One chocolatier goes missing and another turns up dead in his guesthouse?"

Wolf wrapped an arm around my shoulders and squeezed gently. "Always playing the sleuth. You should have been a cop, Sophie. Now get out of here." He turned away.

"Wolf? It may not be anything at all, but when I was cleaning up I found a glass with medicine of some sort dissolving in the champagne."

"Show me."

He followed me down the steep stairs and into the kitchen.

I pointed at the box, and Wolf peered into it.

"Maybe it's a good thing you were here. Most people would have dumped it. I'll have the forensic guys take a look. Can you leave the rest of the glasses until we're done?"

"Sure."

"Now go home so you won't trample any evidence. Man, I hate these nighttime crime scenes. I'll pick up the list of guests from you tomorrow morning, okay?"

I walked down the stairs, grabbed my little card holders and my briefcase, and hightailed it out, but not before I saw Dan watching me from a window in the main house.

I trudged home thinking about Arnaud. It should have been a happy time in his life. Expanding his business to

America had to be a big deal. But then I wondered if he was always a smarmy lush who tried to pick up women. I guessed being a drunken cad wasn't mutually exclusive with being a fine chocolatier. Had he crossed the wrong woman? If his behavior toward me was standard, a wife might have been driven over the edge. Or maybe he was single and totally inept with women. Maybe I was being too hard on him. The poor man was dead.

I unlocked my front door, scooped Mochie up, and held him tight. His purring calmed my nerves.

Exhausted as I was, I had trouble falling asleep that night. I kept thinking of the tomato-faced man and wondering what had happened to Joe.

I had almost drifted off when I sat bolt upright in bed. Cheryl Maiorca and Lori Speer! The two recipe winners claimed to have returned to the site of the party. What if one of them killed Arnaud while the others left? It wouldn't have been difficult. There were so many of them! It would have been easy enough to hang out in the guesthouse and kill Arnaud during the party or the cleanup. No one would have noticed a thing.

~~~

In the morning, the sun shone in a clear blue sky, making the events of the night before seem impossible. I knew they were true, though.

I lingered in the shower, glad that I didn't have to rush off anywhere. The contest winners had the day off to explore the area on their own. Dressed in a sleeveless pink cotton shirt, a white skirt, and cushy sandals, I walked downstairs with Mochie and put on the kettle for tea.

Mochie sat next to his food bowl, watching me with interest. I debated whether his look meant fish or chicken and decided shredded chicken in gravy sounded good. I was spooning it into his dish when I heard tapping on the window of my kitchen door.

Nina was early. I hadn't even started the quiche yet. She had probably heard about the murder and wanted to know more.

I swung around with a big grin but stopped dead when I saw Mitch Ross peering through the window in my door.

CHAPTER SEVEN

Dear Natasha,

I bought chocolates for my girlfriend on the anniversary of our first date. I thought it was a very romantic gesture. But I found most of them in the trash a few days later and overheard her telling her girlfriend that they weren't very good. What gives? Chocolate is chocolate.

—Confused in Chocolate Bayou, Texas

Dear Confused,

Are you a coffee drinker? You probably have a favorite coffee. Like coffee, chocolate starts from beans, which can vary in flavor and quality. Chocolate goes through a long process before it ends up in a pretty box. Sugar, milk, cream, and other ingredients are added because raw chocolate is bitter. Your girlfriend probably has a refined palate like me. Next time, pony up for the expensive stuff and don't be swayed by the prettiest box!

—Natasha

Glad I wasn't still in my bathrobe, I walked to the door and opened it.

Mitch's Adam's apple bobbed, and he appeared uncomfortable. He tugged at the collar of his navy blue golf shirt. "I apologize for dropping by unannounced."

"No problem."

"You can't imagine what we've been through with Joe missing. I'm afraid none of us are at our best right now."

I invited him in.

The kettle whistled. "Would you care for a cup of tea?"

"Yes, thanks. Don't worry, I won't stay long."

I poured tea for the two of us. "Milk, sugar? Lemon?"

"Milk and sugar, thanks. I don't think I've ever been in this house. I like the old fireplace in the kitchen. Gives it a special touch. Seems like no two houses in Old Town are alike."

I handed him a mug of tea and perched on the edge of a chair next to the fireplace.

He sat opposite me in the matching chair. "I'm told that you're pretty good at solving murders."

I didn't respond. I barely breathed as I waited to hear what he wanted.

"I'd like to hire you to find Joe."

Didn't see that coming. In fact, I found it rather interesting that he wanted me to locate Joe, but he didn't mention the murder in Joe's guesthouse. And then I realized what he had implied. "You think Joe has been murdered?"

Mitch held up his forefinger. "Now, I didn't say *that*. We just want to find him."

"I'm not a private investigator." The truth was that I would probably snoop around anyway, if nothing else, as a courtesy to Joe. It wasn't every day that someone hired me and then disappeared.

"That's okay. I don't care if you're licensed as long as you locate Joe. We're all, well"—he gulped air—"the truth is that we're falling apart exactly when we need to struggle to save Amore's reputation. The idiot who murdered Arnaud on Joe's property better not ever run into me." He clenched his fist in anger. "Someone must want to make Amore look bad. The irony is that if he weren't dead, I would think it was Arnaud himself who was the killer."

I didn't quite follow and frowned at him questioningly.

"You know, to make Amore look bad by murdering someone at Joe's house so people would think one of us is the killer. And during our big anniversary week! This will get more press coverage than the anniversary."

Was he worried that a member of the Amore family *had* killed Arnaud? Or was I just trying too hard to read between the lines? I could feel my jaw clenching. "Why are you keeping Joe's disappearance quiet? I thought it was better to go public with these things in case someone saw him."

"Our first concern is kidnapping. We're told it's prudent to not broadcast anything so a kidnapper won't know we went to the police and so that annoying copycat types won't get involved and confuse the situation."

Those thoughts had never entered my mind. I could see the point, though.

"Was there a ransom note?"

Mitch held up his open palm. "We haven't found one. I hear they usually make a phone call with demands. In addition, it sounds just awful, but there's also the business to consider. Perhaps you are familiar with the saying *there is no bad publicity*?"

I nodded.

"It's not true." He held up his hands and moved them apart in the air as though depicting a headline. " 'Joe Merano Disappears on Sixtieth Anniversary of Amore Chocolates' is the worst imaginable publicity. At least I thought it was. Turns out 'Amore Competitor Murdered in Merano Guesthouse' is far worse. We are *not* having a great anniversary."

"I'm very sorry, Mitch—about all of it. But I'm not in the

business of investigating crime. I've just gotten lucky a couple of times. That's all." I couldn't possibly take money for it.

Mitch gazed around my kitchen. "I could pay you quite handsomely."

By Old Town standards, my house was huge. But in comparison to Joe's place, it was a very ordinary home. I could tell he was searching for my weaknesses.

"I would be perpetrating a fraud if I took your money. Really, you need to go to someone who knows the ropes. There are a lot of private investigators around. I'm sure one of them would be thrilled to help you out."

He glanced up at the portrait over the fireplace.

Mars's Aunt Faye had left us the house, and I had bought out Mars's share in our divorce. I kept Faye's portrait over the fireplace in honor of her memory.

Mitch cocked his head a little bit. "For Nonni and Coco?"

Now I felt a smidge of guilt. He had hit on the one thing that I knew to be true. Coco was a wreck.

But at that moment, Wolf knocked on my door.

Mitch gazed at me. "What's *he* doing here?"

"I promised I would print out the guest list of the people at the tasting last night."

Mitch stared at me for a long moment. "Yes, of course. Of course you would think a guest killed Arnaud!" He sounded relieved.

I tried to hide my surprise. Clearly he did *not* think a guest had been the culprit. So that's how it was. He thought a family member murdered Arnaud. Was that why he hadn't asked me to find the killer?

I opened the door for Wolf.

After a polite exchange of greetings, Mitch moved toward the door. I followed him out on the little stoop. As he left, he said, "I hope you'll reconsider. We could use your help."

He strode away, crossing paths with Nina, who ran toward me still wearing her bathrobe. "What's going on?"

She seized my arm and whispered, "What's Wolf doing here? I saw him drive up."

"The new chocolatier is dead."

"Huh? When? Where? How?" demanded Nina.

We entered the kitchen, and Wolf asked, "Did he want you to find Joe?"

So much for keeping their secrets.

"Joe Merano is missing?" cried Nina. "I wondered why he didn't make an appearance at the chocolate tasting."

Wolf stared at me. "You're not going to do it, are you?"

"Of course not. Well, maybe a little on my own. Joe was very good to me."

"Stay out of this, Sophie," growled Wolf. "I'm serious."

I raised my hands. "No problem. Tea all around?" I put the kettle back on and took two more yellow mugs out of a cabinet. "I was planning to make a quiche, Wolf. Want to stay for brunch?" Inspired by a dish I had tried the night before, I mixed batter for indulgent chocolate raspberry muffins.

"Thanks for the invite but I've been up most of the night."

"I'm sorry, I haven't printed off the guest list yet. It will only take a moment." I popped the muffins into the oven and excused myself.

When I returned a few minutes later, Nina was pouring water into the mugs, including mine. "How could you not tell me about the murder?"

"It was late."

"I *cannot* believe that I didn't know about any of this," she muttered.

I handed Wolf the list and thanked Nina for preparing the tea.

She sat down next to Wolf and perused the list of names over his shoulder. "Who had a beef with Arnaud?"

I preheated the oven and pulled ingredients for the crustless quiche out of the fridge. "A beef with him? Who even knew him?"

I chopped salty ham and a couple of slices of leftover

bacon. Using my vegetable peeler, I cut thin slices of savory Asiago cheese. And for a little veggie in the mix, I sliced three tiny baby zucchinis that had grown in my own garden. After whisking the eggs with salt, pepper, sage, and garlic powder, I greased a glass pie dish with sweet butter and scattered everything except the eggs in it. I mixed milk and a splash of heavy cream with the eggs and poured it gently over the ham, cheese, and zucchini so they wouldn't be dislodged. For the final touch, I sprinkled Parmesan cheese over the whole thing. I slid it into the oven next to the muffins.

"Do you two really think you can find Arnaud's killer by looking at a list?" I joined them at my kitchen table.

"I recognize a lot of these names," said Wolf.

"Oh! I almost forgot to mention that two of the winners, Lori Speer and Cheryl Maiorca, came back to Joe's last night. At least that's what they claimed. Either one of them could have been hanging around the whole time, I suppose."

"The killer coming back to the scene of the crime, eh?" asked Nina.

Wolf snorted. "You watch too many crime shows on TV."

"Are you saying they don't come back to the scene of the crime?" asked Nina.

"Would you?" asked Wolf.

"Maybe. If I was nervous and wanted to know what was going on and whether I was a suspect."

"Is it definite that he was strangled?" I asked.

Wolf sipped his tea. "We won't know for sure until the autopsy report comes back, but that was how it looked to me. We did a pretty thorough search but didn't find much in the way of items that might have been used to strangle him."

"No ropes?" asked Nina. "Doesn't everyone have rope somewhere around the house?"

"Nothing that matched the marks. A rope often leaves a pattern that reflects how it was twisted or braided. Sophie, do you remember if he was wearing a tie?"

"Ordinarily, I might not recall, but it was very

distinctive—a cream-colored background, covered with a print of truffles and chocolates. It was hanging around his neck loose when I saw him." I thought back. "He didn't have it on when we found him."

Nina cried, "That's it, then! That's what the killer used to strangle him."

"Or he took it off," said Wolf wryly.

The muffins filled my kitchen with the scent of chocolate. I took them out of the oven, placed them in a basket lined with a yellow napkin and set it on the table with plates.

Wolf and Nina helped themselves immediately.

"I bet it was someone in the Merano family," mused Nina. "You know, getting rid of the competition. Especially since he made such high-end, famous chocolates." Her expression changed to a pout. "Bummer, though, I always wanted to try one. They were supposed to be incredible."

"What was so special about them?" asked Wolf. "Chocolate is chocolate."

Nina laughed at him. "You neophyte! You can't be serious." She watched him. "You are! Really? You can't tell the difference in flavor and texture?"

Wolf shrugged. "I know these muffins are good. And I learned not to eat unsweetened baking chocolate. I did that once when I was a kid. Yuck. That was a bitter mouthful." He chuckled at the memory and wiped his mouth with a napkin. "Guess I better get going. Thanks for the muffin, Sophie."

"You're not staying for brunch?" I asked.

I could read his expression all too well. It was best if we didn't socialize anymore. Sad as it made me, I realized that he was right.

Wolf took the list, opened the kitchen door, and looked back. "Stay out of this, Sophie, you hear me?" He closed the door.

"Wait!" I jumped up and went after him. "Wolf! Let me see that list again." Standing just outside the door with Wolf, I scanned the names as fast as I could. When I didn't see the name I was looking for, I read through it again. "There's no Arnaud on here. He crashed the tasting."

"Good catch, Soph."

"So that kind of eliminates a planned murder, doesn't it? No one knew he would be there."

Wolf grinned at me and kissed my cheek. "Thanks for the list, Sophie."

And right behind him, Alex was crossing the street, headed for my house. His chest heaved, he closed his eyes momentarily, and he left, walking far too fast for me to catch up.

Not again. But then it dawned on me that maybe it was a good thing, because he had seen me with two different former flames. Clearly, what he had seen was meaningless. Alex would probably realize that himself when he got over being huffy. I returned to the house. "Arnaud wasn't on the guest list."

Nina's eyes were big. "That doesn't make sense. How did he know about it?"

"It was advertised everywhere. And he was staying in the same hotel as the contest winners. I'm sure they talked about it publicly. He probably went along with a group of them and no one thought anything of it. I should have insisted Randy take the tickets."

"It was one of the Meranos." She gazed at me with big eyes. "I bet Joe killed Arnaud!"

I pulled the quiche out of the oven. "Joe's entirely too nice. You know, when we realized the body was Arnaud, Mitch said that people would think the Amore family had killed the competition. I guess he was right. That was your first reaction."

I checked the time. "Shall we eat outside before it gets too hot?"

"I'm not even dressed yet." Nina flapped her hand. "Aw, who cares? No one will see me in your backyard. I'll help you carry things."

We loaded a couple of trays with food, cutlery, napkins, a tablecloth, and tea, and headed outdoors into the cool morning.

As we walked along the side of the house, Nina said, "This is the best time of the day in the summer. No humidity, not hot yet—"

She stopped walking so abruptly that I nearly smacked into her.

"There's someone out there," she hissed.

CHAPTER EIGHT

Dear Sophie,

I'm so frustrated. I'm trying to bake brownies but every time I mix the melted chocolate into the other ingredients it gets little hard specks in it. What am I doing wrong?

—Slumber Party Diva in Bakersville, Florida

Dear Slumber Party Diva,

You're probably trying to mix warm melted chocolate with ingredients that are too cold. Ice-cold ingredients will make the butter fat harden. Make sure all your other ingredients are room temperature before mixing in the warm chocolate.

—Sophie

Most people might just be surprised to find someone in their backyards, but Nina and I had been through some scary times together and had learned to be cautious.

Nina stepped to the side so I could peer around the corner
of my house. In my outdoor room, a tiny woman sat in a
lounge chair with her feet up. Nonni!

"It's okay," I said to Nina as I headed toward the covered
patio. "Good morning, Nonni!" I called.

She clapped her hands. "You bring me breakfast? Umm,
such a lovely smell."

"I hope you'll join us. We have plenty."

Nina muttered, "I'll grab another mug of tea."

I glanced around. "Is Coco with you?"

"No. I walk here."

It wasn't a long distance for me but Nonni was a good bit
older. "That's quite a walk."

Nonni smiled. "Is nothing. In Italy we walk everywhere.
Not like here. Coco takes the car two blocks. Is good to
walk. Healthy."

She was living proof of that. "Have you been here long?"

"Not too long. Is very pretty, your garden. The birds sing,
butterflies sit on flowers. I see zucchini and tomatoes growing."
She swung her legs off the chaise longue and settled at the table.

"When I come, Mitch is in your house. I decide to wait
until he is gone."

I threw the Riviera blue Provence-style tablecloth over
the table and unloaded the trays. Nina returned with tea, a
plate, and extra cutlery before I was finished.

"You didn't want Mitch to see you?" I sat down and cut
the quiche.

"Mitch is like, hmm, how you say, *gallo*."

I glanced at Nina, who shrugged.

"Is big bird on farm," said Nonni.

"Turkey?" asked Nina.

"Noooo. Like turkey but smaller. In the morning he says
chicchirichì."

"Rooster!" I guessed.

Nonni pointed at me. "Mitch is rooster." She raised her
elbows as though her arms were wings and thrust out her

chest. "Mitch makes a lot of noise and walks around like he thinks he is pretty—but he has no teeth." She laughed and then sighed. "But Mitch loves Coco. He would do anything for his Coco. Dan has made a better choice. Stella is very nice to me."

"Mitch isn't nice?" I asked, worried.

"Oh yes. But he is bossy." She pointed her finger around. "Like the rooster, always telling everybody what to do."

"How is Coco?" I asked. "Is she still upset?"

"That girl. She loves her father. Joe is a good man. When we come to America, Joe was just a little boy. We had nothing. His father and I work every day in our store. Every day! And Joe, he work with us, sweeping and learning how to make chocolate."

"You must be very proud of him."

"I am! But I worry about him."

Nonni ate her quiche with gusto. "The zucchini is from you garden?"

"It is!"

"*Delizioso!*"

"Nonni, somebody told me that Nonni means grandfather and not grandmother. He's wrong, isn't he?" asked Nina.

Nonni laughed. "Mostly Nonna is grandmother, but little Coco always call me Nonni and now everybody does."

I had a strong hunch that Nonni hadn't walked all the way to my house in the hope she might find brunch waiting for her. But I let her take her time in getting around to what she wanted.

She finished her quiche before she said, "We have big problem in family. Maybe you can help again?"

Oh boy. It would be a lot harder to turn down sweet Nonni. I leaned toward her and said very gently, "You need to hire a professional to find Joe."

She blinked hard. "My heart, it is broken. I tell myself Joe will come home. No, no. Is problem with Coco. The man who died, Arnaud Turnèbe? This is not his real name."

CHAPTER NINE

Dear Sophie,

My girlfriend and I have a bet about which country pro-
duces the finest chocolates. I say it's Germany, and she
thinks it's England. Who's right?

—Chocoholic in London, Ohio

Dear Chocoholic,

The two countries that vie for the title of best chocolate
are Belgium and Switzerland.

—Sophie

"Are you sure?" Nonni had been clear as a bell so far. But
now I had to wonder if she was confused.

"I recognize him. Coco, too."

"But his wallet. Didn't his identification say Arnaud
Turnèbe?"

Nonni shrugged. "He is Arnie Turner from England.

Many, many years ago he was in love with Coco. He left her, breaking her heart. But now he comes back! Surely out of love for Coco, but he is killed, and their love will never be."

"That's so sad!" Nina sagged in her chair. "Imagine the love of your life coming back for you after all those years. But now he's dead."

"Is tragedy," Nonni shook her head.

For a minute, I thought Nina might cry. I wasn't quite as moved. Of course, I'd had a slightly different experience with Arnie, if that was his name. Granted, he was mightily intoxicated, but I had to wonder if a man who returned to see his long-lost love would have bothered trying to pick up a stranger in a hotel.

"How do you know the dead man is Arnie?"

"He look like Arnie. Older, no more beautiful blond hair. Big belly." She smiled. "Not the pretty Adonis of his youth. But Coco isn't the slender signorina she was, either."

Nonni stretched her arm toward me and clasped my hand in hers. "For me and for Coco. You find Arnie's killer. Yes?"

"Sophie, we have to." Nina cocked her head like a puppy pleading with me.

Nonni and Nina were incurable romantics. I didn't dare tell Nonni how Arnie had acted toward me. There was no point in ruining her fond memories of him.

I didn't want to upset her more, but the odds were pretty good that a family member had offed Arnie.

I swear a mischievous twinkle came to Nonni's eyes. "The policeman, he likes you. I see it in his face."

Nina burst out laughing. "They used to date."

"He likes her cooking. This is how I won my husband. I make you a deal, Sofia. You help me find Arnie's killer and my Joe, and I teach you to make tiramisu."

How could a girl pass up an offer like that?

Nina nearly bounced out of her chair. "Yes!"

"You don't even cook," I pointed out.

Nina eyed me. "But I eat."

I made sure Nonni knew I wasn't a professional, she wasn't hiring me to do anything, and that sometimes the truth wasn't what we wanted to hear.

In the end, I agreed to do a little snooping around. Who could possibly turn down that adorable little lady?

By the time we were finished, the sun was high in the sky, and it was way too hot for her to walk home. I insisted on giving her a lift.

Before we reached Joe's house, Nonni made me stop the car.

"I walk from here."

"I can drive you right up to the house, Nonni."

She clutched my hand with cool fingers. "Is better if Coco does not see me with you."

"Does she live at Joe's house?"

"No. But she is always around—and she might be upset that I tell you the story of Arnie."

She hopped out and waved good-bye.

As I drove home, I considered the situation. It seemed to me that in order to find out who might have had a beef with Arnaud or Arnie, I should find out for sure if he even was Arnie. Nonni could very well be mistaken.

I drove home, parked the car, and trotted across the street to the house catty-corner from mine. Bernie must have seen me coming. He opened his front door before I could knock.

"To what do I owe this lovely visit?" He bowed and gestured for me to enter with a graceful swing of his arm.

"I guess you heard about Arnaud Turnèbe?"

"An ugly business, that. He seemed a decent chap. We spoke for a bit at the tasting last night. He was supposed to come by the restaurant for dinner tonight."

I followed Bernie into his kitchen.

"Iced coffee?" he asked. "I was just making some for myself."

"Sounds perfect. Bernie, I realize this will sound insane,

but when you talked with him, did you think he was Belgian?"

"Funny you should ask that. He mentioned spending a lot of time in England. Knew some of the places I like in London. I thought it was because he had a store there."

"Any chance he was really a Brit?"

Bernie ran a hand through his sandy hair, ruffling it. "You mean faking the Belgian accent?"

"I guess so. It sounded French to me."

Bernie handed me a tall glass of iced coffee and led the way to the shady side of the porch that wrapped around his house. We settled into rocking chairs, watching the world go by from a slightly elevated viewpoint. His three cats lounged on the railing.

"Arnaud used some words that Americans don't typically say. He called potato chips *crisps*, for instance. But I assumed that came from spending more time in England than in the United States."

"You were talking about potato chips?"

"He said it's all the rage to mix them into chocolate. You know, that sweet-and-salty thing that's so popular."

"Do you know anything about changing a name in England?"

"I don't recall it being a big deal. My mom went through quite a few surnames what with all her marriages."

"So Arnie could have just called himself Arnaud Turnèbe." I slumped a little bit. "How will I ever be able to confirm that?"

"Let me get this straight. You think Arnaud was British, not Belgian, and that his name was really Arnie?"

"Right."

"You could ask Wolf."

"Like he would tell me."

"He will when it's public knowledge."

I sat up straight. "You know what? I'm not sure it matters.

If Nonni and Coco think he was Arnie Turner, then other people probably did as well."

"Good point. People have been killed before because of a mistaken identity. Wonder if he has a British passport?"

I emptied my glass. "Feel like taking a walk down to Célébration de Chocolat with me? I bet some of the employees are gathering there today as they hear the news."

"You're on. Scoop up Snowball, and I'll bring in the other two pusses. I don't like to leave them outside when I'm not home."

Snowball, Bernie's long-haired white cat, stared at me with big blue eyes but didn't protest when I picked him up. In fact, I thought he might have been happy to sit on my lap and snuggle with me.

With the cats safely indoors, Bernie locked up, and we walked down the steps to the street.

Nina ran toward us from my house. "Sophie! Sophie!"

She caught up to us and bent over panting. "I've been looking everywhere for you." Her chest still heaved when she straightened up. "I think I know where Joe is!"

CHAPTER TEN

Dear Sophie,

I went to a lot of trouble to bake a German Chocolate Cake for my new mother-in-law, who is from Germany. She was very complimentary but insists that there is nothing German about German Chocolate Cake! Is she already jerking me around or is she off her rocker?

—New Bride in Germantown, Tennessee

Dear New Bride,

She isn't jerking you around, nor is she loony. It was originally called German's Chocolate Cake in honor of Sam German, who developed a dark baking chocolate. The possessive S in *German's* has been dropped, leading many to think it's a cake of German origin when it was actually the creation of Mrs. George Clay of Dallas.

—Sophie

"Now promise you won't be mad at me." Nina tilted her head.

"That's a fine way to start," I grumbled. "What did you do?"

"Remember when you sent me into Joe's house with the signs?"

I nodded.

"Well, I might have sneaked up the stairs for a little peek."

"Nina!"

"Don't get upset. Nobody saw me. Although Dan's girl-friend, Stella, nearly caught me. But maybe it was a good thing I snooped because I think they've locked up Joe!"

"Right," I said sarcastically. "Why would they lock him up?"

"I don't know *why*. I'm just saying that they have some-one locked in a room upstairs."

"You tried the doorknob to go into a room?"

"See? There you go making it sound like I did something awful when it was really quite innocent. I just wanted to peek in the bedroom. I dodged into another room when Stella walked out. But when she went downstairs, the door was locked, and I'm certain I heard someone inside."

"Maybe it was someone who was changing clothes, Dan for instance, and was saying 'go away,'" suggested Bernie.

"It wasn't like that. More like someone moving around. I didn't really think much of it at the time. I was more con-cerned about being caught, so when I heard the noise inside the room, I skedaddled back downstairs fast. I didn't give it any more thought until this morning."

I frowned at her. "But that doesn't make sense. If they know where he is, why would Coco be so upset? Why would Mitch ask me to find him?"

"Unless Coco is upset because she's afraid someone will find out," suggested Nina. "Or maybe Mitch doesn't know that Nonni locked Joe in a room."

"Nina! She's the cutest little old lady. Nonni wouldn't do

anything like that. Besides, that would mean Coco was playacting the whole time. Somehow, I doubt she's that good an actress."

Bernie squeezed one eye almost closed. "How do you know it wasn't their dog or cat? They might have locked him in for the party so no one would accidentally let him out."

"That's right! They have that beautiful Maine coon cat. I saw him after everyone left but not during the tasting. I bet that's it." I let out a big breath of air. "You had me scared for a moment!"

Nina sagged. "You're probably right. But I still think we should find a way to sneak into the house and see. Just to be sure."

Bernie pretended to knock on a door. "'Ello, Mrs. Ross. Confined Person Inspector here. I've just dropped by to see if your old dad is still locked up."

Nina wrinkled her nose at him. "All I know is that Joe is missing and something was locked in a room upstairs. Sophie can figure out some way to get inside."

"Sophie will do no such thing," I said. "We're headed over to Célébration de Chocolat. Want to come?"

Nina checked her watch. "Sure. I'm picking up a foster dog in an hour, but she's in that direction."

We walked the few blocks. A crowd gathered around the store. Above their heads, cream lettering on a dark chocolate background proclaimed *Célébration de Chocolat*.

People murmured reverently. I heard a few people ask if the store would still open. No one seemed to know.

We wiggled our way through the little crowd. I gazed through the glass door in search of an employee. Nothing moved. The interior colors were reversed. Cream walls and cases showed off an incredible selection of chocolates. Simple shelves on the walls held chocolate-shaped dogs and bunnies as well as chocolate bars in brightly colored wrappers. The most amazing part of the shop, though, was the glass cases where chocolates were displayed in a seemingly endless variety of shapes. It appeared they were ready to open the door and sell their wares.

Bernie nudged me.

I looked where he was pointing. A sign on the front window read *Monday's Grand Opening has been cancelled.*

"He died two days before he opened the shop," said Bernie.

"Kind of makes you wonder if someone wanted to prevent him from opening. A rival, perhaps . . ." whispered Nina. And then she squealed.

Still whispering, she tugged on the tail of my blouse. "Sophie! Don't those look an awful lot like the chocolates you've been getting?"

They did. A chill shuttled over me. "So the chocolates were a promotional thing after all?"

"Why didn't he label the chocolates?" asked Nina.

"Nonni and Coco must have recognized Arnie's chocolates at my house. That's what they were talking about in their kitchen yesterday. They knew he was here. They just didn't know Arnie was Arnaud."

"Looks like one of them did," said Bernie.

"How so?" asked Nina.

Bernie's eyebrows shot up. "Somebody wanted to get rid of him. One of them must have known his real identity."

I steered them away from the storefront so other people wouldn't hear us. "Someone else might have murdered him for being Arnaud, or Arnie, for that matter. We don't know that it was someone connected to Amore."

"Sophie!"

I turned to see Lori and Cheryl waving at us. We joined them, and I introduced Nina and Bernie, who immediately gushed about Cheryl's chocolate cake recipe.

"Are you having fun on your free day?" I asked.

Lori Speer quickly said, "Cheryl's cousin died."

"I had planned to attend the grand opening of Célébration de Chocolat," said Cheryl. "It was perfect timing for me to come here because the owner is a distant cousin. Now, since I'm already here, I'm the one who's been tapped to make arrangements for Arnie—Arnaud's body."

"So you knew that Arnaud was really Arnie?" Nina elbowed me.

"Oh, sure. We were second or third cousins. Our families visited a few times. I remember him as the annoying kid who tried to kiss all the girls." Her lips pulled back in disgust. "I was only in grade school. I'm sure you remember how revolting boys could be at that age."

"Apparently, he didn't change much," said Lori.

Cheryl flushed. "Arnie was a worm."

"He was your cousin!" Nina exclaimed in a scolding voice.

"Worms are usually related to someone. I'm afraid Arnie was the black sheep in the family."

"Tell them what he did," Lori egged her on.

"It's so embarrassing. He scammed everyone in my family who had two dimes. Never paid them back one penny. *Avoid Arnie* was the big joke in the family. I'm sad that he's dead—no one wanted that—but his unscrupulous behavior caught up with him in the end. The irony is that no one wants to pitch in for his final expenses! I hope he had some cash I can access."

"He probably had a will," I said. "Surely it provides for his final expenses."

"Can his company pay?" asked Bernie.

"No one knows yet. I may need to stick around after Amore quits paying the bill," said Cheryl. "The hotel is beautiful but too expensive for *my* budget."

"We checked out the Honeysuckle B and B a couple of blocks from the hotel." Lori pointed in the general direction. "It's very cute."

"So Arnaud really was Arnie?"

Cheryl nodded. "When you're a slime weasel, things catch up with you. At least that was the guess in my family.

Belgium isn't very far from England, but it must have been far enough to start fresh. They say his chocolates were fantastic."

"I don't think they could have been better than Lori's!" I said. "I could hardly tear myself away from them."

"Thank you. My family has always enjoyed them. My brother came up with the original recipe. I've just updated some of the fillings."

"Your brother is a chocolatier?" asked Bernie.

"He was." She gazed off in the distance. "Chocolates can be a pretty ruthless business. He's a school counselor now."

Cheryl regarded her with curiosity. "Why didn't *he* enter his chocolates?"

"I guess you could say the whole business left a bitter taste in his mouth. He makes them for the holidays and special occasions but just for the family. He didn't want to enter anything in the contest. But I love to travel, and I know how great his recipe is so I jumped at the opportunity."

I was still reeling from the fact that Cheryl and Arnie were related. "Cheryl, did you have a chance to talk to Arnie before he died?"

"No. More's the pity. I figured I would see him at his grand opening. Besides, I was having such a good time being wined and dined and entertained by the Merano family that I didn't think about Arnie."

"I think you might have been staying at the same hotel," I said.

"You're kidding! Gosh, talk about a small world. I wish I had known."

Nina looked at her watch. "Ack! I'm going to be late for my appointment. Nice meeting you." Nina waved as she hurried away.

"We'd better get back to the hotel. We're meeting up with some of the others," said Cheryl.

Amid a flurry of good-byes, they left Bernie and me standing on the sidewalk, watching them walk away.

"Would you have admitted to being related to Arnie?" I asked Bernie.

"You mean if I had killed him? Maybe she thinks it's better to get that fact out in the open so people won't think she has something to hide."

A good twenty yards away, Cheryl and Lori stopped walking.

Lori turned suddenly and jogged back to us. "Pretend you're writing your phone number and giving it to me." She handed me a pen and a piece of paper.

"Do you *want* my phone number?"

"Might not hurt. I really came back to tell you that, much as I like Cheryl, she's lying about not talking to Arnie earlier. There is no doubt in my mind that she had a heated exchange with Arnie in the hotel garden on Saturday morning."

CHAPTER ELEVEN

Dear Natasha,

I've noticed that a lot of chocolate cake recipes call for coffee. Doesn't that make them mocha cakes?

—Baking Diva in Coffee City, Texas

Dear Baking Diva,

You're my kind of gal. What an astute observation! Some people claim a little bit of coffee enhances the chocolate flavor without being noticed. Those of us with exceptional palates know otherwise. Thank you for asking this question and giving me the opportunity to clarify this misconception.

—Natasha

"You saw her with Arnie?" I asked, just to be clear.

"Oh yes. And whatever they were saying was not of a friendly nature. She was furious. Red as a beet. I better go before she gets suspicious." Lori wiggled her eyebrows at us. "I'll be in touch if I learn anything more." She jogged back to Cheryl.

"Think Cheryl felt that dagger twisting in her back?" asked Bernie.

"I feel kind of sorry for her. Lori's an ex-cop. Cheryl might not even realize that she's being interrogated."

A hush fell over the people nearby. Solemnly, but without making a production, Coco walked to the door of Célébration de Chocolat, followed by Randy. Coco adhered a framed picture to the glass, and Randy positioned a wreath of white roses on a stand beneath it.

"I guess that settles it," I whispered to Bernie. "Nonni's story must have been true."

Coco stood before the wreath in silence for a moment but when she turned to leave, she spotted Bernie and me. Coco motioned to Randy, and they strode our way.

"I'm so sorry, Coco. I hear you were once very close to Arnie."

She dabbed at her eyes with a tissue. "If I had only known he was in town. Well, I mean, I knew Arnaud was here, I just didn't realize that Arnaud was Arnie. How I would have loved to catch up with him. Hear how his life turned out."

"From the looks of his store and everything I've heard about him, I'd say he was very successful." I spoke in what I hoped was a comforting tone.

Randy patted her on the back. "He had a good life, Coco. Even if it was too short."

"Nonni said you were quite smitten with him," I prompted, eager to learn more about him.

"Arnie was my first true love. When he dumped me I thought my life was over. It was a good thing Daddy was tough and insisted I go back to college. Oh my. It was all so long ago."

"Speaking of your father, any word from Joe yet?"

Coco stiffened. "Is it only me, or have you ever noticed that disasters seem to arrive in bunches? I can hardly deal with all the crazy things that are happening. No. We haven't heard a word from Daddy. We have all of our phones set up with recording devices, just in case someone calls with a ransom request. Honestly, I can't imagine what happened to him." Coco clutched her tissue to her chest, shaking her head. "I'm worried about Nonni, too, bless her heart. She dotes on Daddy so. We've decided to tell her he went on a business trip. I don't know if she could take the stress of the truth."

I wondered what Nonni thought of that. Somehow I didn't think it was that easy to deceive her. "Are you certain that she doesn't know where he is?"

"Oh, honey, no one wishes that more than I! If I thought she had the first clue, I would be badgering her. He just . . . vanished in the night. One day he was there and the next morning, there wasn't a sign of him."

"You know Sophie has solved a few"—Bernie paused and flicked a desperate glance in my direction—"cases. Maybe she should come by and have a look around Joe's house?"

I sagged with relief that Bernie hadn't said *murders*. There was always hope until a body was found.

Proving that was true, Coco leaped at Bernie's offer. "Why don't you come with us now? Maybe you'll notice something that we missed."

Bernie raised his eyebrows at me. I knew what he was thinking—this was my chance to get inside and find out if Joe was locked in a room upstairs. I made a face at him. Coco would never have invited me if that were the case. Unless they drugged him. What was I thinking? The Meranos weren't the kind of people who would do something like that!

"Sure. I'd be happy to have a look around." It was highly unlikely that the police had missed anything. Still, it was a chance to go inside. Maybe we would find something helpful. We walked the few blocks to the house.

Coco opened the unlocked front door. "Dan?" she called. The four of us filed into the cool foyer, a welcome respite from the heat. The foyer and adjoining living room were painted yellow with white woodwork.

"Stella? Dan? Did anyone call while we were out?" Coco turned toward me. "We're not leaving the phones unattended just in case someone calls about Daddy."

Dan sauntered out of the kitchen, a half-eaten chicken leg in his hand. "Nobody called."

"I thought Stella was here with you."

"She went to church with Nonni. They should be back soon."

"Sophie, Daddy's room is at the top of the stairs on the left."

As I walked up the old staircase, almost every stair creaked a bit when I stepped on it. One thing was for sure. No one could sneak out of this house down these stairs without some noise.

I could hear Dan downstairs asking Coco what was going on.

Bernie was right behind me. We turned into the first room.

For a man whose home and business were worth millions, Joe's bedroom was as simple as the man himself. True, a large oriental rug spanned the floor. Mostly cream and blue in the center, with several red borders tracing the edges. But the rest of the room was somewhat simple in taste. Nothing overly ornate or extravagant.

Old-fashioned wallpaper in cream and light coffee-colored vertical stripes surrounded us. It was very subtle and worked well in the large room. A king-sized bed was neatly made with a white matelassé spread.

Next to the white marble fireplace, a comfortable club chair covered in a cream and blue plaid fabric sagged slightly from use. A matching footstool rested against it. A giant carved wardrobe stood against a long wall. A huge mirror in the middle of it reflected us. On each side of the mirror were carved doors and drawers. A carved cornice swept across the top in a delicate arch.

A long colonial-style mahogany dresser with brass drawer pulls filled a niche near the door.

I perused the reading material on the small table by the chair—the latest thriller, a book on managing a family-owned business, and Winston Churchill's memoirs. I picked up the book on family-owned businesses and thumbed through it. No notes, nothing underlined.

It did fall open to a chapter on continuity through generations. That wasn't terribly surprising. Joe had to be around seventy. I could well imagine that he was concerned about retirement and who might take over at the helm of Amore. I closed the book and dared to peer inside the immense wardrobe.

Suits hung in an orderly fashion. I checked the pockets but found nothing. On the bottom, shoes lined up like little soldiers. Joe was an organized man. That came as no surprise. It fit with the image he projected.

I wandered over to the dresser. A small tray with brass corners sat on the top, empty. "Bernie, where do you keep your wallet?"

"In my back pocket." He walked over to me. "Ah. You mean when I'm at home. I have a similar valet in my bedroom where I place it."

I pulled open each of the top drawers one after the other. Each was dedicated to a type of clothing. Dress socks, boxers, sport-style socks, and the last one contained a number of lotions, combs, and brushes. I felt a little bit guilty going through his drawers. Poor Joe. He probably never imagined that someone would poke through them. But in the bottom right drawer, underneath neatly folded sweaters, I found a picture.

Creased in the middle, it showed signs of age. The hopeful face of a girl stared back at me. Around twelve years old if I had to guess.

Bernie peered over my shoulder. "Coco when she was a kid?"

"Probably." She wore her dark hair straight and long and

grinned with enthusiasm. "Why would he keep this in the bottom of a drawer?"

"He probably just stashed it there and forgot about it."

"I don't think so, Bernie. Look at the edges. Someone has handled this picture a lot over the years." I tucked the photo away where I had found it.

Bernie and I performed a quick scan of the remaining drawers. All of them were as immaculate and tidy as the rest of the room. No sign of a wallet, though.

"Looks like he has his wallet with him." I said heading for the bathroom.

Bernie frowned. "What does that mean? That he left intentionally with someone he thought was a friend?"

"Or that he never made it back up here that night and still had his wallet in his pocket."

Beautifully updated in white marble, the bathroom yielded nothing of interest. His toothbrush and toothpaste were even there, reinforcing the belief that he hadn't intended or planned to leave.

"Suppose he has a home office?" asked Bernie.

"In a house this size? I think we can count on it."

Bernie followed me into the upstairs hallway. "Think that's the door Nina tried?" he murmured.

A quick glance around confirmed that it was the only closed door. The rest were wide open. "Probably."

We tiptoed along the corridor. I looked back at Bernie. "Why do I feel so guilty? Like this is wrong?" I whispered.

"What if Nina is right, and they've locked Joe up?"

"I hardly think they would have invited us to come look around if that were the case."

"Just try the door handle," he hissed.

I grasped it in my hand and turned it down. A soft moan issued from the room. There was no mistaking the hollow sound of footsteps on a hardwood floor.

CHAPTER TWELVE

Dear Sophie,

I see the prettiest shaved chocolate curls decorating cakes. How can I do that at home?

—Loves to Bake in Shaver Town, Tennessee

Dear Loves to Bake,

It's so simple you won't believe you didn't think of it. Use a vegetable peeler!

—Sophie

Bernie seized my hand and pulled. The two of us stumbled toward the stairs in haste and clattered down them like naughty children—right into Mitch.

"Find anything of interest?" he asked.

I sought something, anything, to say. "Joe certainly is a tidy man."

Evidently my response caught Mitch off guard. He studied me, as if he was thinking. "Yes. Yes, he is."

Bernie choked out, "Does he have a home study? A place where he might have kept papers or documents?"

Mitch nodded. "Sure. Follow me."

He led us into a magnificent library. Three walls were paneled in fine cherrywood. The fourth wall featured floor-to-ceiling windows, trimmed in the same cherrywood.

A giant rolltop desk brimmed with tiny drawers that could hide a million little items. Family photos cluttered the top. Most of them were candid shots of Coco and Dan with their dad or Nonni. One professional photo stood out in an elaborate gold frame. A stunning woman with hair the color of espresso teased into a large fluff, 1960s-style, posed in a beaded gown with pearls around the base of her neck.

"That's Coco and Dan's mom," offered Mitch.

"I see them in her face. She looks very kind, doesn't she?"

"It's her eyes and the soft angles of her face. You take the right side of the desk," said Bernie, "and I'll take the left."

"What are you looking for?" asked Mitch.

"Anything that might tell us where he is. A calendar or date book. A note from someone. Who knows?"

"You should come by the office tomorrow. You could have a look around his desk there, too."

I glanced back at Mitch. He was serious. He seemed genuinely worried about Joe.

Half an hour later, we knew where Joe kept paper clips, pens, pencils, envelopes, stamps, staples, and every other kind of office item imaginable. But we weren't any closer to understanding what had happened to him.

We found Coco and Randy at the kitchen table, nibbling on leftover cake from the tasting. Coco wiped a crumb from the corner of her mouth. "Well? Did you find anything?"

"Have a seat," offered Dan. "Coffee?" He poured coffee into two gorgeous mugs without waiting for our response.

When he brought them to the table, I admired the artistry of the mugs. They had to be handmade and hand-painted. They were shaped like a classic tulip mug, and a rich blue covered the middle. Hearts that looked more like abstract wheat and berries had been painted on the blue. Above and below, ornate rings of lighter blues, reds, and deep yellows circled the mugs. Yellow covered the rims and the rich blue accented the handles.

"They're from Deruta in Umbria," said Dan.

"They're beautiful." I wanted a set of my own but these weren't the kind of thing I was likely to see at a garage sale.

Dan placed matching plates in front of us. "There's a ton of leftovers from the tasting. Please help yourselves. So do you have any ideas about what happened to Dad?"

I sipped the strong coffee. "I'd like to ask you a few questions if you don't mind.

Mitch ambled into the kitchen. "Randy, what are you doing here?"

Coco flicked a worried look at Randy. "He was helping me place a wreath over at Célébration de Chocolat. Okay?"

Mitch appeared chastened. "Good idea, Coco. I should have thought of that. I hope it bore the Amore name somewhere."

"Honestly, Mitch! It's not about the business. It was the right thing to do. Arnie was very dear to me."

"Of course. I forgot. In that case, you're free to go, Randy."

"He can stay for coffee and cake!" Coco said it softly.

"I didn't mean it that way. I just didn't want him to think he had to stick around. He has a life, too, Coco."

Randy hadn't said a word. He didn't seem to be disturbed, which made me wonder if this wasn't the first time that he'd heard this kind of conversation.

"What do you need to know?" asked Dan.

Although there were plenty of chairs around the table, Mitch leaned against the island, his arms folded over his chest.

"After the welcome dinner at the hotel, where did Joe go?"

"Home," said Coco. "With Nonni."

I started with Dan. "Where did you go?"

"I walked Stella to her place, and then I went home."

"Where is your home?"

"I have a house on Lee Street. Stella rents an apartment on North Union, a couple of blocks from me."

"When is the last time you saw your father?"

"When we left the hotel. We said good night, and I never saw him again after that."

"How about you, Coco?" I asked.

"Coco and I walked home together," said Mitch.

Coco stuffed chocolate cake into her mouth.

"I don't know where you live. Did you walk back with Joe?"

"No. We went straight home. Right, Coco? We have alibis because we were together all night."

She swallowed and nodded.

Alibis? Wasn't that interesting? Would I have been worried about an alibi if my father or father-in-law disappeared? I didn't think so. I studied their faces. Coco avoided my eyes and ate a piece of cake big enough to choke a horse. Mitch had no problem meeting my gaze. Yet I knew that one or both of them were lying. I had seen Coco out and about that night.

I faced Mitch. "Why would you need an alibi?"

Once again my question appeared to surprise him. "Well, something bad must have happened to him. It's not at all like Joe to just take off without telling anyone."

He was probably right about that. "So we don't really know if Joe ever came home," I speculated.

"Yes, we do. He came home with Nonni," said Dan.

"Didn't she hear anyone come to the door? Didn't she see Joe leave?" asked Bernie.

Mitch sucked in air and rubbed his forehead. "Nonni isn't all there anymore."

Coco was a little kinder about it. "Once she removes her hearing aid and goes to bed, it takes a pretty loud noise to wake her."

"If Nonni is confused, then how do we know for sure that they arrived home together?"

Much to my surprise, Coco looked at Mitch for an answer. Something strange was going on in this household.

Mitch was quick with an answer. "Nonni couldn't find her way home by herself."

That was odd. She'd had no trouble finding her way to my house.

"And none of the furniture was out of place? No sign of a scuffle?"

Coco shook her head. "Nothing." She buried her head in her hands.

"Does anyone else live here? Is there a housekeeper?"

"A cleaning woman comes a couple of times a week but she doesn't live here," said Mitch.

I was itching to ask about the person in the locked room. Maybe that was better done one-on-one. I sensed some tension between them.

Bernie set his coffee mug on the table. "Does Joe have any enemies? Anyone he ticked off?"

"Absolutely not," said Coco. "Ask anybody. Daddy is loved and respected by everyone. You can come by the office tomorrow and talk to some employees if you want."

"You're welcome to stop by, of course," said Mitch, "but we haven't told the employees that Joe is missing."

Randy, who hadn't said a word, finally piped up. "I imagine they'll find out when the cops come by tomorrow morning to question them about the dead Belgian guy."

Dan nodded. "I guess we'd better tell everyone first thing tomorrow morning."

Mitch stiffened. "I don't know what to tell them."

It wasn't like we had much to go on. I had come to two conclusions, neither of which I would have dared say in front of Mitch. Something odd was going on in the Merano family. Some of them, especially Coco and Mitch, knew more than they were saying, but I would have to speak with Coco alone to get answers. "The only thing I know is that he took his wallet with him. Either he planned to go somewhere, maybe had an appointment to meet someone, or someone came here before he had a chance to go upstairs and empty his pockets."

"An appointment," mused Mitch. "Of course. Why didn't I think of that?"

"I didn't see a cell phone anywhere. Have the police tried pinging it?" I asked.

Mitch piped up. "We're told it's not pinging. The battery probably went dead."

Bernie and I thanked them for the coffee and cake, and Coco walked us to the door. I itched to ask her a few questions but Mitch caught up to us.

"Thank you for changing your mind, Sophie. We all appreciate it."

Bernie and I headed for home. He peeled off to check in at his restaurant, The Laughing Hound. I walked the few blocks home by myself, wondering if there could possibly be a connection between Joe's disappearance and Arnaud's murder.

I wasn't quite to my house yet when I saw Wolf banging the knocker on my front door. I called his name and waved. But the closer I came, the more I realized something was wrong. Wolf was an ace at hiding his emotions. I hadn't seen him so upset in years.

CHAPTER THIRTEEN

Dear Natasha,

What is a Devil's Food Cake and how does it differ from other chocolate cakes?

—New Wife in Devil's Lake, North Dakota

Dear New Wife,

Alas, the distinction has been largely lost. Devil's Food Cake is a very dark color with a deep chocolate taste. It's generally made with boiling water instead of milk, which makes it moist and airy without diluting the chocolate. But other cakes are made in a similar manner today, as well. You will find that recipes vary widely.

—Natasha

"What's wrong?" I unlocked the door.

Wolf and I stepped inside. The air was blissfully cool after my walk in the summer heat.

Wolf followed me into the kitchen. "Iced tea or lemonade?" I asked.

"This isn't a social call." His lips pulled tight. "Okay, lemonade."

I poured two tall drinks over ice, and we sat down.

"When did you meet Arnaud?"

I felt as though I was being grilled. "Thursday night at the hotel."

"What did you say to him?"

"Not much. He was staggering drunk. Loaded."

"Did you go up to his room?"

I burst out laughing. "No! Not that it would be any of your business if I had."

Not even a hint of a smile touched Wolf's face. "Arnaud was murdered. Everything he did is my business. You never met him before Thursday? Are you certain?"

What strange questions. I thought for a minute and responded with great caution because I didn't know what Wolf was getting at. "I suppose it's possible that I passed him on the street or met him briefly at an event and don't remember."

"Did anyone see you leave the hotel that night? Someone who could confirm the time?"

I inhaled sharply as the implication became clear to me. "You think I went up to his room and slept with him. Eww! In the first place, I am not in the habit of falling into bed with strangers. And in the second place, I'm not so desperate that I have to seek out someone who is stone drunk and doesn't know what he's doing."

Wolf gazed at me. "You were overheard telling him to go up to his room, and you would join him."

I laughed with relief. "Oh, that. No big deal. I do it with intoxicated men all the time to get rid of them. I don't go up to their rooms. I thought he was one of the Amore contest winners. I can't be rude to them, even when they're out of line. I figured he'd go up to his room and sleep it off." It was my turn to be miffed. "You know me better than that."

Wolf seemed a little sheepish. "Did anyone see you leave the hotel?"

"Did anyone see me go up to his room?" Hah! They couldn't have.

"Sophie! Answer the question."

"Some of the contest winners were talking in the lobby when I left. I have no idea whether they watched me exit. Does the hotel have a camera on the front door? Maybe that would confirm the time of my departure."

Wolf nodded. He bit his upper lip.

Now what was wrong? "Oh no! They've already erased the tapes, haven't they? Why would I be a suspect? I barely knew the guy. And let me just say that I'm more than a little bit offended that you would even think I would jump into bed with the first revolting drunk who happened by."

Wolf leaned forward, rubbing his palms. "They wanted me to bring you in for questioning. I'm doing you a favor by talking to you personally, Sophie." Wolf turned anguished eyes toward me. "There's something else."

Oh joy. "I didn't kill him. I didn't know him. I didn't even know who he was until Mitch looked in his wallet."

"Then why did he send you chocolates?"

"You mean the mystery chocolates? I honestly don't know. How do you know they were from Arnaud? There wasn't a name or a note."

"Coco recognized them when she tasted one. I think it's kind of farfetched, but I'm told people can tell the difference between brands of chocolate."

"Of course they can. I understand that. So she knew they were Arnaud's?"

"Not exactly. It's kind of a long story. She thought they were made by a guy named Arnie."

"The Arnie who became Arnaud."

He blinked at me, completely poker-faced until he laughed. "That's the Sophie I know. Always sticking her nose into murder investigations."

"Let me get this straight. So when Coco tasted the chocolate, she thought Arnie had made it."

"Right. She thought he must be somewhere in town but didn't connect Arnie to the Belgian chocolatier, Arnaud."

"Why would he send me chocolates?"

"That's my question. You can see why it might appear that you knew him. The guy was sending you chocolates, and you were overheard telling him to go up to his room in the hotel, and you would be there in a few minutes."

I understood what the police had cobbled together to point a finger at me. "Except I did not go to his room. I only said that to get rid of the guy. *And* I didn't have a clue that the chocolates were from him. I didn't even eat one because I had no idea where they came from. You can ask anyone. Nina! Ask Nina. She wanted to try them but I wouldn't let her."

"I hope she backs you up."

"She will. Just ask her if she tried one of the mysterious chocolates."

"Assuming she backs you up, then it would still beg the question, why was he sending you chocolates?"

"Allow me to point out that this seems like a big assumption. Maybe they came from Arnie and maybe not! I honestly don't know why he would send me chocolates. He didn't say a thing about it in the few minutes that I spoke to him."

"Were you involved in the grand opening of his store?"

"Nope. Wolf, you know me well enough to believe me. If I had *any* kind of contact with him, I would tell you so, whether it was business or"—I wrinkled my nose—"embarrassingly sleazy."

~~~~~

Wolf didn't apologize before he left. I knew he was only doing his job and there was no question that I should be grateful he didn't drag me down to the police station to be hammered with offensive questions. Yet it disturbed me that

the man I had dated for so many years could think for even
a moment that I might have behaved in such a coarse
manner.

Weeding was not one of my favorite things, but I was
unsettled enough to want to yank out the pokeweed plant
that had settled in my vegetable garden. I changed into old
shorts, a comfy T-shirt that had seen better days, and flow-
ered garden clogs. Pulling on gloves, I marched outside and
was merciless on the invaders, all the while thinking of Wolf
and Arnaud.

"Is that pokeweed?" asked a gentle voice.

I whipped around. When my backyard had been updated,
a gate was installed between my yard and my neighbor's.
Francie Vanderhoosen wasn't quite as old as Nonni, but she
had lived in Old Town almost as long. A devoted bird-
watcher and gardener, Francie had spent much of her life in
the sun and had the wrinkles to show it.

"Yes. I believe it is."

She *tsk*ed at me. "Birds love those berries."

"Help yourself. It has no business in my garden."

"You're testy today." Francie settled on a bench in the
shade. Her overprocessed blonde hair stuck out like straw.
"Wouldn't have anything to do with that visit from Wolf,
would it?" She chuckled at my surprise. "He asked me if I
had seen you. I hear you're knee-deep in the murder of that
chocolate guy."

I loosened the soil around a dandelion so I could pull it
out with the root. "Apparently so. How well do you know
the Meranos?"

"You think one of them killed him?" She pondered for
a bit. "I don't know. One would think that people who went
through a big tragedy like that would value life and not be
inclined to murder. On the other hand, it could also throw
a person out of kilter altogether."

She had my attention now. I tossed the dandelion into my
trashcan. "What tragedy?"

"Must have been thirty or so years ago. It was winter. The roads were icy, and Joe's father lost control of the car in the dark. He died instantly. I think Joe's wife lingered for a while. It was crushing. You can imagine."

I sat down next to her. "Coco must have been about twenty. Oh, that's awful. Gosh, how do you ever get past something like that and move on with life? Did you know them well?"

Francie fanned herself. "Just to say hello. Amore was where I bought hostess gifts and the occasional birthday present. Everyone did. It rocked the town pretty hard. Nonni moved in with Joe to help with the kids. His son wasn't even out of high school."

"At their party, Natasha was musing that the people who live in a house like that must have perfect lives. Just goes to show that we never know what's going on behind the front door."

Francie laughed. "Oh, honey. That's always been true. You never know what heartache lies behind closed doors."

"You didn't come to the chocolate tasting." It was more of a question than a statement.

"Meh. Four hundred people all reaching for chocolate and no place to sit. Besides"—there was a twinkle in her eyes—"I have this neighbor who likes to bake, and I'm hoping chocolate cake will be on the menu soon."

"You must mean Natasha," I teased.

"Perish the thought! That girl could ruin a decent chocolate cake in a dozen different ways."

"Mars hates her cooking, too. Funny that the people who watch her show seem to like it."

"Someone made her chocolate chip cookies and brought them to the garden club meeting last week. They had chunks of bacon in them! You should have seen everyone raving about them. Yuck. Contrary to popular belief, bacon does not improve everything."

"How about coming to dinner tomorrow night? I'll grill

something, and we can sit out here and enjoy the summer
night."

"Sounds good." Francie stood up. "What can I bring?"

I didn't even hesitate. Francie had great connections.
"Gossip about Arnaud and the Meranos."

She raised an eyebrow. "Is there a chocolate cake at
stake?"

"There is."

"Then you got it, baby!"

I watched her toddle back to the gate. She would hate
knowing how cute I thought she was. I put away my garden-
ing items, and after a quick shower, slid into a cool azure
cotton sheath and white sandals. Now that I had calmed
down, it was time to do a little snooping of my own. But I
needed something to use as a bribe. Well, not a bribe so
much as an inducement.

I opened the freezer and studied the contents. Hmm, the
frozen cupcakes would be thawed and ready to eat by the
time I got there, but they wouldn't smell quite as tempting
as warm chocolate chip cookies. Especially to a guy who
was probably hanging out in a cold basement.

CHAPTER FOURTEEN

Dear Sophie,

I like chocolate chip cookies that are soft on the inside. My mother-in-law says the trick is to lower the heat and bake them longer. I don't believe her.

—Cookie Monster in Soft Maple, New York

Dear Cookie Monster,

I tried baking the same raw chocolate chip cookie dough at 325 degrees, 350 degrees, and 375 degrees. The only difference was how long they took to bake. At 350, they required 12 minutes, at 325, they needed 14 minutes, and at 375, they took only 10 minutes. When cool, my expert taste testers, including Nina Reid Norwood, could not tell any difference between the cookies. And neither could I.

—Sophie

Warm chocolate chip cookies in hand, I strolled over to the hotel where the recipe contest winners had stayed. I'd had enough functions and events there to know my way around pretty well. I strode through the lobby, pushed open a door marked *Employees Only*, and trotted down the stairs to the basement.

As I expected, Jack Houser read a newspaper, relaxing in a chair with his feet up on his desk. Not exactly what a security guard ought to be doing. Balding, portly, and always slightly flushed, Jack was a decent sort who mingled with guests comfortably. Most of them hadn't a clue that he was the house detective.

I rapped on the door as a formality. "Hi, Jack."

His feet thumped down onto the concrete floor. "Sophie!" He sounded relieved. "Come on in."

"Thanks." I settled into the pretend leather chair across the desk from him, the basket of cookies on my lap. "You had a guest named Arnaud Turnèbe staying here recently—"

"Not him again. What now?"

"Oh? Did you have trouble with him?"

"Not really. Wolf came by to ask some questions about him. The guy was a lush. He stumbled around and said inappropriate things to women. That kind of baloney. What is that I smell? Cookies?"

"Was anyone seduced by his come-ons?"

"Besides you?" Jack sat back and laughed.

I didn't even crack a smile. "That's not funny."

"I wouldn't know who else."

"Since when? You always keep an eye on who's doing what. I've seen you in action. I've heard you talking with the other security guys." I leaned toward the desk and set my little basket of cookies on it. "Why don't you check the list in your desk that you keep just in case someone claims the housekeeper stole their stuff when it was really strangers that they took up to their rooms?"

His nose twitched. "Chocolate?"

"Warm and gooey chocolate chip, fresh from the oven."

"You drive a hard bargain." But he laughed, and I could tell he didn't mind sharing his information with me. "I don't have to look. Cheryl Maiorca, also a guest at the hotel, seemed put out with him, so maybe he stole from her, but she was too embarrassed to report it. The one that worried me the most was the blonde."

"Lori Speer?" The former cop whose brother had been a chocolatier?

Jack frowned at me. "Know about her, huh? She pegged me right away and told me she had been a cop. She's a wild one, for sure. We noticed that she kept her eye on our buddy, Arnaud. But it was the other blonde that I was watching."

"Who?"

"Don't know. She wasn't a guest of the hotel. Never engaged Arnaud in conversation that I saw, but we spotted her watching him more than once. Didn't look like a hooker. She wore high heels like one, but so does my daughter. She's gonna break her ankle one of these days. Calls it fashion."

"Age?"

"Seventeen. They think they know everything. Oh! You mean the blonde. Late twenties. Long, straight hair. Pretty as can be. Never saw her smile, though. Not even once."

It could have been any of a thousand women. Of ten thousand women! But I had a feeling it might have been Stella, Dan's girlfriend. "Did she go up to his room with him?"

"Got in the elevator with him. What happened from there, well, I couldn't say."

I scooted the cookies to the middle of the desk and folded back the blue gingham napkin that covered them. The heavenly scent infused the air in the small office.

"I don't know what you're up to, Sophie Winston, but you take care. Hear? I wouldn't want anything to happen to someone who brings me warm chocolate chip cookies." Jack bit into one, and as I left, I heard him grunt, *um-hmm*.

I left thinking about Stella. She seemed so young and sweet that I hadn't given her much thought. Why would she be interested in Arnaud? Could she be a chocolatier groupie? I chuckled at the thought. Did she work in the chocolate business? I must know someone who could tell me more about her. Bernie. Everyone went to his restaurant, The Laughing Hound, sooner or later. I walked the two blocks to the restaurant.

They were doing a brisk business. The outdoor patio was packed. Fewer people lingered in the bar. I asked the bartender if Bernie was around.

He pushed open a swinging door to the kitchen. "Bernie? Someone to see you."

Bernie emerged and smiled at me. "I'm glad it's you and not someone complaining about the food or service."

"Aw, c'mon. I eat here all the time. I bet you don't get many complaints."

"Even one is too many. What's up?"

"Do you know Stella, the woman who dates Dan Merano?"

The bartender overheard my question and drew closer. "I do. Is Stella in some kind of trouble?"

"No, nothing like that. How do you know her?"

"We used to work together at the Amore store. I think she manages it now."

I nodded but didn't tell him how interesting I thought that was. "Do you know where she's from?"

He flicked a glance at Bernie. "Maryland, I think. Or was it Kansas? I'm not sure anymore. All I remember is that her grandmother passed away while we worked together. It was really hard on her because her grandmother raised her. She never knew her parents. They died when she was a baby."

"That's so sad. Poor Stella."

"Did she have siblings?" asked Bernie.

"I'm not sure. I don't remember her saying anything about them. She's really nice, though. Always willing to fill in for somebody or to swap shifts."

"Was she dating Dan then?"

"They probably met there. Dan's a cool guy. He was

always bringing in new flavors for us to try. He always said, 'You can't sell them if you don't know how they taste.'"

I wasn't quite sure how to phrase my next question without sounding very odd. "Did she have a thing for chocolate? Or guys who liked chocolate?"

Thankfully, the bartender laughed. "Nothing weird if that's what you mean. She was a workaholic and really took an interest in the details of making chocolate. Me, I just liked to eat it. But you know, when it's in front of you every day, it loses some of the attraction." He excused himself and strode away to take a drink order.

Bernie walked me out to the sidewalk. "What was that all about?"

"Someone who fits Stella's description was watching Arnaud at the hotel. It's not definite that it was Stella, though. Could have been any beautiful blonde about her age."

Bernie nodded. "Worth following up on."

"Francie is coming to dinner tomorrow night, want to join us?"

"I'll bring the appetizer."

"Deal." I kissed his cheek and headed for home.

I could hear a cat rowling a loud complaint before I reached my block. The wail grew louder as I walked. And there, at my front door, sat my sweet Mochie, protesting at the top of his lungs.

"Mochie!"

He turned his head and ran to me, complaining.

"What happened? Why are you outside?"

He mewed nonstop, as though he was explaining. I picked him up.

Mochie clung to my shoulder, still mewing. He butted his head up against my cheek, letting me know he was glad I was home.

I tried the side door. It was locked. I pulled out my key, inserted it, and swung the door open.

CHAPTER FIFTEEN

Dear Natasha,

I know I'm supposed to melt chocolate in a double boiler, but I end up with a grainy mess every time. I don't understand what I'm doing wrong!

— Inept Chocolatier in Double Trouble, New Jersey

Dear Inept Chocolatier,

Water and steam make chocolate seize. It's possible that your double boiler isn't the right shape. Use a bowl that's larger than the bottom pot, preferably with sides that slant outward. When melting chocolate over a double boiler, wipe the water off the bottom of the top bowl as soon as you remove it so the water won't drip into your chocolate or other ingredients.

— Natasha

"Mars? Natasha?" I shouted. They had a key and were known to let themselves in. Mars would never let Mochie out but Natasha might.

At first glance, everything seemed normal. I tried to unglue Mochie from my shoulder. Nothing doing. He sank his claws into the fabric of my dress.

Leaving the door open in case I wanted to beat a hasty retreat, I peered into the foyer. The closet door wasn't completely closed. I could have left it that way but I usually closed it. I debated calling for help. 911 seemed kind of silly, though. They had real emergencies to tend to. I stood still and listened for a moment. The house was blissfully quiet. Maybe I was overreacting.

I lifted the wall phone and called Mars. If he was home, he could come over in a jiffy. Luck was with me.

Three minutes later, Daisy bounded into my kitchen, and Mars followed. "What's up? You sounded so worried."

I patted Daisy and told Mars about finding Mochie outside.

"That's not like you at all. Have you looked through the house yet?"

"I was waiting for you."

"Okay." He lifted a cleaver out of my knife block.

I made a face at him.

"What? We need a weapon. Where's the Taser I gave you?"

"In the console by the front door." Mars pulled the drawer open and found it. "Okay. Let's see what's going on."

With Mochie still clinging to my shoulder, I ventured into the dining room and living room, which appeared perfectly normal. In my little home office, a light was on. I didn't think I had left it on but that was the sort of thing that one easily forgets.

Mars led the way into the sunroom. "Looks okay in here, but the door's not locked."

"I came in from the garden that way earlier. I guess it's possible that I left the door unlocked." It wasn't like me, but at the moment, I was embarrassed. "Thanks for coming over, I feel pretty foolish." I unsnagged Mochie's claws and set him on the love seat.

He looked up at me and yowled again, ruining my moment of calm.

"Mars," I said, looking around, "that door might have been unlocked but it was closed. How did Mochie get out?"

We trudged upstairs, Mochie clinging to my shoulder again. We didn't find anything out of place. We even checked out the basement.

When we were done and back in the kitchen, Mars sighed. "Sorry, Soph. Either you're getting forgetful or Mochie has figured out how to open doors."

"He can open cabinets and drawers, but I really don't think he's figured out doors. Besides, can't you see how upset he is?"

"Soph, did you notice anything missing? I didn't."

He had a point. "Could it have been Natasha? You know how she loves to let herself in."

Mars groaned. "What's next from her? Soph, I swear it's one calamity after another. She gets so focused on something that she just can't see anything else. She's not like you, Soph."

"Yeah, well, I *hope* I'm not like Natasha. If I ever am, you better straighten me out."

"I'll leave Daisy with you. If anyone comes around, she might alert you. Maybe I should stay over for a few nights. Just to keep an eye on things."

I burst out laughing. "Mars, are you that eager to get away from Natasha?"

He frowned at me, not at all amused.

"Oh my gosh. If it's that bad, you know you're always welcome to stay here. I'm sure Bernie would be happy to have you, too."

"No, she's just driving me nuts with her latest project. She wants to make her own chocolate."

"What's wrong with that?"

"I don't think you understand. She doesn't mean melting chocolate and pouring it into molds. She wants to buy the raw chocolate beans and process them herself to create her own personal line of chocolate."

"Doesn't that require major machinery?"

"See? You have a brain! Yes, they have to be roasted, then a machine has to break out the centers, and then they have to be ground. It's a major process."

"I feel kind of sorry for her."

Mars glared at me.

"All she wants is to be successful at something, but everything she tries is so big and weird that she never succeeds. That must be hard on her. It's one failure after another."

"You're feeling sorry for the wrong person," Mars grumbled. "I'm going home to ask her if she came over here. It would put both our minds at ease if we knew it was Natasha who thoughtlessly locked Mochie out."

He left by the front door, and I checked my e-mail. I had just finished when Daisy howled.

"Do you hear something?" I listened for a siren.

Daisy ran to the front door and barked. Had my intruder returned? I picked up the Taser, just in case, and latched a leash on Daisy so she wouldn't run outside the second I opened the door.

Cautiously, I swung it open. I didn't see anyone but I heard shouting, and Daisy leaped with such force that the leash tore out of my hand. I ran after her. She didn't go far. She ran across the street and straight to Mars's house.

When I caught up to her, she was kissing Mars's face. He lay on his back, sprawled on the brick landing at the top of the stairs just outside his front door. One of his legs was bent at an unnatural angle, like a broken doll. Gold bathroom fixtures lay around him.

"Mars!" I kneeled beside him. "Daisy, sweetie, back up." I gently pushed her aside. "Are you okay?"

"No! A box of something fell out of the air."

The front door opened. Natasha held her hands over her mouth, aghast. "Mars! Can you ever forgive me?" She bent over him and sobbed.

"Did you call an ambulance?" I asked.

Natasha looked at me wide-eyed. "I'm sure it's not that bad. You're not bleeding. Are you in pain, Mars?"

"Ow, don't touch me."

"I think you'd better call for help, Natasha."

The second she went into the house, Mars grabbed the neckline of my dress and pulled me toward him. "Come with me to the hospital. I can't take Natasha's drama."

It would have been cruel to remind him that *he* chose to live with Natasha. "I don't think that's going to happen. I promise I'll take Daisy home and drive over as fast as I can."

Natasha reappeared. "They're on the way."

"What happened?" I asked.

Natasha swallowed hard. "I can't stand having gold fixtures in the bathrooms. They're so outdated. I have an image to maintain. I was taking them out and the box was just too heavy to carry down the stairs, so I . . . I pitched it out of the window."

Mars growled, "Are you insane? You could have killed me!"

"I thought you were downstairs in your office!"

"Didn't we talk about that anyway? Didn't we agree that gold would do just fine? I hate it when you replace perfectly serviceable items."

"Well, you're just wrong about that," Natasha snarled back. "I can't live with them anymore. They're embarrassing!"

I was enormously relieved when the ambulance arrived and the squabbling stopped. I kept my word to Mars, though. After taking Daisy home, I drove to the hospital.

Fortunately, he had a simple fracture. The doctor put a cast on his leg, recommended bed rest with an elevated foot, and sent him home.

It was nine o'clock in the evening when I left Mars under the dubious care of Natasha.

The last I saw of them, he was negotiating the stairs on crutches.

I took Daisy out for a walk. The air had turned lovely, like the gentle kiss of a summer night. It soothed me after the commotion with Mars.

Nina was outside with a darling puppy, who sniffed my feet, her little tail wagging nonstop. I crouched to pet her and immediately received puppy kisses. "Who is this?"

"Truffles. Isn't that the cutest name? She's a *chocolate* Lab."

"She's adorable. You better not get too attached. Someone will adopt this little cutie right away."

"I must be getting too old to deal with a puppy. She slept for a couple of hours and now she's like a little tornado."

"Why don't you walk with us? Maybe it will help wear her out."

I told Nina about Mars's accident and about finding Mochie outside. "When I left just now, I made doubly sure that all of the doors were locked. It's the oddest thing."

"You didn't call Wolf?"

"Nothing was missing. The only explanation is that Natasha was snooping around again." I groaned. "What with Mars breaking his leg, I forgot to ask her!"

"Does Alex have a key?"

"No."

"Really?" She had a gleam in her eye.

"We're not there yet in our relationship, okay?" And the way things were going, there was a good chance we would never get to the point of exchanging keys.

"Look," said Nina, "Truffles is already following Daisy's lead. I should have thought of that right away. Maybe she should stay with you so Daisy can housebreak her."

"Good try, Nina."

We ambled along the brick sidewalks, admiring the colonial-style outdoor lights on the homes. At one narrow beige house, a Maine coon cat sat by a burgundy front door, much like Mochie had waited by my door to be let in.

The cat watched our two dogs walk by without much concern, but Truffles was eager to meet the cat. The puppy wagged her tail and tugged to the left to get a close-up look.

The cat grumbled but didn't budge.

I unwound as we walked. The last couple of days had been stressful. I hadn't even known Arnaud. If my nerves were strained, I couldn't imagine what Coco must be going through.

Nina chattered about Truffles and all the adorable things she had done. And then without any warning, she asked, "Do you think the person who murdered Arnaud also killed Joe Merano?"

I stopped walking for a moment. "It seems like there would be a connection, doesn't it? I hope not. But the Meranos appear to be knee-deep in this."

"Could just be a chocolate-hater. Or someone who is allergic to chocolate."

The dogs tugged ahead. "They're killing people who make great chocolates? Don't you think that would be over-reacting?" I asked.

"They're in the same business. What if it's someone who worked for both of them? Like Lori Speer's brother."

"Because he's the only other chocolatier you've heard of? Besides, would she have had the moxie to come to the Amore celebration if that were the case?"

"Maybe she didn't know her brother intended to kill them," suggested Nina. "Or maybe she was in on it and helped him."

"But why would she stick around? Why wouldn't she get out of town as fast as she could?"

"That would draw attention to her."

I couldn't help laughing. "I hope you never turn to a life of crime. I fear you might be very good at it!"

By the time we circled back to our block, energetic little Truffles had slowed considerably. I had a feeling that Nina might get some sleep that night in spite of her darling companion.

～❦～

The next morning, I woke to the sound of a text jingling on my phone.

Daisy cocked her head at the phone.

I rolled over and flicked it on. A text said, *Bring food. I beg of you!*

Mars was alive and well, if hungry. I texted back, *Okay.*

But I took the time to shower and dress first. I had a feeling it was going to be a scorcher. By the time I walked downstairs in a skirt with an abstract azure and white print and a sleeveless blouse of the same blue, Nina was at my kitchen door.

I unlocked it, and Truffles bounded in so fast that she couldn't stop and slid to a halt at Daisy's feet.

"No coffee yet?"

"Coming right up. Scrambled eggs and fruit salad?" I filled the kettle with water for French press coffee and spooned a rich breakfast blend into the French press.

"Sounds good. I'll make the toast."

My phone jangled again. "That's probably Mars."

Nina peeked at my phone and read aloud. *Bring food. Real food. Am starling.*

"Starling?" I cracked eggs into a bowl, added salt, pepper, and savory garlic powder, and whisked them together.

"Must mean starving. I'm not surprised. Natasha probably made him eat—" She laughed. "It's worse than I thought. Natasha brought him 'eggs poached in grapefruit juice served on top of sea bass with a peanut sauce.'" Nina staggered around the kitchen, laughing. "I shudder to imagine what she did to the coffee."

While bacon sizzled, I cut a cantaloupe in half and sliced the gloriously orange melon into six pieces. I slid a knife just below the gorgeous color and cut the fruit into pieces. Fresh blueberries, rosy raspberries, and a spoonful of sugar went into the bowl, and I squeezed lemon juice over top. A quick stir and it was ready to serve.

The eggs went into the hot pan, where butter melted, mingling with olive oil. "Is it my imagination or are her food combinations getting more peculiar by the day? It's like she doesn't understand basic concepts of what works together."

"It's because she doesn't eat. Have you ever seen her really eat anything? I haven't. All she does is nibble to see how it tastes." Nina scowled. "No wonder she's so thin."

"Maybe she should stick to decorating. How can you cook if you don't eat the food?"

"We have to rescue Mars. He'll pitch himself out the window if he's stuck there for too long."

I poured hot water into the French press. "I guess it would be kind to take the food over while it's still warm."

Nina drummed her fingertips on the counter. "What are you going to tell Natasha when she answers the door?"

"I guess we'll just have to pretend we want to see Mars and say we brought him something." I packed the eggs in a container that came with a warming sleeve. Toast, creamy butter, and a small dish of the boysenberry jam I knew Mars loved went into the tote bag on top of it. Nina added a tall, insulated mug of coffee.

"Really? I'm sure Natasha makes coffee."

Nina shot me a doubtful look. "Probably with ginger and chili peppers in it."

We added a covered bowl of fruit salad and an aluminum foil packet of crisp, warm bacon.

"That ought to do it." I attached Daisy's leash to her collar, and we set off for Mars's house, across the street and a few doors down.

Daisy whined and gazed upward when we reached the front door.

"*Psst.* Sophie! Up here."

I looked up just in time to dodge an athletic bag tied to a silver-gray sheet. Mars leaned out the window, holding the other end. "Quick. Take the dish out and put the food in it."

"The dish?" I grabbed the bag and sure enough, it contained paper napkins wrapped around something. I swapped it for the tote bag we brought and not a minute too soon.

CHAPTER SIXTEEN

Dear Natasha,

In my family it's traditional to make a Christmas gift for everyone. I would like to give chocolates this year. How do I make my own chocolates?

—Thinking Ahead in Choconut, Pennsylvania

Dear Thinking Ahead,

What a lovely gesture. Order chocolate beans from South America. Roast them, then crush them to take out the nibs. Mill the nibs to make cocoa liquor. Add sugar, milk, and cocoa butter. Temper the chocolate and pour into molds. Fill the hardened molds with your favorite ganache, fruit, or nut center. Seal the sides together, place in a handmade box, and tie with a special ribbon.

—Natasha

Mars was still pulling the sheet up when Natasha opened the front door.

"I thought I heard someone out here. I hope you came to visit Mars. He's so crabby. And such a baby."

"Maybe that's normal under the circumstances," I said.

"I'm a little concerned, to tell the truth. He has no appetite!"

Uh-oh, she was going to be looking for that dish. Maybe I could bring it back a little later.

"And I'm not going to get a thing done with him home all the time."

"You look terrific," said Nina.

Natasha's hair was perfect, as always. She had changed her hairstyle, though. Long bangs touched her eyelashes. Her almost-black hair was cut in a sleek new look, barely brushing her shoulders. She wore a tight dress that showed off her figure, and her makeup was perfect.

"Why, thank you. I'm in love with the new colors. This dress is toasted glacier."

It looked like dusty taupe to me. "Very nice. What happened to robin's-egg blue?"

"I know you don't care how you look but I have to keep up, well, really *ahead of* the times. Set the trends, you know. Much as I loved it, robin's-egg blue is just passé." Natasha frowned. "Is it raining?"

I looked at the sky. Not a single cloud. The sun shone. A beautiful summer day.

Natasha twitched. "There it is again. Another raindrop."

Nina shot me a worried look.

"I don't think so, Na—"

At that moment, water poured down on her head, leaving trails of mascara and gullies in her foundation.

Natasha screamed and jumped back but it didn't help. More water drizzled from the ceiling.

I reached for her hands and pulled her outside.

We heard a thump above us, no doubt Mars's cast hitting the floor.

Mars looked down at us from the bedroom window. "What's going on down there?"

"You have a leak," I shouted.

"It must be coming from the bathroom you were working on, Natasha. Turn off the water."

"I'll be right up," she said.

"Not up here. The whole house water turnoff valve in the basement."

Natasha faced me. "What does it look like?"

Mars heard her question. "For Pete's sake. Sophie, there's a flashlight in my office. It's on the back wall near the water heater."

I handed Daisy's leash to Nina. Ducking my head, I dashed through the water and down the stairs. Bad news for Natasha and Mars. The water was already spilling down the steps. I grabbed the flashlight in Mars's home office and ventured into the back of the basement. I found the valve right away. Someone, presumably Mars, had hung a sign on it to identify it. It stuck at first but finally cooperated.

Grasping the handrail so I wouldn't slip on the wet steps, I made my way back up. Droplets still spilled from the second-floor ceiling.

Mars was making his way downstairs with Nina's help. It amused me to no end that he carried the bag containing food. He paused in front of Natasha. "I'll be at Sophie's."

"But, Mars . . ." Natasha pleaded as he continued past her.

He didn't yell. He didn't scold. He didn't even make a fuss. He simply hobbled out on his crutches.

I truly did feel for Natasha. She seldom looked disheveled. Her new toasted glacier dress probably *was* toast. And worst of all, she had no running water in the house. A drywall seam in the ceiling had broken loose above her. The hardwood floor at her feet needed immediate mopping, and her toasted glacier high heels were ruined.

With Nina's help, Mars had already reached the sidewalk. Daisy and Truffles led the way, walking with great patience while Mars hobbled along.

I wanted so much to leave Natasha to her mess and go eat my breakfast. But sometimes you have to do what's right. "Where's the mop?"

"In the kitchen. I'll be back in a few."

"Where are you going?"

"I have to fix my face and hair."

"Natasha Earlene Smith, you go get old towels and help me clean up this mess. Then you will call the plumber and only then will you worry about your appearance. Do you understand me?"

I guess no one had called Natasha by her full name in years. In a totally uncharacteristic moment, she actually complied with my instructions. I mopped while she spread out towels and pots to catch lingering drips. When we finished with the floors and the stairs, she actually thanked me.

"You're my only true friend, Sophie. Even Mars abandons me in times of trouble."

"He has a broken leg. It's not like he can get down on his hands and knees to help."

"I can't believe I broke his leg."

"Maybe you shouldn't have tackled that bathroom job on your own."

"Oh sure. It's definitely a do-it-yourself project. But I do need to make it up to him."

"Uh, Natasha, maybe you could skip the chocolate project."

"He told you about that? I can't believe it. I confided in strictest confidence. Well, now I suppose you'll steal my idea."

"I think you're quite safe there." How could I subtly steer her away from food? "You're much better at decorating anyway." A bald-faced lie since I wasn't a fan of her décor ideas. However, everyone had different tastes, and her TV show *was* popular, so some people loved her style.

"Do you really think so?"

"Yes. Stay away from plumbing and electrical projects, though. Maybe your assistant could handle those. You could be the one in charge, telling him where to put things."

She pouted. "But the Meranos and Arnaud Turnèbe made so much money with their chocolate businesses."

"It took the Meranos three generations, and it didn't end well for Arnaud."

She shoved wet hair off of her forehead, and for the first time, I saw gray in her hair. "Don't be silly. No one would kill me."

I wasn't so sure. After reminding her to phone the plumber, I headed home.

Mars rested comfortably in a chair by the fireplace, his foot up on an ottoman. Daisy at his side, he sipped coffee while Nina poured herself another cup.

"We saved you some eggs," she said.

"Thanks, but I'm running behind. I think I'd better shower and check in with the winners before I eat." I ran up the stairs and made quick work of showering and dressing in a pink sheath and flat black sandals.

I left Nina and Mars to their own devices, walked over to the hotel, and made sure the winners were boarding the bus for their daylong tour of the Amore manufacturing facility located outside the beltway.

When the bus pulled away, I returned home. Nina had set a place for me at the table, complete with a plate of scrambled eggs and toast. A bowl of fruit salad nestled next to it. I gratefully slid into the banquette and gulped coffee. She had thoughtfully fixed it exactly how I liked it. "Thanks, Nina!"

"I can't believe that you helped Natasha."

I let her comment slide. Someone had to help her. I dug into the eggs Nina had warmed.

"I hope you don't mind if I stay over," said Mars.

"After finding Mochie outside"—Nina met my gaze

straight on—"I think it would be best if you had someone with you."

I looked to Mars. "Did you ask Natasha if she was here?"

He nodded. "It wasn't her. I believe her, too. She couldn't have done so much damage to our bathrooms if she was putzing around over here."

A shiver skittered down my back as I imagined someone entering my house while I was gone. It was really the only explanation. Mochie wasn't prone to running out the door.

"Does anyone else have keys?" asked Nina.

"Bernie and my parents. Maybe Mochie escaped through an open window or something." I knew it wasn't true. The air-conditioning was on, and all the windows were closed and locked. "Maybe it would be good to have someone in the house when I'm out during the day."

"If it's all right with you, I'd like to sleep down here on the pullout sofa. I really hated being upstairs all by myself at home. I dislike not being in the middle of things."

"Okay, but don't forget that there's no shower or bath downstairs."

Mars pointed at his cast. "It's not like I'm going to be showering for the next few days. I can clean up in the powder room. I'll call Nat and ask her to bring over some clothes and my laptop."

Nina helped me tidy up, and I invited her to dinner. "It will almost be a party. I'd better be off to the store as soon as I get Mars settled."

I made up the pullout sofa in the small family room between the kitchen and the sunroom. I fluffed huge, square pillows stuffed with down against the back of the sofa and provided a couple for his leg. Throws and blankets were within easy reach. I laid the remote for the TV on the bed along with the landline phone, added some books and the newspaper, and set a carafe of coffee and a bottle of water on the side table. It wasn't perfect, but I figured he ought to stretch a little bit anyway.

Mochie opened one eye when I said I was going to the market. He gave me the distinct impression that I had disturbed his nap.

Nina wanted to walk Truffles for a little socialization, so we took Daisy along, too.

My insulated tote bag on wheels in hand, I locked the door, and we ventured into the summer heat. Three blocks away, I began to rue my decision to walk. Driving to the bigger grocery store out on Duke Street might have been wiser.

But then we spotted Coco stepping out of the Honeysuckle Bed-and-Breakfast. She glanced around furtively.

Instinct forced us to back up and hide behind a tree. A futile effort with two dogs and a cooler in tow. When I peered around the tree, Coco's back was to us as she hurried along the sidewalk on the other side of the street. I didn't think she had noticed us.

Following someone in Old Town wasn't easy. We darted from one tree to another. Coco never looked back, though.

"What do you suppose she's doing at the Honeysuckle B and B?" asked Nina.

"This is the second time I've seen her there."

"She could have a friend staying there."

"I don't know. I feel like she's up to something. Did you see the way she looked around? Oh, rats. She turned the corner. We'll lose her."

We hurried in the same direction Coco had been headed, turned the corner, and walked by the large plate glass windows that fronted the gourmet grocery store.

Nina stopped abruptly and seized my arm. "There she is!"

I peered through the glass just in time to see Coco's back as she walked along an aisle inside the store. I burst out laughing. "How very suspicious of her to go to the store."

"Don't they have tons of food left over from the chocolate tasting?"

"They're probably a little burned out on chocolate, don't you think? Maybe she's picking up fruit or meat."

"Man, but it's hot. I'll grab one of the outdoor tables if you'll bring some water for Truffles and Daisy and an iced coffee for me."

"Deal." I left my tote outside and entered the store, where I bought two puppy waters and three iced mocha lattes in the hope of luring Coco outside so I could ask her a few questions. I stashed them neatly in a box so they wouldn't spill, and sidled up next to Coco, who studied the prepared foods.

"The mango and shrimp salad looks terrific," I said.

Coco looked at me and smiled—except it wasn't Coco!

"I'm so sorry. I thought you were Coco."

"No problem. I get that a lot." She moved on.

How could she look so much like Coco? They even wore their hair in similar bobs. I watched her as she shopped. And then she turned her head just so and it clicked. I hurried over to her. "You're the girl in the picture!"

She flashed me an odd look. "Picture?"

"In Joe Merano's bedroom. It's a school picture. You were about twelve or so. You wore your hair straight and long and were wearing a white blouse. Who are you?" All sorts of crazy thoughts about an illegitimate daughter ran through my head.

She took a step back. "Who are *you*?"

"Sophie Winston. Joe hired me to set up some events for him."

"You've seen him? You know where he is?"

I didn't have the first clue how to handle this woman. All I knew was that I didn't want her to run away. "Could I interest you in an iced mocha latte? I bought an extra one."

CHAPTER SEVENTEEN

Dear Sophie,

What is alkalized chocolate and why do I have to use it? Aren't all cocoa powders pretty much the same?

—Confused in Cocoa Ridge, Georgia

Dear Confused,

Alkalized chocolate, also called Dutch chocolate, has been through a process to neutralize some of the acidity. As a result, it has a darker color and a deeper chocolate flavor and is recommended in many recipes. It is generally paired with baking powder because it doesn't react to baking soda in the same way that natural chocolate does.

—Sophie

The woman who resembled Coco followed me out of the store. Two things were in my favor. Truffles would make anyone except the most coldhearted person feel warm and

fuzzy. She would probably give Nina and me instant cred-
ibility as decent people whom the woman didn't need to
fear. And Nina had unknowingly been wise in her table
selection. It was in the shade but public enough for the
woman to feel secure.

"This is my friend, Nina Reid Norwood, that's my dog,
Daisy, and the little rascal is Truffles."

Just as I expected, the woman sat down and fussed over
Truffles. She didn't neglect Daisy, but the happy, wriggling
puppy couldn't be resisted. "I love chocolate Labs!" she
cooed at Truffles.

Nina shot me a confused look.

"And you are?" I asked.

"Kara Merano. You work for my dad?"

Nina and I gasped. Not the best way to make Kara
comfortable.

We introduced ourselves. "I'm an event planner. Joe hired
me for the events in connection with Amore's sixtieth anniversary celebration. You're Coco and Dan's sister? Or half
sister?"

"They might wish I wasn't their sister but biologically
we're full siblings, no matter how they feel about it."

A sibling squabble of some sort? That might explain why
she wasn't staying at her father's house. It certainly couldn't
be for lack of room. I handed out the lattes, uncovered the
water bowls for Truffles and Daisy, and set them on the
ground near Nina's feet. "Are there any more siblings?"

"No, just the three of us."

"You look so much like Coco," said Nina. "Are you twins?"

Kara smiled. "We always looked a lot alike. I'm two
years younger than Coco."

"You don't work for Amore?" Surely I would have met
her if she did.

"No. I live in Colorado. I came to Old Town when I heard
Dad was missing. Do you know where he is?"

Well, wasn't that interesting? I was pretty sure I saw her

going into the B and B the night he disappeared, which meant she was already in Old Town before her father dropped out of sight. I tried to trip her up. "You heard about that all the way out in Colorado?"

"His administrative assistant, Marla, called me." Kara took a big swig of her latte. "I'd forgotten how hot and humid it is here in the summer."

"How long have you lived out west?" asked Nina.

"A long time. Decades." She focused on me. "What do you know about Dad? Is he okay?"

"I'm sorry if I misled you. I don't know much. He seems to have vanished without a trace."

Her upper body sagged. "Has Coco hired a private investigator?"

Nina's eyes met mine. "Haven't you talked with her?"

"No. Only with Marla, and she doesn't seem to know much."

I sipped my latte. Who came to town and didn't contact her siblings? Especially when their dad couldn't be found?

"Do you have any idea where Joe might have gone?"

"How would . . . No. I don't even know where to start looking. I'm so afraid for him."

"Why?" asked Nina.

Kara blinked at her like she was stupid. "People don't just disappear. Something must have happened to him. It can't be anything good, or his administrative assistant wouldn't have called to ask if he was with me."

"Is there any possibility that he's out in Colorado, searching for you?"

"I don't think so. I've been in touch with my neighbors and coworkers. They're watching for him." She stroked Truffles with a gentle hand and gazed up at me with hope. "You said he has my picture in his bedroom?"

I nodded. "It's pretty worn, like he looks at it a lot." I thought it best not to mention that it was hidden in a drawer under sweaters.

She shielded her eyes with one hand, but it didn't hide the sniffles or the tears that rolled down her cheeks. "I'm sorry. It's just that I never imagined he might . . . die. That sounds so stupid. But now that it's a possibility, it breaks my heart to think I might never get to see him again."

"You think he's dead?" Nina blurted.

Kara wiped away tears with her fingers. "I hope not! But what else can I think?"

She scribbled a phone number on a napkin. "Here's my cell number if you hear anything. I'm staying at the Honeysuckle B and B. I've been away so long that I don't really know anyone in town anymore. Please don't hesitate to call me with any news at all."

I thought I might know one person who would be happy to see her. "Would you like me to bring Nonni to visit you?"

Her head shuddered, and her eyes widened in alarm. "No." She stood up and said, "No! Please don't do that." She walked away, clearly upset by my offer.

Nina watched her go and whispered, "What do you suppose happened?"

"I don't know, but she's lying about coming here because her dad went missing. She was already here that night."

Nina perked up. "Maybe she's in on it."

"You think she kidnapped him?"

"If your estranged kid called you and said she was in town, wouldn't you go to see her?"

"I would." Nina had a good point. "I definitely would. But why would she want to kidnap him?"

Nina shrugged. "Money?"

It wasn't out of the realm of possibilities. Joe and the family had plenty of it and would gladly pay a ransom.

"Think Coco will tell you what the deal is with Kara?" asked Nina.

"Coco or Nonni. Or maybe Dan. We'll have to figure out who might be most receptive. I'm going back inside to buy a few things for dinner tonight."

"Okay. I'll walk Truffles and Daisy home. It's hot out here for them."

I strolled into the store, thinking about Kara and the Merano family. The rest of them still seemed to be together, fairly tight-knit, in fact. The old picture that Joe kept told me that he cared about Kara. But he kept it hidden. What had Kara done to be ostracized?

"Ma'am?" The voice grew louder "Ma'am? You're next."

I looked up and realized the butcher was speaking to me. "Two pork tenderloins, please."

He wrapped them and handed the package to me. I forced myself to concentrate on my shopping. Onions, gorgeous red peppers, and fresh white mushrooms went into my basket. For our lunch, I bought a rotisserie chicken, steamed green beans, and a macaroni salad that I knew Mars liked. I carefully packed the perishable items in my insulated tote, paid, and ambled out the door.

The heat was brutal. Francie might not want to eat outside. We would probably eat indoors anyway to accommodate Mars. I strolled home still thinking about Kara. I would check her out on the Internet, but if the problem arose twenty years ago or more, I probably wouldn't find much. In fact, if it was a family issue, I wouldn't discover anything. No, I would have to find a reason to ask Coco, Dan, or Nonni what had happened.

I stopped by Big Daddy's Bakery for fresh bread. His adorable little granddaughter was running through the bakery at hyper speed. No one cared, except for Big Daddy's assistant, who couldn't catch the energetic little girl.

~~~

While Mars and I ate lunch, I let the butter and eggs for Francie's cake come to room temperature. They were perfect when I was ready to undertake the cake I had promised Francie. I melted dark squares of unsweetened chocolate that reminded me of the three cherubs Dan had carved out of white, milk, and dark chocolate. Had they been meant to represent the three Merano children? Was Kara the black sheep of the family like Arnie had been in his?

The mixer whirred, beating the butter with the sugar. I tossed in local eggs from the farmer's market. The yolks were so golden they were almost orange. The batter thickened and changed color as I added the melted chocolate to it in a thick ribbon. After adding the dry ingredients, I poured it into two round cake pans and slid them into the oven.

Half an hour later, they perfumed the kitchen. I set each of the layers on a rack. They had to cool before I could frost them, which worked perfectly for me. I could get in a little paperwork in my office before checking on the winners and starting dinner. But first, I melted bittersweet chocolate chips from Amore in the microwave so they could cool before I made the frosting.

<hr/>

An hour later, I returned to the kitchen to frost the chocolate cake. I poured the thick chocolatey goodness into my Kitch-enAid mixing bowl, added vanilla, softened butter, and tangy sour cream and mixed them. Beating in powdered sugar brought it to perfect frosting consistency. I scooped a dollop with my finger and tasted. Delicious! I'd better frost the cake and refrigerate it before Mars got wind of it.

Natasha would have criticized me for not cutting the rounded top off the cake. But I thought it looked wonderful that way. I spread seedless raspberry jam across the bottom layer for a surprising bit of fruitiness, then topped it with frosting and set the other layer on it. The frosting swept over the sides smoothly. I mounded it on the top and spread it with artful swirls. Finally, I pressed miniature chocolate chips to the sides to dress it up a bit.

I moved it to the fridge and checked the time. The winners would return soon. I ought to be there when they came back, just in case any of them had a problem or needed something. I brought the frosting bowl to Mars to lick and asked if he needed anything before I left. You would have thought I had handed him bars of gold.

I ventured into the hot summer day again and walked the few blocks to the hotel. I knew trouble was brewing the minute I saw Wolf waiting by the front steps.

"I'm afraid to ask what you're doing here."

"I'm glad to see you, too," he quipped.

"Seriously. Are you waiting for the Amore winners to return on the bus?"

His mouth pulled tight when he nodded.

"I don't suppose you'd care to tell me why?"

Wolf appraised me for a moment. "You'll hear about it sooner or later. Remember the champagne glass you found with the pills in it?"

Oh no. This couldn't be good.

"They were diazepam, a sedative and anticonvulsant. Very dangerous mixed with alcohol."

"Then we're lucky we didn't have an emergency. Wouldn't someone who takes those drugs know not to take them with alcohol?"

"You'd think so. Especially since the person didn't take them."

"What do you mean?"

"Most people swallow pills whole and wash them down with a liquid. They don't dissolve them first, because of the bitter taste."

I scrutinized his earnest face for a moment, unable to grasp what he was getting at. "Maybe he couldn't swallow pills."

"Or maybe *she* wanted someone else to swallow them but the pills didn't dissolve."

"Are you saying someone meant to kill Arnaud with the pills?"

Wolf heaved a sigh. "Have you got a better explanation?"

I didn't. But my mind reeled from the implications. "So

you think Arnaud's killer tried to dissolve the pills in champagne but then they didn't disintegrate fast enough, so the killer strangled him instead?"

Wolf just raised his eyebrows.

"If you're waiting for the bus, then you must know who it was!"

"We found fingerprints on the glass."

"You'd think the killer would have wiped the glass clean."

Wolf leaned against a railing. "Luckily for all of us, murder is exceptionally stressful. It's very rare that the killer doesn't overlook some little detail."

The bus rolled into the driveway. I was feeling pretty stressed myself. "Were they Cheryl Maiorca's? I've heard she had an argument with Arnaud."

"Nope. Your former cop."

"Lori Speer?" I was stunned. Surely a cop wouldn't forget to wipe a glass clean. She was so exuberant, so full of life. As the bus ground to a slow halt, I asked Wolf, "Why?"

"That's what we need to find out."

The winners disembarked slowly, like they'd had a very long day. One weary person after another stepped off the bus and then Lori bounced out, cheerful and giddy.

"Hi, Sophie!" she sang. She stopped beside me as though she was waiting for someone.

Cheryl joined her just in time to see Wolf flick out his badge and hear him say, "Lori Speer? I'd like you to come to the station with me to answer some questions, please."

Lori looked at me. "What's this about?"

I didn't dare say anything lest I clue her in. I kept quiet and let Wolf do the talking.

"Arnaud Turnèbe."

"Sure!" She sounded excited. "I'll see you guys later."

As she walked away with Wolf, I heard her say, "You know, I really could tell you everything at the bar."

Wolf muttered, "I'd prefer that you were sober for this."

Still shaken by the new development, I trotted up the

stairs to the lobby, where many of the winners still mingled, to remind them about their television appearances the next day. "Get a good night's sleep, everyone."

Just to be on the safe side, I stopped by the hotel manager's office to ask if there were any problems. She assured me everything was going well.

Back home, Daisy and Mochie greeted me at the door. Mars shouted to me from the sofa bed. "Is that you again, Natasha?"

I peeked in at him. "Natasha?"

"Hope you don't mind. She came over to take a shower. Turned out to be a huge mistake on my part, though. She's wildly jealous of your green and black tile because you're ahead of the trend. 'It's the new gray,' " he said, mimicking her. "I have a very bad feeling that our bathrooms are being demolished as I speak."

"The black and green tile in the bathrooms must date back to the 1950s. What's that saying? *Everything old is new again.*"

His cell phone rang, and I retreated to my office to phone the limo company and the people who would be escorting winners to their various appearances. No one had forgotten and everything was on track.

I made two mugs of tea, handed one to Mars, and settled in the cushy armchair next to him, curling my legs underneath me.

Bored after a day of hanging around the house, Mars ate up the information about Lori Speer.

"She's the one who made those incredible chocolates, isn't she?"

"They were amazing. She said they were her brother's recipe."

Mars looked at me in surprise. "Didn't she tell you something about her brother giving up because it's a ruthless business? Could she have killed Arnaud as some kind of revenge?"

CHAPTER EIGHTEEN

Dear Sophie,

Can I melt chocolate in the microwave? Natasha says it burns.

—Skeptical in Melton, Missouri

Dear Skeptical,

It won't burn if you're careful. Microwave chocolate on medium, stirring every 30 seconds. Or microwave it on high, stirring it every 15 to 20 seconds.

—Sophie

"What?" I nearly spilled my tea.

"Sure. It all fits together," said Mars. "I was standing next to Dan and overheard Coco say Lori's chocolates tasted like Arnie's chocolates. Maybe there's a connection."

"If I recall correctly, she said her brother is now a school counselor."

"A lie to cover up the truth. We'll see what everyone thinks at dinner tonight. By the way, I invited Humphrey. He called while you were out."

I prodded Mars to help me with dinner. He limped into the kitchen on his crutches, sat down at the table with his leg up, and most agreeably proceeded to slice potatoes and dip them in Parmesan cheese.

Meanwhile, I preheated the ovens and poured water into a huge pot for the ears of fresh corn. I took a minute to make a basil-garlic butter for them.

Mars and I were discussing Arnaud's murder when Daisy ran to the door and wagged her tail.

Alex looked through the glass at us. I wanted to dig a hole and crawl into it. Why did he keep catching me with Mars and Wolf? It was always as innocent as possible, but Alex didn't see it that way.

Taking a deep breath, I smiled, and opened the door.

Alex took one look at Mars's cast and asked, "What happened to you?"

"Natasha tried to kill me," joked Mars.

Alex glanced around. "Are you . . . are you *staying* here?" *Oh no.*

Mars must not have felt the awkwardness I was experiencing, because he very casually said, "Temporarily."

I hurried to add, "They don't have running water right now, and there's no bed on the main floor of their house."

Alex gazed at Mars for a long moment. "Could I speak to you outside, Sophie?"

I followed him out the door, dreading what I knew would come.

Alex picked up my hands and held them in his. "Sophie, I was hoping we might have something special. So far, mostly we just seem to butt heads. I can't deal with Wolf and Mars in your life. You're obviously still devoted to them." He glanced at the house. "Too fond of them, actually.

Call me when you've finally closed those doors." He released my hands and turned to leave.

"Alex?" I said.

He stopped and looked back just enough to see me.

"They're my friends. They're part of my life. I will never close any doors on them."

"Then you're slamming one on me."

How could I make him understand that I would never turn my back on my friends? I returned to the kitchen, where I chopped tomatoes for the salad with a slight vengeance.

Mars looked a little concerned when I minced garlic with the cleaver too vigorously. "Everything okay?"

I said yes and laughed, mostly because I didn't want to talk about Alex with him. After slicing the two pork tenderloins lengthwise, about three-quarters of the way through, I slathered them with pesto, rolled them up, and browned them in oil.

Mars had filled two baking sheets with potatoes. I slid them into the oven.

"We're almost done. Shall we eat in the dining room or outside?"

"I'd rather eat right here in the kitchen, if it's okay with you."

I assumed he didn't want to lurch around on his crutches too much, so I readily agreed and threw a blue and yellow tablecloth over the table. I set the table with square peacock blue plates, sunflower yellow napkins, and cutlery. I would serve the food on my blue majolica serving dishes with the bright lemon pattern.

I took a minute to turn on music but made sure it played softly, at a background level.

"Peach sangria or lime margaritas?" I asked Mars.

He gave me a funny look but smiled. "Natasha never asks what I want. Definitely peach sangria."

"You're on." I placed water and sugar in a pot on the stove for the syrup. Peach schnapps, frozen peaches, sliced fresh peaches and strawberries, a squeeze of lemon juice, and sparkling wine went into a large glass pitcher. I popped it in the fridge. "Do you want to invite Natasha? Does she have running water yet?"

"It's going to be a couple of days. They have to rip out drywall to get to the leak. She's out tonight, though. Some kind of business meeting."

"Oh?" I took the syrup off the stove to cool.

"I have no idea what it's about. You know Nat. Always working on something new."

I had a bad feeling it might involve her new chocolate manufacturing idea but chose not to butt in. There wasn't anything Mars could do about it at the moment anyway.

Daisy lifted her head and swished her tail across the floor.

A moment later, Francie and her golden retriever, Duke, showed up with Humphrey, Nina, and Truffles. Bernie was a minute behind them.

My kitchen filled with chatter as they expressed their concern about Mars and asked questions.

I stirred the cooled sweet syrup into the pitcher, then lined up large wine glasses painted with summery flowers in shades of yellow, orange, and red.

Nina pulled colorful markers out of her pocket and promptly drew an abstract flower on Mars's cast.

Bernie opened the box of appetizers he'd brought from the restaurant. I placed the shrimp summer rolls on a majolica platter. Peachy-colored shrimp and green cucumbers showed through the thin rice paper wrappers.

They took turns drawing on Mars's cast, munching on the appetizers, and trying out the sangria.

I took the meat out of the oven and let it rest before slicing it.

Nina drew cute cartoonish sketches of the dogs on the cast with canine messages of sympathy. Not to be left out,

Mochie jumped in Mars's lap and appeared to demand inclusion, which brought on a round of laughter.

Bernie accommodated him by adding a kitty face to the cast and signed Mochie's name for him.

Humphrey carried platters of food to the table, and I took the chocolate cake out of the fridge. I left it on the counter to take the chill off so the flavor would develop. We sat down to eat, but it wasn't long before dinner conversation gave way to gossip and speculation about Arnaud's murder.

"Get a load of this!" Mars filled them in on Lori Speer's fingerprints and his theory that she might have some connection to Arnaud because her brother's truffle recipe tasted like Arnaud's.

Bernie stopped eating. "Mars, are you taking strong medicine for the pain in your leg? Because you're really stretching with that crazy notion."

Francie frowned. "Have I met this Lori Speer?"

I smiled at my elderly neighbor. "See what you missed by not coming to the chocolate tasting?"

"Bah! I don't think I missed a thing. Mars, I hate to offend you, but your theory sounds unlikely to me. Aren't there other suspects?"

"Nina, pass me one of the markers, please," said Mars. "Sophie, do you have a notepad in the kitchen?"

I rose to fetch a little notebook that I kept by the phone.

Mars wrote *Arnaud* at the top of the list. Underneath, he jotted, *Lori Speer, makes chocolates like Arnaud's.* "Isn't there another suspicious winner?" asked Mars.

"Cheryl Maiorca. She and Lori both came back to the Merano garden after the chocolate tasting. Cheryl was Arnaud's cousin. Apparently he was a mooch. She said he took money from relatives but never paid them back, even when he was doing well."

"*Hmmph*," grunted Francie. "There's a motive for you."

"We can't forget the whole Merano family," said Nina.

"Starting with Coco. Most of them share the same motive. Fear of competition from Arnaud."

Mars wrote the names of Coco, Mitch, and Dan. "I suppose we can eliminate Nonni and Joe?"

"Nonni is a delight. There's no way that sweet little lady could ever kill anyone." Bernie ate a bite of potato.

Francie snorted. "She's tougher than you think. Nonni might look adorable, but I'm pretty certain there's a fierce woman underneath that darling façade."

I sipped my refreshing peach sangria. "Francie, do you honestly think she would have had the physical strength to strangle Arnaud?"

"She could have talked Dan into doing the dirty work for her."

"Don't forget Kara," said Nina. She looked around the table at surprised faces. "You guys don't know about Kara!" She told them the story of meeting Coco's sister.

"Francie, have you ever heard of another sister?" I asked. "I had no idea."

Mars added Nonni and Kara to the list. I was skeptical about Nonni, but it was his list.

"Doesn't anyone else think it's suspicious that Joe disappeared around the same time?" I asked. "Both of them are chocolatiers."

"What if Joe went into hiding to kill Arnaud?" asked Bernie.

"How would that work? He'd still need an alibi when he showed up again," said Mars.

But I noticed him adding Joe to his list, too.

CHAPTER NINETEEN

Dear Sophie,

I'm crazy for white chocolate. My wife insists that she can't just substitute white chocolate in a recipe because it won't work. I think that's because she prefers dark chocolate. Who wins this bet?

— White Chocolate Fan in Whitelaw, Wisconsin

Dear White Chocolate Fan,

I'm afraid your wife is correct this time. You can bake with white chocolate but it cannot be substituted for other baking chocolates because it is very high in butterfat and will not act like other kinds of chocolate.

— Sophie

"Any leads on Joe?" asked Humphrey. "He was always so nice to me. I hate to imagine that harm came to him."

"The only thing I know is that Kara was in town the night he disappeared," I said. "I wish we knew more about her."

"You could ask one of them," said Francie. "I know I'd be willing to tell you just about anything for a piece of that chocolate cake."

We took the hint. Bernie helped me clear the table.

I put on hot water for tea and coffee. "After-dinner drinks, anyone?"

"Yeah, sure," said Bernie. "I'm not headed back to work tonight."

Nina jumped up from the table. "I've been itching to try Chocolate Covered Berries. Everybody game?" She dashed into the dining room and returned with Chambord, Godiva liqueur, and six cordial glasses with identical stems but bowls of different colors and shapes. Retrieving Baileys Irish Cream from the fridge, Nina asked, "Who would benefit most from Joe's death?"

It was a horrible question but one well worth consideration. Maybe Joe's disappearance had nothing to do with Arnaud's death.

"Wouldn't the three children inherit equally?" asked Humphrey. "Or do you think he left Kara out of the will?"

"I suspect it's more complicated than that." I cut slices of cake and passed them to my friends. "Amore is a closely held, family-owned corporation. Aside from inheriting Joe's personal assets, I wonder who would be in control of the company. Joe had a book in his room about ensuring the continuation of family corporations."

"Wouldn't that be Coco and Dan?" asked Francie.

Bernie handed out mugs of coffee and tea.

"Depends on how the stock ownership is set up. And who would inherit Joe's shares." Mars nabbed a knife from the table and slid it under his cast. "*Ahhh*," he groaned with relief. "I can see why Joe would have been worried about it."

"I thought Mitch was second in command after Joe," said Nina. "Wouldn't he continue running the company?"

Mars wiggled his eyebrows. "Depends on who his boss is. If Coco, Dan, and Kara are the shareholders, I guess he'd better kiss up to them."

"A chocolate kiss?" Nina chuckled as she tried her berry concoction. "Ohh, not bad. I like this drink. Kara told us her family wouldn't speak with her. Do you think Mitch is trying to win her over?"

I sat down again. "Wouldn't it have been easier to win over Coco?"

"Maybe that's why he's kissing up to Kara. He's afraid of being burned by Coco and Dan when her dad turns over the reins," suggested Bernie.

"Would that be a good enough reason to get rid of Joe?" I asked.

"Probably, but then why would Mitch come to you about looking for him?" asked Bernie. "Maybe it's Dan who thinks he'll be out. Or Kara, though if she was written out of the will and everything else, it probably happened a long time ago, so why turn up now?"

The conversation turned to Nina's delicious drink and the moistness of the chocolate cake I had made for Francie. But while they raved, I was thinking that I needed to know more about Kara. Maybe Joe's administrative assistant, Marla, knew the scoop.

Nina stayed behind to help clean up when the others left. Truffles raced around the kitchen underfoot. She yapped at Mochie, who stalked out of the room with feline indignation. She yapped at Daisy, who didn't even bother to lift her head.

"Feel like another walk tonight?" Nina asked.

"Sure. I have to take Daisy out anyway." Besides, Nina wouldn't get any sleep unless Truffles worked off some of that energy.

With the dishes done, we left Mars reading a book with Mochie on his lap, and ventured out into the night. I was glad

Nina had suggested a walk. The balmy air of the summer night lifted my spirits, evoking memories of vacations. Little Truffles followed Daisy's lead. We practiced heeling, and the little cutie seemed to understand when she was supposed to sit.

"So how does it feel to have Mars home again?" asked Nina.

"Stop that. I hope you don't say things like that to other people. You'll give them all the wrong idea."

"I noticed he didn't insist you invite Natasha to dinner."

"She was busy tonight. And he's obviously still very miffed with her."

"So—how's it going?" Nina elbowed me.

At that moment, Coco crossed the street not too far from us.

Nina and I exchanged a look. Without another word, we picked up our pace and turned the corner to follow her.

Coco paused at a small gray town house with a blue door. She unlocked it and let herself in.

"*Hmmph*, somehow I don't think that's where Coco and Mitch live," said Nina. "I imagined them in a much bigger place."

"I don't think so, either. Could it have been Kara?" I looked for some clue to the residents. No cutesy flowerpot with the family name on it. No mailbox, either. There was a slot in the door.

To the left, a wrought iron gate to the old service entrance was barely wide enough for one person. Although streetlights and the outdoor lantern by the front door imparted a charming glow, the tiny passageway along the side of the house wasn't lighted at all.

"Think one of them is hiding Joe here?" asked Nina.

"I hope not! What would possibly posses them to do that?"

Nina shrugged.

I committed the house number to memory. "I can check the land records tomorrow to find out who owns this place."

I stepped back a little to see if the lights had turned on upstairs.

A woman screamed like the world was ending.

Daisy strained against her leash and tugged me straight to the gate.

"Are you sure it came from this house, Daisy?" I asked.

"Maybe we should knock on the door and ask if everything is all right," said Nina.

I nodded. That seemed reasonable. But Nina hadn't even rapped on the door when we heard someone screaming, "No. No! No!" The wail of sorrow that followed made Daisy and Truffles howl in sympathy.

Nina banged against the door. "Coco? Kara?"

"Forget the door," I said. "Call the cops."

Nina pulled out her cellphone and pressed the numbers.

"Why didn't we bring a flashlight?" Of course I knew the answer. Who would have expected to have to run into a dark passage?

Daisy pawed at the gate, and Truffles whined. I opened the gate and wedged inside.

"Sophie! Are you nuts?"

I hoped not. But I could hear someone crying. "Coco?" I called. I thought I would only take a few steps. That I would remain in the area lighted by the streetlamps. When my eyes adjusted, it didn't seem quite so frightening, though. The glimmer of a light at the end of the passage gave me hope. But what if I came upon someone wielding a knife or a gun? I might be trapped. "Coco? Coco?"

"Back here!" Her voice sounded tearful.

Daisy lunged forward, forcing me to move faster. We jogged through the shadowy passageway. It opened to a narrow backyard. Under the light of a lantern mounted by the back door, Coco leaned over someone in a patio chair.

My heart plummeted. It had to be Joe. "Coco?" I spoke gently.

"I can't find a pulse." Her voice wavered with hysteria. "I think he's dead," she whispered. "He must have had a heart attack."

She stepped aside for me to see him. The light from the house was enough for me to make out Randy, the Amore employee who had helped Coco with the memorial wreath. I paused in surprise and shock for just a second before feeling his wrist for a pulse.

Coco watched me hopefully. "Anything?"

I desperately wanted to tell her that he would be okay. But the truth was that I couldn't find a pulse at all. I moved my hand to his throat.

A siren sounded very close by.

Coco's eyes grew large. "I can't be here. Sophie, cover for me, please?"

At the sound of boots on the brick passageway, Coco glanced around in panic. "I'll go out through the house. You never saw me, okay?"

Before I could object, and before Coco could escape, it was too late.

Three EMTs calmly set about their business, examining Randy and asking questions. "Does he have a history of heart disease?"

Coco wasn't much help. "No. Not that I know of."

"Did he complain of pain or shortness of breath?"

"I just got here," said Coco. "This is how I found him."

I didn't know what she was afraid of, but Nina and I could back up her claim that she had just arrived. I slid a reassuring arm around her.

The EMTs started CPR. I reeled Daisy in close and noticed that a glass had fallen on the brick pavers where Randy had sat. It hadn't broken. Maybe it was plastic.

I could hear Coco softly reciting a prayer.

Nina and Truffles showed up. Even the little puppy seemed to understand that it was a somber time.

Coco clutched my hand and motioned toward the house

with her head. She led the way inside through a dated kitchen to a sizeable living room. Nina and I followed with the dogs.

Coco was so distraught she could hardly speak. She sat down on the sofa, placed her face in her hands, and sobbed.

Curiously, the room featured two identical fireplaces. I had noticed the historical plaque outside. It must have been two rooms decades ago when fireplaces were used for heat. White built-in bookshelves filled the space in between. No curtains hung on the windows. White interior shutters blocked passersby from seeing inside.

I retraced my steps to the kitchen in search of tissues and returned with a roll of paper towels. They would have to do.

Coco tore one off and dabbed her face. "I know this is asking a lot," she blubbered, "but I need you to give me an alibi."

Nina's worried eyes met mine.

"You don't need an alibi, Coco," I assured her. "We saw you enter the house. There's no way you could have killed him that fast without a knife or a gun."

"You think Randy was murdered?" Coco choked and fell into a coughing fit.

I fetched a glass of water for her. "I'm so sorry, Coco. You must have been close to Randy."

Her head snapped up. "Please," she begged, "I came here with you." She frowned at me. "What *are* you doing here?"

I sought a reason, not wanting to confess that we had followed her.

Nina piped up. "Just happened to be out walking the dogs when we saw you."

That was true! I signaled Nina with my eyes. *Good thinking!*

"All right." Coco's eyes searched the room frantically. "I walked with you because"—she looked around again—"we were looking for Bacio, and your dog ran into Randy's backyard." Coco closed her eyes and nodded. "That'll work."

"Who is Bacio?" I asked.

She opened her eyes. "My dad's cat. He's never left the

garden before. And now," she wailed, "we can't find him anywhere!"

I sat down next to Coco and hugged her.

An unfamiliar man entered the room and took Coco aside.

We overheard him say, "I'm so very sorry for your loss. Does Mr. Hicks have family we should notify?"

"He has a son in the military but I don't know where he is," said Coco. "I'll try to locate him."

"Do you know if Mr. Hicks had a particular funeral home in mind? We'll be taking him for an autopsy but we need to know to whom the body should be released."

That broke Coco up again.

I suggested the name of the mortuary where Humphrey worked. "If his son decides differently, she'll let you know."

Nina had a brief conversation with him while I tried to comfort Coco. We heard van doors closing outside. Nina returned and sat down in an easy chair.

I was painfully aware of the silence now that everyone had left.

Coco wiped her eyes and blew her nose. "It had been so long since I had seen Arnie that his death seemed surreal, but now to lose Randy, too—it's almost too much to bear. Randy was such a kind soul. He was a sous chef at a restaurant and got fired for punching out a man who was beating his wife in the parking lot. Daddy saw the whole thing and hired Randy on the spot." She burst into sobs again.

I gazed around the room. Randy's taste was decidedly masculine. He opted for comfort over style, choosing brown leather furniture and utilitarian tables of hefty wood. But here and there I spied signs of a feminine hand. An Italian pottery cookie jar took center stage on a bookshelf. An elegant garnet throw that looked to be cashmere hung over the end of the sofa. A chunky gold bangle bracelet lay on an end table, as if someone had taken it off and left it there. I thought I recognized the bracelet . . .

CHAPTER TWENTY

Dear Natasha,

My husband is wild for chocolate liqueur. I thought it would be fun to make some for him. Is that possible?

—Loving Wife in Boozeville Mountain, Georgia

Dear Loving Wife,

It's actually easy to make chocolate liqueur. Add cocoa nibs and sugar to a bottle of vodka. Or dissolve unsweetened cocoa powder and sugar in hot water and add it to a bottle of vodka. The water may dilute it a bit so the nibs might make a stronger chocolate flavor. Spark it up by adding vanilla, raspberries, or coffee! Let it stand until the flavors develop.

—Natasha

I extricated myself from Coco and wandered into the kitchen. A box of chocolates lay open on the counter. They looked exactly like the mysterious anonymous ones I had received. Six chocolates in crimped white paper had been in the red box. Only one remained uneaten. I examined the box. No company name or logo. Plain as could be. Had Randy been getting the chocolate delivered to him, too?

Near the stove I found what I was looking for—a telltale aluminum macchinetta just like the one at Joe's house. I opened a cabinet and discovered Italian pottery dishes and mugs. And, as if there was any doubt left in my mind, on the refrigerator hung a selfie of Randy and Coco being cozy at the beach.

They were an unlikely couple. I never would have put the chubby handyman and the socialite together, but evidently they had found something in each other. No wonder Coco needed an alibi. She wasn't worried about being accused of murder. She was afraid of Mitch finding out about her affair.

I returned to the living room. "Mitch doesn't know about your relationship with Randy?"

Nina jerked forward in astonishment, her eyes wide.

Coco sank back, dabbing at her nose with a paper towel. "We worked hard at keeping it a secret. Mitch dotes on me. He would have fired Randy."

Nina sputtered, "Oh, come on. Mitch isn't stupid. He must have noticed that you weren't home."

Coco sighed. "We've been living apart in the same house for years. Separate bedrooms, separate lives. Mitch doesn't want a divorce because we're Catholic. He won't hear of it. I might have gone ahead with a divorce anyway, but it would probably kill Nonni if I did. So we pretend to be a couple. I don't keep tabs on him, and I come and go as I please. When he asks, I tell him I'm going to Dad's house or out to some meeting."

"Did you come here the night your dad disappeared?"

Coco winced. "No. I went home with Mitch. But he could easily have left without me knowing it. I moved up to the third-floor suite a couple of years ago, and he uses the second-floor master bedroom." Her fist coiled into a ball around the paper towel. "It's my fault. I should have moved home with Dad and Nonni. I would have been there that night. I would have known what happened to Dad."

Coco looked from Nina to me. "There hasn't been a word from him. Not a hint of what might have happened. How can that be? How can a person disappear without a clue?"

How indeed? Nonni had called Mitch a rooster. I wondered if she would really have been upset by a divorce. Maybe so. Coco's revelation that they hadn't been together the night Joe vanished, as Mitch had claimed, made me wonder if he had a hand in it.

There was so much I wanted to ask her. But it wasn't really fair to take advantage of her at the moment. I feared that inquiring about Kara might make things worse. I went for an answer to one other thing I hadn't been able to ask her in front of Mitch.

"Coco, who is in the locked room upstairs in Joe's house?"

Coco blinked at me. "How did you know about that? Oh right, you went upstairs to look around Daddy's room. Of course, you probably heard her. It's my mom."

"You keep her locked up?" Nina was aghast.

Coco sighed. "You make it sound so awful. It's not like that. It's for her own safety. Mom was in a terrible car accident a very long time ago. She's been an invalid ever since. Brain damage left her unable to speak much or to reason. A few years ago, she managed to propel her wheelchair to the top of the stairs when the nurse wasn't looking, and Mom very nearly toppled down them. She would have broken her neck. After that near miss, we decided that it would be wisest to keep the door locked." She scowled at Nina. "The nurse brings her downstairs. It's not as though she's locked up. We try to take her outside every day. Weather permitting, she sits in the garden with Bacio in her lap."

"There's always a nurse with her?" I asked.

"We wanted to keep her at home. Someone is with her around the clock. At first it was Nonni and me." Coco lifted a weary hand to her face and massaged her temple. "My grandfather, Nonni's husband, died in the same accident. Arnie had just left me, and I thought my life was over. I tried to put on a brave face but I spent hours weeping in my room, just devastated. Daddy finally insisted that I go back to college, which was a blessing for me. I felt like a traitor at the time, like I was giving up on my mom, but Dad was right. He hired nurses and that's how it has been ever since."

"Then there must have been a nurse in Joe's house the night he went missing."

Coco nodded. "She didn't hear a thing. Not the doorbell, not a knock on the door, not the phone ringing, nothing. She was as shocked as everyone else to learn he was gone."

"Your mother didn't come to the chocolate tasting," observed Nina.

Coco bowed her head. "Heavens no. She would have been terrified and confused. She lives a very quiet life."

"I'm so sorry, Coco. It must have been terribly hard on you."

"The most awful time in my life . . . until now. Why did Randy have to die? They say trouble comes in threes, you know."

She didn't say it but she didn't really have to. She was thinking her dad was probably dead, too.

"Coco, you shouldn't be alone tonight. Would you like to come home with me?" I asked.

"That's very kind of you. But no, thanks." Coco slipped on the bracelet that lay on the side table. "I need a little time to pull myself together. It will do me good to walk to Dad's house. Then I'll have to break the news"—her voice wavered—"to Nonni, Dan, and Mitch."

The three of us and the two dogs filed out the front door. Coco turned off the lights and locked up. It felt horrifically final, like she was closing the door on Randy's life. Coco headed for Joe's house while Nina and I walked slowly back to our street.

"How come you didn't tell me they were having an affair?" asked Nina.

"I didn't even suspect it until we were inside Randy's house."

"You know, now that I think back, Randy did seem to be around a lot. He didn't say much, but he sort of hovered near Coco. Do you think Mitch suspects?"

"I don't know. Coco said he dotes on her."

Nina *tsk*ed. "I bet he knows."

"What worries me more is how quickly Mitch insisted that he was home with Coco the night that her father vanished. Coco doesn't really know where he was. How convenient."

"So he felt he needed an alibi," murmured Nina. She stopped walking. "You looked in the wrong house!"

"What?"

"If Coco doesn't pay attention to Mitch, what's to stop him from hiding Joe at their house? Or worse, burying Joe in their garden?"

I wanted to say that was ridiculous. That her imagination was running wild. But I wasn't at all sure that was such a preposterous suggestion. "Surely Coco would have noticed something like that. Chances are that Joe left with someone he trusted or went to meet someone he trusted."

"If Mitch had asked Joe to come to the office or meet him somewhere, wouldn't Joe have gone?" asked Nina. "I bet he would have. So we find out where Mitch and Coco live, and you figure out how to get inside the house."

"I love the way you always say *I'll* figure out how to get in. No way."

"We can walk by at least. Check the windows."

"You think Joe put up a sign that says, *I'm being held captive*?"

"We can look in the garden to see if any dirt has been freshly turned over."

We had reached our block. "Okay. We might not be able to see it at all, but we can give it a try."

We said good night, and I ambled home with Daisy leading the way.

Mars appeared to have dozed off. I moved his book to the table and turned out the lights in the family room. Daisy and I were in the kitchen before Mochie showed up, stretching as though we'd interrupted a great catnap. He didn't seem to mind, though, when he realized that sliced turkey dinner for cats was being doled out.

It had been a rugged few days. I poured myself half a glass of white wine, added a little cranberry juice and topped it with sparkling water. I carried my drink into the sunroom and turned on only the tiny lights strung overhead against the glass.

Everything seemed so calm as I gazed out at my garden. It was hard to imagine that Randy was dead. At least he hadn't been murdered. Unless . . . the stress of being involved in Joe's disappearance or Arnaud's death had been too much for him and led to his heart attack. Stress could bring on a heart attack, couldn't it?

I sat there for a long time, thinking about Coco and the tragedies in her life. You just never knew what kinds of burdens people carried. From the outside Coco seemed to have it all, but tangible things hadn't prevented her from suffering more than her fair share of sorrows. She lost her grandfather. Her mother had survived but spent her days locked in a room. Coco's marriage was over. Her lover had died, and her first love had been murdered. I hoped her father wasn't dead, too. How much could one person endure?

☙

The next morning, Mars still slept when I rose. I let Daisy out and back in, and fed Mochie. By the time I had showered and dressed in a pleated navy blue skirt with a forgiving waistband, that—*oof!*—was getting to be a little less forgiving, a white sleeveless cotton blouse, and white sandals, Mochie and Daisy had gone back to bed with Mars.

I made a cup of tea and grabbed a leftover muffin for breakfast. Closing the door quietly behind me, I locked it, and set off for the hotel in the gloriously refreshing summer morning.

Happily, all my escorts were present and waiting. Groups

of winners would be going to various studios for television appearances.

I spied Lori Speer, looking none the worse for her encounter with Wolf. "Good morning!"

Lori bubbled with her usual enthusiasm. "Isn't it a hoot that I'm a suspect?"

"Not everyone would feel that way."

"The real killer must have dumped those pills into my champagne glass after I set it down. That's the only logical explanation."

It was a good explanation. And plausible. "But why?"

Her eyes narrowed and a breeze lifted her wild hair. "That's what I've been wondering. Either to throw everyone off track, or he intended to poison Arnaud but something went wrong, and he had to strangle him instead. I figure it must have been someone who is married. You know, someone whose spouse or lover might have found the pills so the killer couldn't dispose of them at home."

"You've been giving this a lot of thought."

"You bet. The old cop in me loves a puzzle like this." Lori paused and motioned me away from the rest of the winners. "Arnaud Turnèbe ruined my brother's life by stealing his chocolate recipe. Arnaud made a fortune, and my brother got nothing out of it at all. Nothing. He left the business he loved, the career that was meant for him, and it was because of Arnaud and his sleazy tactics. I didn't kill him, but I'm not surprised that he got his comeuppance from someone. Arnaud was a cheat. He crossed one too many people, and it finally caught up with him."

I watched her board a van. She was right about Arnaud. I barely knew him but so far the only nice thing anyone had mentioned were his chocolates, which, if one believed Lori, were really the creation of her brother. Maybe Mars wasn't off base with his ideas about Lori.

The vans pulled out, and I found myself standing alone

on the sidewalk in front of the hotel. Confident that everything was on track, I took a little hike down to Amore head-
quarters. After all, Mitch had suggested I check out Joe's
office. It wouldn't be polite of me not to talk to Marla while
I was there . . .

The building was oddly quiet. Vince, the ponytailed
handyman who had helped Randy, walked through with his
head bowed. I suspected all the Amore employees would
feel melancholy today.

The receptionist in front recognized me and forced a
feeble smile.

"I'm so sorry about Randy," I said.

The receptionist burst into tears and reached for a box
of tissues, which was empty. Wiping her face with her fingers, she said, "I can't believe he's gone. We're all broken
up about it."

"I hate to be a bother, but Mitch asked me to come by."

"Sure," she sniffled. She waved her hand toward the
stairs. "You know the way."

I walked up the steps, listening to her soft sobs. On the
second floor, I passed the glass partition that enclosed the
conference room and stopped at the door with Joe's name
next to it.

Marla Eldridge looked up from her work. A dimple took
shape next to her mouth when she smiled. Her highly
streaked hair wasn't as perfectly coiffed as usual. In fact,
she appeared a bit disheveled, as though she hadn't bothered
to run a brush through her hair that morning. A half-eaten
sandwich in an open foam box lay on a console behind her.
"Sophie! What can I do for you?"

"Mitch asked me to stop by and have a look around Joe's
office."

"Mitch?" Her slender hand moved to the phone and rested
on it.

"A little surprising, I know. He thought I might notice
something that had been overlooked. He's worried about Joe."

Her hand slid off the phone, and she chewed her lower lip. "Okaaay." She stretched the word out as if she wasn't sure.

"Why don't you come into his office with me? That way you'll know what I'm doing."

"All right. You go ahead, I'll be with you in a minute."

She picked up the telephone and smiled at me.

I walked into Joe's office but left the door open. I could hear her ask someone, "Where's Mitch?" After a few seconds, she said, "Call me the minute he comes back."

She watched me from the doorway, fidgeting with the belt on her dress. In her forties, she was slender and attractive. I'd seen her eyes light up with laughter in the past but she was some kind of nervous today.

"Was that so we can skedaddle out of here when Mitch returns?"

Marla flushed as red as a raspberry. "I'm sorry."

Nonni had called him a bossy rooster. "Don't be. I'm sure he can be pretty intimidating."

"He didn't really ask you to come here, did he?"

"Actually he did." I pulled open the top drawer of Joe's desk. Pens, paper clips, ordinary office items. I knelt on the floor.

"What are you doing?"

I glanced at the underside of the middle drawer and the side drawers. "Just checking to see if he taped anything to the drawers to hide it from view."

"I never thought of that. I'm worried sick about him."

I flipped through his daily calendar. Except for the welcome dinner, he didn't have anything noted for the night of his disappearance. "Not into a computer calendar yet?"

"He keeps both. He relies on that one on his desk, though. Some old habits die hard."

"I heard you called Kara." I said it as casually as I could.

She gripped the doorframe. "Mitch made me call her."

The phone rang in her office. Marla excused herself to answer it. I heard her gasp.

CHAPTER TWENTY-ONE

Dear Sophie,

My sister was going to bake some brownies but we didn't have any baking chocolate. Is there a substitute that can be used in case she tries to use that excuse again?

—Skeptical Little Brother in Sisters, Oregon

Dear Skeptical Little Brother,

Next time suggest she try using three tablespoons of unsweetened cocoa powder plus one tablespoon of butter or vegetable oil for each ounce of baking chocolate.

—Sophie

"Thank you for letting me know," said Marla. It took a few minutes before she returned to the door. Her hair was a bigger mess than before and something in her eyes had changed. They were restless and wary.

"Everything okay?" I asked.

Her mouth twisted, and she didn't answer me right away. "Fine."

"Why didn't Mitch call Kara himself?"

"She hasn't communicated with the family in years," said Marla. "He thought she would hang up on him."

"Why?"

"I didn't work here then. I don't really know many details. Joe said once that it was the biggest regret in his life."

"What did he regret?"

"That she ran away, I guess. I think he felt it was his fault."

"Why wouldn't she keep in touch with Coco, Dan, and Nonni?"

"I really don't know. I don't dare mention her name . . . and there's really no reason to."

"Where did you get her phone number?"

"Joe's desk. Lift the blotter," she instructed.

I lifted the edge of it and found a simple sheet of paper. "Is this Joe's handwriting?"

Marla nodded.

It didn't say much, just Kara's phone number and an address in Colorado. I lowered the blotter and straightened it.

"Do you think Kara could have anything to do with Joe's disappearance?"

The surprised expression on her face told me she hadn't even considered such a thing. "Oh my word! That seems unlikely."

I scanned the items on his bookshelves. They reflected Joe's simple tastes. Pictures of his family, Italian ceramics, chocolate awards, and a display of the packaging for Amore chocolates. I stood there for a moment, musing that they summed up Joe's interests and life fairly well. He was a devoted family man, proud of his Italian heritage, and a workaholic determined to make the most of the family chocolate business. I turned to Marla.

"Did anything out of the ordinary happen recently? Unusual phone calls to Joe? Anything like that?"

She shook her head in the negative.

"What about Arnaud? Was there any contact between Joe and Arnaud Turnèbe?"

"Not that I'm aware of. His name came up, naturally. There was some concern that his new store would cut into sales at our local store. But it wasn't anything outside of a normal business context."

"That's the store Stella manages?"

"Right."

I pointed toward the array of boxes. "Is there any other packaging in use by Amore?"

"Not that I know of." She frowned at me. "I'm not following. Other boxes?"

"Do they have a line, say, without the name of the company embossed on the box? Maybe small red boxes for the hand-dipped gourmet line?"

She licked her top lip. "No. I don't think so."

"What do *you* think happened to Joe?"

She hesitated a second too long. She knew something. Or suspected something. "I don't know," she replied in a whisper. Speaking in a normal tone again, she said, "Thanks for coming by. You know what? I believe I'll walk downstairs with you to get some lunch."

I didn't say a word about the sandwich on the console that she hadn't finished or that it was still early for lunch.

She collected her purse in a rush and held the door open for me. She chattered about the weather on the way down the stairs. Outside on the sidewalk, she waved good-bye and hurried along the street.

I followed her for a few blocks to a parking garage. She pulled out a minute later, driving a white Toyota RAV4, far too fast for Old Town.

There was nothing more to do but walk home.

While Mars and I noshed on leftovers for lunch, a wicked

summer storm arose, complete with thunder, lightning, and torrential rain. When it wound down to a rhythmic patter, we both hit our computers and worked from home.

The rain had almost stopped when I took Daisy with me to check on the Amore winners. They had all returned, giddy about their television appearances. Daisy was thrilled with all the attention, wagging her tail nonstop. Mars and I spent a quiet evening at home, speculating about the Meranos, Arnaud's death and Joe's whereabouts. We always came back to the same question—what had happened to drive Kara away?

In the morning, I skipped breakfast to get an early start. But I took the time to cut a quarter of the chocolate cake and wrap it in cellophane, tying it off with a lime and white gingham bow. I walked over to the hotel to check on the Amore crowd first. Coco had arranged for them to visit the Inner Harbor in Baltimore. They boarded buses, looking a little tired after the stress of the previous day.

From there, I walked over to Joe's house.

I rang the bell and Nonni answered the door.

"Sofia! I am thinking about you. Come, come." She swept her hand inward.

I followed her to the kitchen and handed her the cake.

Nonni untied the bow and sniffed it. "Is beautiful. You drink coffee with me. Yes?"

She didn't wait for an answer, and poured coffee into two of the stunning Italian ceramic mugs. "Please, sit. Now, you tell me who kill Arnaud."

"I'm still working on that but I need some information, please."

Dan stumbled in looking tousled and tired. He gave Nonni a kiss. I thought he had a place on Lee Street but it appeared that he had spent the night at Joe's house.

"You excuse me. I get breakfast for Danny."

"Nonni! I told you not to do that. Sit, I can get it myself."
Dan smiled at me. "Good morning! When I stay over, Nonni
always pampers me like I am still a kid."

Nonni shook her finger at him. "He thinks I cannot hear
the telephone at night."

Dan made a little face. "Nonni, when you take out your
hearing aids you don't hear a thing." He glanced my way.
"In case we get a call about Dad."

I sipped my coffee. It was strong and hot. Nonni had
added milk and sugar to it.

Dan ambled to the stovetop and shook his head. "You
made me eggs." He looked up at me. "I can't keep her from
waiting on me hand and foot. Would you care to join me?"

"No, thanks. I just wanted to ask a few questions."

Dan brought his plate to the table. "Don't let me interrupt."

I was hesitant. I'd hoped to get Nonni alone. They would
share anyway, so I forged ahead. "Could you tell me about
Kara?"

Dan stopped chewing. His fork clattered to his plate.

Nonni appeared to stop breathing.

"Are you all right, Nonni?" I asked.

"Why you ask about Kara?" Nonni demanded.

Dan heaved a huge breath and released it in a long
whoosh. "I think it's pretty obvious, Nonni. She's figured
out the connection."

"Kara has nothing to do with this. No one kill Arnie
because of something that happens thirty years ago."

"It might help if I knew what transpired," I suggested.

Dan had forgotten about his food. He ran his hands
through his hair and shook his head. "Coco and Kara were
in love with the same man."

CHAPTER TWENTY-TWO

Dear Sophie,

I hate to be so clueless, but I'm always seeing desserts with ganache. It seems to be the latest thing. What is it exactly?

—Starter Cook in Start, Louisiana

Dear Starter Cook,

Ganache is simply chocolate mixed with cream. It can be used as a glaze, an icing, a sauce, and even a filling. It has a beautiful sheen that is very attractive.

—Sophie

"Kara and Coco were both in love with Arnie?" I asked.

Nonni's sweet mouth pulled tight. "Was horrible. Two sisters who were so close."

"Arnie ruined our lives. He took a family"—Dan pretended to twist something in his hands—"and broke it into a million little pieces. We've never been the same. It's all his fault. Arnie was two-timing them. Can you imagine? It's bad enough to two-time any women, but sisters?"

"So what happened?"

"I remember the screaming and crying like it was yesterday." Dan screwed up his face and winced at the memory. "Arnie took off, like a worm. He ran away from the problem." Dan glanced at Nonni before he continued. "Kara raced after him in her car. It was a cold winter night. Very icy with snow coming down like crazy. Everyone was in an uproar. Mom and my grandfather, Nonno, went after Kara. It wasn't very far, just up the road to the airport. It wasn't as developed up there as it is now. Somehow, Kara caught up to him. She must have been driving like crazy. She stopped her car, jumped out, and she and Arnie argued in the middle of the road. Arnie knocked her to the ground. My grandfather, Nonno, must not have seen them until the last minute because of the snow. He slammed the brakes, and swerved to avoid hitting them. The car rolled over and landed in the Potomac. Nonno died, and Mom has been an invalid ever since."

"That's why Kara left? Because she felt it was her fault?"

"Was the fault of no one!" said Nonni emphatically.

Dan turned sad dog eyes toward me. "The next day, Kara pursued Arnie anyway. Mom was in the hospital, Nonno hadn't even been buried, and Kara took off again to be with Arnie."

I was stunned. "She chose Arnie over her family."

"She was foolish young girl in love. She thinks she has found her man." Nonni leaned toward me, waggling her finger. "But Arnie, he really loves Coco. This is why he comes back now."

"Was there a rivalry between Coco and Kara?"

"They were good sisters, sharing everything," said Nonni.

Sharing a man wasn't quite as easy as borrowing a sweater. I thought I knew the answer to my next question but I wanted to hear their version. "Have you been in touch with Kara? Didn't she ever come home?"

"She left us to deal with cleaning up the disaster she wrought on us." Dan's jaw twitched as though he couldn't control it. "She ruined our lives, our family. I was only fifteen when we fell apart. Nonno was gone. Mom was still with us, but barely. Coco cried all the time. Dad hid at work. I don't know what would have become of us if it hadn't been for Nonni."

She reached over and patted his hand. "You food is cold!"

Dan swigged the remainder of his coffee. "It's okay, Nonni, I'm not that hungry."

"What happened to Kara and Arnie?" I asked.

"We never heard another thing about Arnie," said Dan. "And Kara was dead to us."

"Dan! You no talk about Kara that way." Nonni reprimanded him sharply. "Kara never returns home again."

The family had lost a lot and spent years suffering. No wonder they didn't talk about Kara.

I gazed around the kitchen. "Did you ever find Bacio?"

Nonni clasped her hands together. "Joe's wife misses Bacio. We all do. You know what it means, *Bacio*?"

I shook my head.

"Kiss. Is Italian for kiss." She leaned over and kissed Dan's cheek, ruffling his hair like he was still a little boy. "You must forgive you sister."

"I forgave Coco a long time ago."

"Is not what I mean."

"Coco is the only sister I have, Nonni." Dan rose from the table and walked out.

Nonni wrung her hands like she was washing them. "No one forgives Kara. It was wrong to leave us. To chase this man. But she was young and foolish." She leaned toward me and grasped my hand. "Sofia, you must let the old wrongs go. There is no good in hanging on to them."

She saw me to the door and thanked me again for bringing the cake. I strolled home, feeling like I'd been run over by a bulldozer. How would I have coped if my sister abandoned our family in favor of a two-timing louse? Granted, Kara had been young, and we all made poor judgments when we thought we were in love.

Obviously, Joe had kept tabs on his daughter. Dan resented Kara to this day. Nonni wanted to forgive her. I wondered how Coco felt about her sister after all these years.

I stopped at Mars's favorite deli to pick up sandwiches for lunch and ran into Humphrey and Francie.

"We were just talking about you," Francie exclaimed.

Humphrey beamed at me. "I was going to call you as soon as I picked up my lunch." He lowered his tone and whispered, "I've been dying to tell you since yesterday. You know Randy? The Amore handyman? He didn't die of natural causes."

CHAPTER TWENTY-THREE

Dear Natasha,

I love your show. Your taste is so exquisite. I've painted every room in my house high-gloss gray like you advised, and it's never been more stunning. I need to make a showy dessert for guests. Would you do an episode on how to make chocolate trifle?

—Your Biggest Fan in Greystone, West Virginia

Dear Biggest Fan,

Your home must be terribly elegant. Send pictures! I hate to disappoint you, but a proper trifle is made with custard, fruit, and sponge cake, never with chocolate.

—Natasha

"Are you sure?" I asked.

Humphrey nodded. "I was at the medical examiner's office yesterday. They were all buzzing about it, but I couldn't tell you until it was official. There was no sign of a heart attack, so they ran some tests and found phytolac-catoxin."

"What is that? I've never heard of it."

"American pokeweed," said Francie. "The same plant you pulled out of your garden. Very toxic stuff. I've seen recipes for cooking the berries, which I find odd, because the stalk and roots are deadly. Personally, I wouldn't take a chance on the berries."

"They're everywhere. I see them all the time when I'm driving by wooded areas. I had no idea they were so poison-ous." I leaned against the wall. "I can't believe this. It couldn't have been accidental. No one would eat a weed like that. Why? Why kill Randy?"

"Maybe he murdered Arnaud," said Francie.

"And someone knew," suggested Humphrey.

"Coco." It was the barest whisper but they heard me. "Coco was, um, close to Randy. He did a lot of errands for her."

"They were having an affair?" asked Francie, cutting to the chase as usual. "Hah. Never would have suspected them as a couple."

"That's not what I said," I insisted.

"We're all adults." Francie shook her head. "We know what that means."

"You can't tell anyone!" I hissed. "Mitch doesn't know."

"Someone better tell Wolf," said Humphrey.

I felt terrible for Coco. She was doing the wrong thing by having an affair, but since her marriage was essentially over, I didn't really blame her for seeking love elsewhere. And now the truth would come out. If Randy had died of natural causes, Mitch might never have been the wiser.

"How do we know that Mitch isn't having an affair, as well?" asked Francie. "These things often work both ways when a marriage is on the rocks."

"What if it's not because of the affair at all?" I asked. "Maybe someone murdered Randy because he knows where Joe is."

We left the deli and went our separate ways. Had Mitch found out about Coco's affair? Wouldn't he have been the one most likely to kill Randy?

Stunned by the news, I wound my way home past Célé-bration de Chocolat, the shop Arnaud hadn't lived to open. He'd only died on Saturday and poor Arnaud was nearly forgotten. Only Coco's wreath still marked his passing. He might have been a two-timing letch, but he deserved to be remembered.

As I stood there looking at his storefront, Natasha walked by inside the store. I blinked a few times and peered through the window for a closer look. It was definitely Natasha. I rapped on the glass.

Natasha pushed the door open. "Mars isn't with you, is he?"

I stepped inside. "You broke his leg, remember?"

"That doesn't mean he can't walk."

"Well, yeah, it kind of does. But he's not with me. What are you doing here?"

"I'm going to rent this place. Isn't it beautiful?"

"Rent it?" I screeched. I coughed and tried to control my voice. "For your chocolate business?"

"All I have to do is change the name in the front to *Natasha*. Well, that and order new boxes that say *Natasha*. It's almost ready to go."

"Have you ever made chocolates in your entire life?"

She averted her gaze. "Don't you love the display cases?"

"Natasha! Are you out of your mind?"

"You're just jealous. You wish you had thought of this."

"Don't turn this around and make it about me. Honey, this place has got to cost a fortune. It's in a prime location. Shouldn't you try making chocolate first? Maybe take a class or spend some time working at Amore before you invest money?"

"This is why I didn't want Mars here. He would try to spoil my brilliant idea, too."

"Because this is insanity, Natasha!"

"Shh, here's the Realtor. Don't embarrass me."

I greeted the real estate agent as he emerged from a back room. While they talked, I took a look around. It was a pity that the store had never opened. Arnaud must have signed a lease. How could they be renting it to someone else already?

I walked into a small office. On a shelf to the left were boxes that solved one mystery conclusively. They were identical to the boxes in which the mysterious chocolates had arrived at my house. I picked them up and examined them to be absolutely sure. They bore no company name or logo.

Nonni and Coco had recognized Arnie's trademark chocolates when they tried them. Even Wolf took their word for it that the chocolates must have come from Arnie. And now it seemed they were all correct. But why did Arnie send *me* chocolates? And why use unmarked boxes when the Célébration de Chocolat logo on an elegant cream background was on everything else?

I ambled behind the desk and glanced through the Day-Timer. Someone had been using it for a while. *Opening day* was marked in huge letters. Someone had made a notation on Saturday that said *Amore Tasting.* Near the blotter lay an invitation to the tasting. The wording was exactly right. I had written it, so I knew what it had said. There was one problem, though. The paper was wrong. I gently lifted a corner and ran my finger under it. I'd had them printed with the Amore logo embossed at the top and a raised edge around the side. This one appeared to be ordinary cardstock run through a printer.

CHAPTER TWENTY-FOUR

Dear Sophie,

My boyfriend's dog always drools when we eat something chocolate. I know chocolate is bad for dogs, but haven't I seen chocolate dog treats somewhere? Do they use artificial flavoring or something?

—Still Just the Girlfriend in Dogs Corners, New Jersey

Dear Still Just the Girlfriend,

You are absolutely right. Chocolate can kill a dog. However, dogs can eat carob. It comes from the pod of a tree. The flavor is not as strong as chocolate but it's an excellent substitute.

—Sophie

Someone had made up an invitation and sent it to Arnaud. Why would anyone do that? No wonder he showed up. He wasn't crashing the party. He thought he had been invited.

A chill enveloped me. Someone wanted to see him. Someone intended to kill him.

I had to tell Wolf. Using a pen, I flipped the invitation over. On the back, three tiny telltale ink smears had been left by the printer. None of the real invitations bore that kind of amateurish mark. I scooted the invitation under the blotter so no one would touch it or throw it out before I could tell Wolf about it. Maybe he could find fingerprints on it.

I hurried out to the front of the store, where Natasha engaged the Realtor with her crazy plan.

"Excuse me, but didn't Arnaud or the Célébration de Chocolat company sign a lease?"

The real estate agent smiled. "Yes. But given the circumstances, the owner of the building is lining up a replacement tenant. You understand. Just in case Célébration de Chocolat doesn't have the resources to pay the rent. They would probably appreciate being off the hook if they don't intend to keep the store."

Too bad. I was hoping to find a reason to discourage Natasha. I made up a lie to prevent her from taking any more steps toward committing herself to renting the place. "Mars called. He's asking for you. He's having some kind of emergency."

Natasha apologized to the real estate agent but promised to swing by his office as soon as he had drafted the lease. *What a nightmare!*

We walked home together as the midday heat started to bear down on Old Town.

"Sophie," said Natasha, "do you know what my greatest fear is?"

"Food? Calories?" I joked.

"No, I have that under control. *You* might be wise to fear them, though."

"Thank you. That makes me feel much better."

"I'm only telling you for your own good, honey."

I gritted my teeth. "So what's your greatest fear?"

"Not being successful. I'm not getting any younger, and I still haven't achieved my dreams."

"Natasha, you have a popular TV show. Your fans adore you. I've seen them fawn over you."

"They're wonderful to me. It's true that I have fans. But I wanted to be the Martha of the South. I don't have a magazine. I don't have any products for sale. I don't even have cookbooks. And my show is just local. Go out of town and no one has ever heard of me."

"Sure they have. They read your column."

"Then why do I feel like such a failure? All I do is spin my wheels. I never make any progress. I don't know how to move forward."

"And you think having a chocolate shop is the key?" A brilliant thought came to me. "Martha doesn't have a chocolate shop."

Natasha stopped dead. "She doesn't! That would set me apart from the rest. Good point, Sophie."

I couldn't believe that backfired on me.

"Goodness!" cried Natasha. "No wonder Mars needed me. What's going on?"

I shifted my focus to the street. We were still a good distance away from our block, but there was no mistaking a commotion in front of my house. I took off at a run, leaving Natasha behind in her five-inch heels.

A little crowd of neighbors had gathered before my home. The gate to the backyard hung open. I recognized an unmarked police car, probably Wolf's. But parked right in front of it was a white car ominously marked *Police*.

I was out of breath but fear propelled me forward. I staggered up the few steps to my kitchen door and flung it open.

Mars stood in the kitchen, leaning on crutches. Daisy rushed to me, wagging her tail.

I was so out of breath that I bent to breathe and hug Daisy at the same time.

Wolf stepped out of my family room and pulled me into

a hug. He pressed me to him, his chin nuzzled my ear, and he whispered, "It's okay. Everything will be okay."

He released me so fast that I nearly lost my balance.

The door opened behind me. A man built like a brick wall stepped inside. His head was shaven and a lush mustache hung over his top lip. "Sophie Winston? I'm glad you decided to come back."

Come back? I lived here. "Who are you?"

"Sophie, this is Sergeant Wolchik. He's a new investigator."

I held out my hand to him. "Hi, nice to meet you."

Wolchik ignored it. "I'd like to speak with you privately."

I looked around. There was no one else in the kitchen besides Daisy, Mochie, Mars, and Wolf. "That's not necessary. What's going on?"

"Have a seat please, ma'am."

My breath was coming more naturally again but my heart pounded. I sat down on one of the chairs next to the fireplace.

Wolchik crossed his arms over his chest and stood too close to me, with his feet apart. A menacing stance if ever I saw one.

Daisy, the most easygoing dog in the world, pulled her long lips up to show her teeth and growled at him.

Mars sat down in the chair nearest me and called her over to him.

"Nice house for a single woman," said Wolchik.

The words could have been complimentary, but I understood them as questioning my possession of a big place. I looked over at Wolf, who shrugged. I didn't dignify the veiled suspicion with a response. "What do you want, Sergeant Wolchik?"

"Where were you yesterday?"

"What? Why do you care? Am I some kind of suspect?"

Wolf settled on the banquette, behind Wolchik. Wolf rotated his hand in a gesture I took to mean *just play along and answer him.*

"Okay. I went to the hotel to check on the Amore guests. Then I stopped by the Amore offices, came home—"

"Stop right there. Who, if anyone, did you see at Amore?"

If anyone? Did he think he was a prosecutor in a trial? "The receptionist, that new guy, Vince, and Marla, Joe's assistant."

"What did you want with Marla?"

I hesitated to admit that I hoped she would know the story behind Kara's estrangement from her family. "Nothing. Mitch had suggested that I stop by Joe's office to have a look around."

"Why?"

"He's worried about Joe."

"And he thought you would find something the police, who are trained, would overlook?"

I played his game. "I can't tell you what *Mitch* thought."

His face grew darker and grim. "Don't get sassy with me. You're in a lot of trouble. I suggest you answer respectfully."

I didn't dare look straight at Wolf lest this creep toss him from the room. But out of the corner of my eye, I could see Wolf getting miffed, something that rarely showed on his face.

"When is the last time you saw Marla Eldridge?"

"When I left the building. She walked out with me. Said she was going to get some lunch." If he had been nicer to me, I would have told him that she drove away, but he was such a pill that I did not want to cooperate. Besides, I could tell Wolf after this annoying cop was gone.

"Why are you asking about Marla?" I sucked in air. "Oh no! Is she dead, too?"

"Aha! Why would you think that?"

"There *have* been a couple of murders."

"Where did you go after that?"

I was slowly putting things together. "First Joe, then Randy. And now Marla?"

"Where did you go after that?" he shouted.

"Home." I spoke very quietly to calm him down. "I came home."

"We'd like to see your car. Do you have any objection to that?"

"My car? Whatever for?"

It finally dawned on me that he thought I had Marla in my car. "I walked. I haven't been in the car for days. You can ask Mars. He was here." I didn't mention that he was in the family room, which didn't have a window that looked out on the detached garage.

"Did you murder Randy Hicks?"

"What?" I jumped out of my seat just in time to see Alex open the kitchen door and walk in. "What are you doing here?"

"I called him," said Mars. In response to my angry glare, he added, "I thought we might need him."

Right in front of everyone, Wolchik stepped into my face. He was a good foot and a half taller than me, and his complexion had gone fury red. "Look, we know you murdered Randy Hicks. We've got your prints on your box of poisoned chocolates. Wolf can't save you this time, and neither can a slick-talking lawyer. I'm going to ask you one more time, did you murder Randy Hicks?"

I stepped back intending to look him in the eye, but I fell into the chair, not exactly the impression I wanted to give. "Poisoned chocolates? I have never murdered anyone. Ever!"

"Then explain your fingerprints. Explain the poison we found in your backyard."

Alex stepped up to him. I wouldn't have called Alex puny, but Wolchik had a good six inches and sixty pounds on him. "Let's see the search warrant."

I caught the hint of a smirk on Wolf's face.

Wolchik stormed out of my kitchen.

"Quick," said Alex. "Give me a dollar."

Mars pulled a buck out of his pocket and handed it to me.

"What's this for?"

"Hire me before Godzilla comes back," Alex whispered.

"I don't need to hire anyone. I didn't do anything."

Wolf groaned. "For pity's sake, Sophie. Just do it."

I snatched the dollar from Mars and handed it to Alex, who said, "Thank you, ma'am, you've just hired yourself a lawyer."

I flicked a hand at him. "I don't care about that." I walked over to Wolf. "What's going on? Is it because my fingerprints are in Randy's house?"

The kitchen door opened, and Natasha strolled in. "I've been talking to those nice policemen. Sophie, I think we should serve them some refreshments."

CHAPTER TWENTY-FIVE

Dear Natasha,

I love your recipes. It's so refreshing that you don't stick to the same old tired dishes that I've seen one hundred times. I'm supposed to bring dessert to a function where my ex-husband will be. What would knock his socks off?

—Who's Sorry Now? in Exie, Kentucky

Dear Who's Sorry Now,

Homemade chocolate cannoli. They will be gorgeous, taste fabulous, and it will only take you about five hours to make them.

—Natasha

"Not now, Nat." Mars focused on Wolf. "Is she really in trouble?"

Wolf ran a hand through his hair and sighed.

"You can't tell us? Why did they send that horrible man?" I asked.

"There are people who think I can't be objective because I'm too close to you," Wolf explained.

"I'd agree with *that*," said Alex.

I shot him a look of daggers. "Wolf, I don't understand. I thought Randy died from pokeweed poisoning."

Wolf blinked at me. "How do you know these things?"

I wasn't about to rat on Humphrey. "Can you tell us what happened to Marla?"

"Sophie," trilled Natasha, "where do you keep the coffee?"

"In the freezer."

Wolf nodded. "You're the last person who saw her. She never went back to the office yesterday after she left with you. She didn't turn up for work this morning, either. She's not at her home. No one can locate her."

"Well, thank heaven she's not dead! Something scared her, Wolf. When we left the Amore building, she got in her car and took off like the devil himself was chasing her."

"What did you two talk about?"

"Joe and his daughter Kara."

Wolf's eyebrows rose, "Kara?"

Alex interrupted. "Do you really have poisonous plants in your backyard?"

"Lots of people do. They just don't know it. Pokeweed is pretty common."

"I've never heard of it," he insisted.

"You've seen it, I'm sure. In the fall, the plants have bunches of beautiful dark purple berries on curving fuchsia stems, kind of like currants or tiny grapes but poisonous. I'm not sure the berries are poisonous, but the rest of the plant is."

"And you have this in your backyard?" Alex drew away from me as though he was appalled.

"One had grown in my garden, so I yanked it out, but then I went to the hotel for something and didn't throw it away. It should still be out there if the evil cop didn't take it."

"If it's such a common plant, then why are they focusing on Sophie?" asked Alex.

"Because her fingerprints were on the box of poisoned chocolates that killed Randy," said Natasha, as though she was talking about the weather. "Sophie, where do you keep your jalapeños and truffles?"

"Chocolates? What chocolates? How do you know that?" I asked.

"If you were nice to the police, they might tell you things, too." Natasha poked my shoulder. "The jalapeños, where are they? I'm baking chocolate chip cookies. I can't do it at home because there's no running water."

I ignored her. "Is that true, Wolf?"

He nodded his head. "They found a box of poisoned chocolates at Randy's house with your fingerprints on it."

"But I haven't made any chocolates or bought any." I fetched the giant box of chocolates Alex had sent and brought it to the table. "These were a gift from Alex."

"And the hospital still has the unidentified boxes of chocolates, right?" Mars opened a box of the Amore chocolates from Alex and tried one. "Is it just me or did these used to be better?"

Alex tilted his head. "Really? That's how you disparage me? You have to put down the chocolates I bought for Sophie?"

Men! I hurriedly ate one of the chocolates. "They're delicious!" But I understood what Mars meant. They weren't quite as good as they used to be. The chocolate tasted different. It didn't have that silky, melty feel on the tongue that I remembered. I didn't mention it, though. Alex would have gone through the roof, and he was plenty mad at me already.

I hastened to change the subject. "I guess the hospital lab still has the mysterious chocolates. All except the last box that arrived the day after Coco's collapse. I stashed it in my desk so no one would accidentally eat any."

Mars used one of his crutches to point in the direction of my office. "Go get it."

I didn't see the point in that, but I was so shocked by this odd turn of events that I did what he said.

Except it wasn't there.

I was certain that I stashed it in the lower right drawer. I checked all the other drawers. It was nowhere to be found. In a little frenzy, I looked around my tiny office. Not on the desk, not on the sofa, not on the printer or the bookshelves.

I could hear Mars's crutches as he made his way to my office.

Alex poked his head in the doorway. "Something wrong?"

"I can't find it. I know I put it in the bottom drawer out of the way so no one would be tempted to try them."

Wolf stepped past Alex and pulled open the desk drawer. "Think back. Was anyone in here?"

"Mochie!" blurted Mars.

Alex and Wolf stared at him like he'd lost his mind, but I knew exactly what he meant. "The day I found Mochie outside! Someone *was* in the house."

Wolf frowned at me. "Why didn't you call me? Did you report it to the police?"

"We thought Mochie might have slipped by me. Mars went through the house with me and nothing was missing or out of place."

Wolf studied Mars. "Is that true? Can you verify that?"

"Sure. You should have seen Mochie, he was very upset. He's an indoor cat, and I think he didn't like being left outside."

We walked back to the kitchen, where Natasha was sliding cookies into the oven.

"Let me see if I have this straight," said Wolf. "Under your scenario, someone broke into your house and searched for the mysterious chocolates, which just happened to be poisoned with the same deadly plant that is in your backyard. Then the chocolates were given to Randy, who ate them and died."

"Think Wolchik will buy that?" asked Alex.

I realized how unlikely it sounded. "But that *must* be what happened. You know *I* didn't kill him! How else could a box of chocolates with my fingerprints have turned up in Randy's possession? And seriously, let's say I *had* intended to murder Randy, don't you think I would have worn gloves to handle the box in the first place? I could have gotten rid of the chocolates after he died, too. It would have been easy to remove them from his house after the ambulance left."

"Nina or Coco would have noticed," Mars pointed out.

Thank you, Mars. Whose side was he on?

"Wolf," I said, "check the inside of the box for fingerprints. I never opened it. I was busy and just stashed it away. I never looked inside of it."

"The cops are gone." Natasha sounded melancholy about it.

Did she not realize what was going on?

"Wait! They left one behind. Great!" Natasha held up the French press plunger. "I don't get this gadget. Where does the coffee go?"

"You need boiling water." She was doubly confused when I added ground coffee right to the pot.

"Is the cop with you?" Alex asked Wolf.

"No. Wolchik must have left someone behind to make sure Sophie doesn't destroy evidence." Wolf settled at my kitchen table and looked down, deep in thought.

When Natasha took an *I-heart-police* mug out of my cabinet, Alex and Mars were appalled.

"Why do you still have that?" asked Mars.

"You see, Sophie? This is what I'm talking about," grumbled Alex. "You can't let go."

Wolf just grinned.

I tried my best to ignore all of them. At the moment, my love life looked like the smallest problem on my horizon.

Natasha poured the coffee, placed some fresh-from-the-oven cookies on a plate and took them out to the officer.

I poured coffee for the guys and set the creamer and sugar

on the table. Holding a less controversial English bone china mug painted with pink, purple, and blue morning glories, I sat down at the table with them. "Nothing fits together," I complained. "I thought there might be a tie between Joe and Arnaud because they're both chocolatiers but the main connection seems to be Kara and Coco."

Wolf's head snapped up. "Tell me about Kara."

Natasha returned, laughing and giddy.

While I told the story of Arnie, Coco, and Kara, Natasha placed a platter of fresh chocolate chip cookies on the table along with napkins and sat down with us.

"That's so sad," she said. "From the outside, it looks like they have the perfect life. But it's really messed up and tragic. My heart breaks for them. They've lost almost half their family."

I cupped the coffee between my hands. "In a way, Arnie ruined their lives. Everyone in the family must have resented him enormously. If he hadn't dated Kara and Coco at the same time or even if he hadn't run off in the snow like a coward, their lives would have been different."

Alex drummed his fingers on the table. "That's what comes of dating more than one man at a time. I mean woman, of course."

Oh! That was aimed at me! I scowled at him.

Natasha tilted her head. "You could say the same thing about Kara. She didn't have to run after him."

Mars pulled out the list he had made. "Joe, Nonni, everyone in their family had a reason to kill Arnie. Even Coco and Kara."

Alex glanced at his watch. "I've got to go. I have a client coming to my office in fifteen minutes. Sophie, call me if anyone arrives with a search warrant." He rose to leave and bent his head to kiss me.

I ducked. "After all the jabs you made at me? No, thank you. Besides, isn't there some kind of rule about not kissing clients?"

Alex heaved a sigh. "I have no idea what I see in you, Sophie Winston." He opened the door and turned, "But I still want you to call me if Wolchik turns up again."

Wolf stretched his legs. "I'd better go, too. There's no telling what Wolchik is up to now."

I saw them to the door. As soon as they left, I said, "I have an errand to run. Call me if Wolchik or another cop shows up."

"But it's time for lunch," Mars protested.

I stared at him. Only then did I realize that I never bought anything at the deli. "Lucky for you that Natasha is here." I couldn't help grinning as I closed the door and hurried away before he could protest further. Maybe I'd bring some takeout back with me.

Mars's observation about the quality of Amore chocolates had been dead-on, and it worried me. They took such care with their chocolates. I hoped the box at my house had been an aberration, but if it wasn't, then something was up.

I walked straight to the Amore retail shop on King Street. A couple occupied the small white wrought iron table and chairs outside the brick building. A giant chandelier sparkled inside. Boxes wrapped with bright bows and summery adornments like faux flowers and pairs of miniature flip-flops had been artfully stacked in the window. The *Birth of Venus* statue that Dan had carved was front and center. The masterpiece appeared to lord over all the smaller chocolates.

A bell rang merrily when I opened the door. The mouthwatering scent of chocolate wafted in the air. A friendly employee asked if she could help me. I selected a few of the truffles and specialty chocolates in the showcase, as well as three different boxes of chocolates. "Is Stella in today?"

"She's in the back. Stella! You have a visitor."

Stella emerged from a rear room. She wore her blonde hair pinned up in a bun. Not a single strand fell into her pretty, young face. "Sophie, right?"

"Yes. I needed a few things and thought you might have a minute to chat."

"That was nice of you." To the clerk she said, "Give her the family discount."

"No, no. That's not what I meant at all. I just wanted to talk with you for a minute."

Stella's expression turned fearful. "Follow me."

I walked behind the counter and through the doorway into an office.

Stella closed the door and leaned against it. Her chest heaved as she took deep breaths. She focused worried eyes on me.

I needed to say something to make her relax! But what? I hardly knew the girl. And then I saw her shoes. Thick soled and comfortable, her thong sandals were fashion forward with fountains of tiny amber beads sprouting from the tops.

"FitFlops?" I asked.

She knew exactly what I meant. "Yes! I'm on my feet most of the day and these are like walking on a cloud. I can't usually afford them, so I buy them off season when they're on sale."

I was partial to them myself. "I know exactly what you mean. Especially in Old Town, where we walk so much."

She looked down at her feet, and when her gaze returned to me, she said, "I hear you're the last person who saw Marla."

"That's what they tell me. Do you know where she is?"

Stella held her hands behind her back and studied the floor.

She hadn't invited me to sit down, even though three basic office chairs crowded the room. Various advertisements for Amore had been pinned to the walls. The guides to flavors of Amore chocolates were the most vibrant. The desk was cheap fiberboard, worn on the edges so that the pressed material underneath showed through. A laptop computer resided in the middle of the desk, the cover open. A printer sat on a console to the side with a stack of pink paper fliers announcing a sale. I picked one up. "A sale in honor of the anniversary? That's nice!"

She spoke in a hurry, words tumbling from her lips. "I don't know where Marla is, but I fear for her and Dan."

I hadn't expected that.

She held her hands over her mouth. "I'm so afraid for them."

"Not for yourself?"

"Gosh, no!"

"Why them and not yourself?"

"Joe, Arnaud, Randy . . . I don't know who's next. I thought it would be Dan because they're all men, but now Marla is gone." She thought for a moment. "Arnaud was an awful man. There must have been people all around the world who would have liked to do him in. It's so sad that he's dead and no one mourns him," she whispered. "He stepped on everyone and cared for no one. Can you imagine being that kind of person? What happened to him? What makes a person be like that?"

I had no answers. "It must have been hard on Dan when his mother was injured."

"I think he would have killed Arnaud himself had he known who he was." She gazed up at me in horror. "Not that he did! I don't mean that at all. Dan is so kind."

"What do you know about Kara?"

"I've never met her. Dan speaks angrily about her. He blames her for . . ." She stopped abruptly.

"It's okay. Dan told me what happened that night."

"Then you know how angry he is. But I think part of him would still like to have his sister back."

"I heard you lost your parents quite young. That must have been awful for you."

"My mother died when I was only three months old. I never knew her or my father. But I had a wonderful grandmother who raised me. And I'm so lucky because Joe

Merano has been like a dad to me." Stella's eyes brimmed with tears.

"What do you think happened to Joe?"

She answered in a whisper. "Whoever killed Randy murdered Joe first."

"And you fear Dan is next?"

"What would you think?"

I had never considered that possibility. "Why not Mitch?"

Her mouth drew tight and her eyes grew wide.

"You think Mitch killed them?"

"I never said that."

I asked her to call me if she thought of anything that might shed light on the murders, paid for my purchases, and left the store. When I reached the sidewalk, I realized I was still holding the pink sale flier. I folded it to tuck it into my shopping bag and stopped dead.

On the back were three little dots, exactly like the ones on the back of the fake invitation to Arnaud.

CHAPTER TWENTY-SIX

Dear Natasha,

I am a huge fan of your show. I love that you're always a step ahead of the other lifestyle divas. I'm baking brownies for my book club, and I wondered if I should add bacon like you do in your fab chocolate chip cookies.

—Your #1 Fan in Browns Corner, Maryland

Dear #1 Fan,

Why not surprise them with something new? Chop up some mouthwatering jalapeños, and toss them into the brownies for the delicious kick that everyone loves.

—Natasha

I turned around and gazed through the store window.

Stella waved at me.

I raised my hand, but she no longer seemed such a sympathetic person. Had she created and mailed an invitation to Arnaud? I walked away slowly. Why would she want him to be at the chocolate tasting? Did she have anything to gain by his presence? She had spoken so fondly of Joe and Dan. Why would she risk upsetting the family if she knew who Arnaud really was? Maybe, just maybe, she thought it appropriate to invite the chocolatier who was new to town, and had taken it upon herself to do so. It could have been a simple act of generosity. Or not.

I stopped by Mars's and my favorite barbecue place for pulled pork. Armed with coleslaw, baked beans, and pork, I headed for home.

Daisy and Mochie rushed me at the door. I petted, hugged, and kissed both of them. There was no sign of Natasha or Wolchik.

From the other room, Mars shouted, "I hope you brought food. I'm starving."

I carried the takeout into the family room, where he sat on the sofa bed working on his laptop, his leg propped up.

"Natasha didn't make lunch?"

"She did."

"Then why are you hungry?"

"Because Natasha cooked lunch."

"It's in the trash?"

"Bingo! You better take out the trash before she comes over again."

It sounded like an order but I knew he meant well. Neither of us wanted to hurt her feelings. I spread out the food and fetched iced teas for both of us. When I sat down to eat, I asked, "What are you going to do about her? She wants to rent the chocolate shop that Célébration de Chocolat was going to occupy."

"I'm not cosigning a lease. If she gets herself into a mess with a store, I can't help her. Where were you off to so fast?"

I told him about my meeting with Stella.

"You mean that bag is full of chocolates?"

I laughed at his excitement. "It's dessert, but also a test.

I totally agreed with you about the Amore chocolate this morning. I just didn't want to offend Alex. Something isn't right."

When we finished the barbecue, I made hot coffee with fair trade coffee beans from Colombia. Caffeinated for me and decaf for Mars.

We set the chocolates I had bought at Stella's store on a tray. Boxed chocolates on one side and individual gourmet chocolates from the store on the other. Mars read the sign on the cover of the box and lined up similar chocolates boxed and fresh. I cut each one in half, and we sampled them.

Neither of us spoke except Mars, who said the name of each as we tried them. "Champagne truffle, raspberry, Grand Marnier, Irish cream, and salted caramel."

It was the most gloriously, ridiculously indulgent thing I had ever done. When we were finished, neither of us had finished our boxed chocolate versions but we had gobbled up the individual fresh gourmet chocolates.

Mars examined the tray. "I think we have our answer."

I nodded. "Something's not right with the boxed chocolates. They taste less chocolatey and feel kind of waxy."

"I couldn't have said it better."

"So what do you make of it?" I asked.

Mars sipped his coffee. "Ahh, invite me any time you need to taste chocolates."

"Seriously."

"I'm not in the business, but I'd say someone is cutting corners on the ingredients in the boxed chocolates."

"That's my take, too. Would that be reason to murder someone?"

"Mitch?" Mars asked.

"I doubt that Randy ordered the ingredients."

"So, you're suggesting that Mitch got rid of Joe?"

"Then why would he have come over here to ask me to look for Joe? You'd think he would have been thrilled that the family was keeping it so low key."

"Good point."

I filled him in on Stella's fake invitation to Arnaud. Mars sat up straighter. "Why would she do that?"

"I don't know. I'm afraid she's up to her pretty little neck in this mess. But a notion crossed my mind earlier today." I checked my watch. Just enough time. I cleaned up the chocolates, made a cute little packet of some of the extra gourmet ones, and stashed the rest safely out of Daisy and Mochie's reach.

I hurried back to my computer. A quick search brought up a picture of Stella with Dan at a social event. Just what I hoped for. I printed it out.

Peeking in at Mars, who was comfortably snuggled with Daisy and Mochie, I told them I was heading out again and left.

I hoofed it over to the hotel to check in on the winners of the chocolate contest. They had the day off tomorrow and then a gala farewell dinner in the evening with the Merano family at Bernie's restaurant.

Many of them lounged in the foyer when I arrived. I paused to chat, and they shared humorous stories about their television appearances.

All in all, it sounded like everything went well. I excused myself and was about to go downstairs when I saw Jack, the hotel's detective, outside on the terrace by the swimming pool.

"Did you bring me more cookies?" he asked.

"Not this time. But I do have some chocolates for you." I handed him the package of truffles I had wrapped.

"What are you buying this time?" he joked.

I handed him the photo of Stella and Dan.

He looked at it. Without moving his head, he eyed me from the side. "You want to know if I've seen her?"

"Yes."

He nodded. "Hard to miss that pretty little lady. She's the one who was watching Arnaud here in the hotel."

"You're absolutely sure?"

"Positive."

"Thanks. Enjoy the goodies."

I walked home convinced that Stella knew a whole lot more than she had told me. Arnaud had a reputation for chasing women. Surely he hadn't dumped her and broken her heart. Had she traveled to Belgium or England? Where had she met him? At a chocolate conference? In any event, she had her eye on him.

Maybe she planned to jump ship? Had he contacted her about managing his store? I felt better. That made perfect sense. Slimy Arnaud may have wanted to steal the competition's manager. That explained everything, including her reason for sending him an invitation. Maybe he even asked her if she could wangle an invitation for him. Given his reputation, it wouldn't have been unlikely that she heard something about what a jerk he was. Maybe she was watching him to see for herself before she signed on with him. And it only stood to reason that she wouldn't want to tell the Merano family. They'd been so good to her.

Still, Wolf had to know about the invitation. I pulled out my phone. Why did I feel like a traitor when I dialed his number? Probably because I wanted so much to like poor Stella. When Wolf answered, I told him about finding the invitation and how the ink blots on the back matched Stella's printer.

I blew out a huge breath of air when I hung up. Stella seemed so sweet and kind. I didn't want the poor child who had lost both her parents at such a tender age to be a killer. Still, I didn't know that he had tried to steal her to manage his store. I couldn't jump to that kind of conclusion.

But if it wasn't Stella, who was Arnaud's killer? Which member of that family finally reached a breaking point?

I paused at the entrance to the B and B where Kara was staying, wondering if she would ever reconcile with her family, when she bounded out.

"Have you heard something about Daddy? Did they find him?"

"I'm so sorry, Kara. No. I don't have any news about him at all. I was just on my way home."

Her crestfallen expression tugged at me. How would I feel if it were my dad? "It must be so hard on you, being out of the loop and not knowing if anything has happened."

"It is. I can't reach Marla anymore, either. Do you know anything about that? Has she shut me out like the rest of my family?"

I felt for Kara. Even though her family was in Old Town, she couldn't go to them. She must have felt very alone. "You're not being shut out. It's kind of a long story. Let's get out of the sun. Could I interest you in some iced tea? It's hot out here."

"Yeah, sure. Why not?"

When I started for home, she stopped me. "Aren't the shops and restaurants that way?"

"They are. I thought you could come to my house." I grinned. "I have chocolates!"

Kara laughed. "The one thing in the world I never had enough of growing up!"

She fell in step with me, and we were home in no time. I opened the kitchen door. "Mars! We have company!"

Daisy and Mochie gave Kara a warm welcome, leading me to believe she couldn't be all bad. Little Truffles waggled head to tail on seeing Kara.

"If it's Natasha, tell her he's not here." Nina's voice came from Mars's quarters.

"I apologize," I said to Kara. "He broke his leg and he's a little cranky."

Kara followed me to the family room.

At the sight of her, Mars sat up straight. "Good heavens. You're the image of your sister!"

"So I'm told."

Francie was visiting with Nina and Mars. Comfortably

nestled in an armchair, she peered over her glasses. "I would have taken you for Coco any day."

I fetched tea and chocolates while they talked.

I placed five tall glasses of iced tea on a tray with the most adorable napkins. They reminded me of Arnaud's tie because they were printed with images of all kinds of chocolates. I located the bag of chocolates I had stashed away and carried it into the family room along with the tray.

"Mars was just telling us about your experiment." Nina eyed the bag. "Can we try?"

"Sure. I don't know if I'm up to another round of taste testing, though."

"If anyone knows how Amore chocolates used to taste, it would be Kara," said Mars.

Kara held her hands up in protest. "It's been a long time. They may have altered the formulas over the years."

Mars re-created the experiment on the tray.

One bite of a boxed chocolate and Kara recoiled. "They're adding some kind of waxy substance."

Nina savored them. "I think they're heavenly. But the gourmet ones are better. The chocolate on top of the filling is richer. It has a deeper chocolate flavor."

Kara nodded. "This is more like what I remember from my childhood."

Francie tried one of each and concurred with their assessment.

"I can't imagine that Daddy would allow the quality to suffer like this." Kara studied a chocolate, breaking it open. "We've always prided ourselves on a top-notch product. This is edible but hardly Amore quality."

Nina didn't care. She happily selected chocolates to try.

Francie focused on Kara. "So where have you been living all these years?"

"Colorado."

"Seeing as how Arnie turned into Arnaud of Belgium, I guess things didn't work out between you two," said Francie.

I froze. Francie might be pushing it. I didn't want to frighten Kara away.

Kara stared at the chocolate in her hand for a few seconds before responding. "He dumped me for a blonde. Two weeks—that's how long we lasted. It took only two weeks before he was interested in someone else. I hung on. I tried to make it work but two weeks later, he left us both, me and the new blonde. I don't know where he got the money, but he flew back to England and that was the last I ever saw of that miserable rat." She paused as if remembering. "I was eighteen, waitressing, and couldn't even cobble enough money together for rent. I was out on my bottom in no time."

"But, sweetheart, why didn't you come home? Or at least call your father for money?" asked Francie.

"How could I? I was a stupid foolish child to leave my mother in her time of need. She wasn't even out of the hospital when I left. I missed my own grandfather's funeral just to be with Arnie. It took me a few years of growing up before I came to grips with how everything could have happened the way it did. I finally realized that Arnie didn't care about Coco, or me, or the blonde. He didn't love any of us. Nonno *died*, but Arnie didn't care. I doubt that he ever really loved anyone."

We sat in painful silence for a moment.

"Did you find a nice man, I hope?" asked Francie.

I marveled that she could get away with asking personal questions of someone she had only met half an hour ago.

Kara took a deep breath. "I never trusted another man. I don't think I ever will." She smiled. "But I'm not unhappy! I have an active life with a lot of friends, who are like family to me."

"Child," said Francie, "you make up with your family before someone else passes, and it's too late."

"I'd like to see my dad. I'd like to apologize but, just as you said, Francie, it's probably already too late. It breaks my heart to know that I waited too long. Was too involved in my own shame and anguish to reach out to him. And now, my only contact isn't taking my calls. Sophie, do you know what happened to Marla?"

"I wish I did. I stopped by Amore yesterday. Marla seemed fine, if a little anxious. Right about the time I was leaving, she said she'd go with me to pick up some lunch. But I could see her lunch in her office. And then she took off in her car like she was afraid of something."

Francie's brow wrinkled. "Think harder, Sophie. You must have said something that upset her."

At that moment the kitchen door opened. I rose and took the three steps to the kitchen just in time to see Natasha close the door behind Coco.

"Mars!" Natasha sang. "You have company!"

A knot lodged at the base of my throat. "How thoughtful of you to drop by, Coco. Natasha, this isn't a good time."

"Nonsense. He's just lying around like a slug."

"No, really!" I sought anything that might stop them. "He's not decent."

Natasha blinked at me. In an accusatory voice she demanded, "Why would Mars be undressed, Sophie?" She barged past me into the family room.

Coco gave me a wild-eyed look and whispered, "Oh, Sophie! How could you?" as she flew by me.

CHAPTER TWENTY-SEVEN

Dear Sophie,

People are always giving my mother chocolate bars as gifts. Consequently, she uses them to bake with instead of baking chocolate. I think that's unwise but she won't listen to me. Will you tell her?"

—Bossy Daughter in Candy Town, Ohio

Dear Bossy Daughter,

I'm afraid I have to agree with you. Chocolate bars intended for snacking contain different amounts of fat, sugar, and chocolate. If she sticks with unsweetened, bittersweet, or semisweet chocolate meant for baking, she'll achieve better and more consistent results.

—Sophie

I wanted the floor to open up underneath me. The War of the Meranos was about to commence in my tiny family room. I braced for the onslaught.

It began with gasps. They turned into shrieks. And then the screaming started. It didn't take long for Coco to self-eject from the family room. She paused in my kitchen just long enough to point at me and spit, "You're fired. Don't ever show your face at Amore again. Not even as a customer."

Kara was on her heels, though, and followed Coco out the door. I peered through the bay window and saw them as they turned onto the sidewalk. Coco walked as fast as she could in fashionable flats. Kara kept pace without any trouble in sneakers.

They stopped and faced each other. Even though they were shouting, I couldn't quite make out what they were saying. Nina, Natasha, and Francie crowded behind me, watching. Even Mars managed to hobble into the kitchen in a hurry.

Coco and Kara's hands flew in wild gestures. They didn't alternate speaking, like one does in normal conversation. They were so heated they just kept raising their voices and shouting over each other.

And then Coco threw up her hands and marched away. Kara followed her, two paces behind. The war hadn't ended, it was just moving to another location.

"Well!" Natasha patted her hair into place. "I knew Mars couldn't be interested in you, Sophie. Imagine Coco thinking such a thing for even a second. Undressed! Ridiculous!"

"Thanks for your vote of confidence," I muttered wryly.

"Did I hear her say you're fired?" asked Natasha.

"You did. The big farewell banquet is tomorrow night at The Laughing Hound." I flapped my hand through the air. "That should be a snap for Coco to handle." I forced a smile at them. "I guess I have some unexpected time off."

But inside, I felt as though I had done something wrong. I hadn't, of course. On one level I knew that. Still, it bothered me.

Francie seemed to read my mind. She ran a comforting hand across my back. "It wasn't pretty, but it was important for them to be face-to-face again. You just wait and see. Something good will come of it. I think I'll go call my sister."

Every one of us looked at her in shock.

"You have a sister?" asked Nina.

"I don't talk about her much. She's a crotchety old blabbermouth. Always asking questions that are none of her business. Drives me batty."

Thankfully she left before the laughter broke out. I hoped she couldn't hear us.

"I believe I could use a drink," said Nina. "Is it cocktail time for anyone else?"

Mars was game but I declined. "That horrible cop Wolchik might return. I think I'd better keep my wits about me."

"Now you've gone and taken all the fun out of a little stress reliever," Nina complained.

"Sorry. I need a strong cup of hot tea. Anyone else?" I asked.

"How can you drink anything hot in this weather?" Natasha gazed around at us. "It's summertime! The livin' is supposed to be easy."

It was anything but easy. I set the kettle on the stove, wondering where she had been.

"If the police are coming back, I'd better bake something for them."

Mars groaned and drew a hand over his face. "Spare me."

"I think it's a great idea." With any luck she would chase them away.

While my tea steeped, I poured more iced tea for Nina and Mars and handed the glasses to them.

Natasha bustled about my kitchen.

I added milk and sugar to my tea and settled at the banquette. "It all started with Joe. No, it didn't. It started with Kara. She came to town, and then Joe disappeared."

Nina wrinkled her nose at me. "I don't think Kara had anything to do with that. Seriously, what would it accomplish?"

"Maybe she harbors some deep psychological resentment and killed him," suggested Mars.

"Wouldn't that anger be toward Coco? Why Joe?" I moved on with my thoughts. "Not even twenty-four hours later, Arnie—Arnaud was murdered. Stella put it pretty well when she said people all over the world were upset with him. If all the Meranos had motives, who had opportunity?"

"Everyone in attendance. The only one that eliminates is Kara." Mars sounded discouraged. "We're going at this all wrong. What he did to Lori Speer's brother, and to the Merano family, and to Cheryl and her family—all of that was in the past. No one bothered killing him for it over the years. I hardly think they'd do it now. Who had a current motive?"

Nina tapped her fingernails on the table. "Stella. Mars told us about you finding the invitation she must have sent to Arnaud for the chocolate tasting. She wanted him there for some reason."

"I hoped she sent it because he was going to hire her . . ." But as I spoke, the theory fizzled along with my words. "She was watching him at the hotel."

"Aha!" Mars sat forward. "Now we're getting somewhere. Looks like Stella might be our culprit."

I raised my eyebrows. "Because she was watching him?"

"Yes! Don't you see? She must have known who he really was and had some interest or possibly contact with him before his death."

"You don't know that. Maybe she was observing him because she knew he was Arnaud. And I might also point out that Cheryl Maiorca knew he was really Arnie, the slimeball relative," I pointed out.

"That's right!" Nina spoke with excitement. "And she baked that incredible chocolate cake. Maybe she thought she would inherit Arnaud's chocolate business!"

"People have certainly killed for less." Mars stretched. "I wish I could get up and run around."

"Really? Where would you go?" I sat up, hoping he had a great idea.

"Well, now that we know something's wrong with the chocolate, I think it's safe to assume that the murders, including possibly Joe's, had something to do with that. In Arnaud's case, the killer had a lot of guts to strangle him right there when anyone could have seen him."

"But no one did," Nina observed.

Natasha stopped chopping chocolate. "I did. I saw that other handyman, Vince, going into the guesthouse."

Nina groaned. "Oh, please. I was in there, too. That doesn't mean anything."

Natasha pouted. "He worked with Randy. Maybe he wanted Randy's job."

Vince. I'd never given him any thought. "Does anyone know anything about Vince?"

Natasha preheated the oven. "I can see that I will have to make inquiries now that Sophie has alienated the entire Merano clan."

"What are you baking?" I asked.

Mars leaned toward me and whispered, "The repair guys kicked her out."

That came as no surprise. "So that's why she's hanging around here."

Natasha dried her hands on a towel. "I was so shocked by your lack of staples"—she counted them off on her fingers—"no jalapeños, no mustard greens, no oysters, no truffles of the mushroom type—"

"Good heavens," Nina blurted. "No wonder poor Mars is always over here sniffing for food like a starving dog."

"I don't have eye of gnat or toe of rat, either. What are you baking?"

Natasha looked as though she'd been slapped. "Don't be

ridiculous." But she gazed at Mars with a worried brow. "You could defend me, you know."

"Nat," he said gently, "you try too hard. Caviar isn't special on top of ice cream."

Natasha shook her forefinger at him. "That's not true. That pregnant lady loved it."

"It's just that sometimes people like to eat food that's familiar and comforting. Chocolate chip cookies don't have to be spicy. Mac and cheese doesn't need chocolate chunks in it, and let's not mention the seaweed lasagna."

I thought Natasha might break down. She was getting some tough love.

She raised her chin, though, and explained, "You don't understand that as a lifestyle authority, I am expected to be on the cutting edge of new trends. I can't just prepare the same old thing. Then I would be like"—she glanced at me—"everyone else. I have to forge ahead and find new flavor combinations. Though I will admit that the seaweed lasagna was a mistake."

Nina screwed up her face. "You're the one with a sophisticated palate, Natasha. Why don't you bake with things like bourbon?"

Mars seemed much happier. "I love bourbon. What's more Southern than bourbon?"

"Do . . . you . . . have any bourbon, Sophie?" asked Natasha.

I brought her three bottles.

Nina perked up. At first I thought it was the bourbon that picked up her spirits, but then she said, "We never did go over to check Mitch's yard for signs of recent digging."

"Oh puh-leeze, Nina! Like Coco wouldn't have noticed if Mitch dug up the yard?"

"What if she's protecting Mitch? What if she's in on it?"

"I'll grant you that she might have murdered Arnaud. But if her dad was murdered—and isn't just missing—I can't imagine her being involved in that. Besides, we don't know the address."

"I do."

I shot her a questioning look.

Nina shrugged. "So I asked around. It's worth a look. Come on."

The sad truth was that we didn't have any better ideas. We left Truffles and Daisy with Mars and walked over to Mitch and Coco's house. Not surprisingly, it was an impressive house built in the colonial style favored in Old Town. Not as majestic or large as Joe's house, but quite lovely. The historic plaque by the front door left no doubt about its age or authenticity. Although the windows that fronted the street were huge, we couldn't see inside.

"Not that I would ever say *I told you so* but—"

Nina lifted the latch on the gate in the brick fence next to the house.

"—you'd better be careful. A lot of those gates are weighted with a cannonball to make sure they swing shut. They make an incredible racket," I hissed.

"Look at this garden. It's beautiful!"

It was lovely. A smaller version of Joe's garden, ancient trees and thick bushes lined the perimeter just inside the brick fence. A round brick seating area in the middle offered benches and chairs with plush cushions the color of yellow daffodils. Tables inlaid with blue and yellow tiles that must have been Italian were bunched with colorful tall vases and planters overflowing with blooms.

Nina jabbed me. "Look," she whispered, pointing to a freshly dug flower bed. "It's the right size for a body."

CHAPTER TWENTY-EIGHT

Dear Sophie,

My wife says some diva authority told her she can't make chocolate trifle. Please tell her that ain't so!

—Disappointed in Greystone, West Virginia

Dear Disappointed,

Of course she can make chocolate trifle. She could use chocolate cake instead of a white cake, or she could make a chocolate custard, or she could do both!

—Sophie

"Big enough for Nonni maybe. Certainly not for a man," I whispered.

Undeterred, Nina crept forward.

I nabbed the back of her dress. "Are you nuts? We're trespassing, and it's broad daylight."

"I should have thought of that. We'll come back tonight with shovels."

"We'll do no such thing! Coco is already furious with me, and that idiot Wolchik wants to nab me on something. Let's get out of here."

"Give me just a minute more."

"No! I'm going." I turned tail and hurried out of the gate, trying to look like I belonged there, just in case anyone was walking by.

And I rushed right into Nonni.

I was horrified, but she wrapped her arms around me like I was her own child. "Sofia, Sofia. You bring my Kara back to me."

That was putting the best spin on it. "Nonni, Marla called her. I didn't have anything to do with it."

She let go of me. "Now Marla is gone. What is happening to us, Sofia? It's the curse!" She lifted her forefinger and little finger again.

"What curse, Nonni?"

"Curse on the Meranos. One good thing happen, and one bad thing happen together. Always it is like this."

A muffled scream came from the backyard. If Nonni noticed it, she didn't let on. I, on the other hand, was cringing inside. Nina had been caught.

"Now Kara is back, and Marla—poof!" Nonni linked her arm into mine. "Come with me. We greet Kara."

"Kara is here? At Coco's house?"

"Is wonderful!"

"Nonni, I don't think so. Coco is very angry with me. You go ahead and have a nice reunion with Kara."

Coco's front door opened, and Nina stumbled out, followed closely by Lori Speer and Cheryl Maiorca. Coco's face blazed with fury.

"There you are!" Nina exclaimed. "We lost you."

She was trying to send me some kind of signal with wide

eyes but I couldn't quite read it. I figured it meant, *Play along and get me out of here because they caught me.*

"Coco, I'm so sorry."

Coco helped Nonni up the few stairs to her door. "About spying on me or about secretly meeting with Kara?"

"We weren't spying on you." I wished I had sounded more convincing.

Nonni tottered inside, and I could hear her shrieking with joy.

Coco turned a cold face to me. "It's funny. My dad had total confidence in you, but Mitch didn't trust you. I usually side with my dad because he's a good judge of character, but this time, he was dead wrong."

She walked inside and closed the door. The lock clicked with ominous finality.

I hoped Joe was only wrong and not dead, too. Well, we got what we deserved for snooping. I was horrified, embarrassed, and ashamed.

Lori and Cheryl breathed heavily.

"What were *you* doing in their garden?" I asked.

"Lori thought we might find Joe." Cheryl shook her head at Lori. "I told you that was a bad idea. And the Meranos have been so nice to us, too."

Lori wasn't quite as undone as Cheryl. "We went over Joe's garden very carefully. I honestly thought Coco and Mitch might have buried the old fellow over here."

"See?" muttered Nina. "It wasn't such a dumb idea after all. Did you see where the dirt had been recently dug?"

"We did!" Lori was in her element. "I even lay down beside it as a measurement but it's too short to be Joe."

"And that was when Coco saw us." Cheryl grimaced at the thought. "I've never been so embarrassed in my life."

"You'll get over it. What's a little embarrassment when your cousin was brutally murdered?" asked Lori. "Who knows what might have happened to Joe."

I motioned them to move along the sidewalk so Coco

couldn't overhear if she happened to open a window or a door. It seemed wrong to discuss her family right in front of her house. "Are you suggesting that one of the Meranos murdered Joe?"

Lori pushed her hair out of her face. "I'm not suggesting anything. I'm considering possibilities. All the winners think Joe's disappearance is bizarre. It's not unusual to have power wars within a family, especially when a big business like Amore is involved. I hope Joe is still alive. He's a lovely man. But I can't help wondering if someone in his own family is behind his mysterious absence."

I hoped she was wrong. Lori and Cheryl went on their way, with Cheryl still yammering at Lori about her bone-headed idea of sneaking into Coco's yard.

I could relate. But I couldn't really blame Nina. I had gone along with her.

Nina joined Mars and me for dinner that night. They chattered about their theories, but I tuned them out while I sliced mushrooms for a simple pasta sauce. The two of them gabbed nonstop during our linguini and mushroom main course with a summer salad topped with creamy homemade ranch dressing.

My mind was on the Merano family, too. I felt terrible. Coco hated me. I'd been fired from my job, a first for me. I felt like I had let them all down. It finally dawned on me that there was one thing I could do to help them. I could bring Bacio, their cat, home.

~~~

After the kitchen had been cleaned up, and Nina had gone home, I left Daisy with Mars so she wouldn't scare the cat.

Streetlights glimmered in the night. Large windows glowed with warmth in the old houses that nearly sat on the sidewalk. Crickets chirped in the quiet night.

I stopped across the street from the house in question. The cat sat on the stoop as usual. Someone must have turned off a light upstairs, because the windows went dark.

A minute later, the front door opened.

A man stepped out, bent to scratch behind the cat's ears, and went on his way. Could he be Joe? The cat followed him, and so did I.

For three seconds, I got a better look at him as he walked under a streetlamp. There was no doubt about the long gray ponytail and baseball cap. I stopped midstride. It wasn't Joe at all. It was Vince, the Amore handyman.

Given the time of night, he was probably headed to a bar. Still, I followed him in the hope that he might lead me to some kind of clue about what was going on.

To my surprise, Vince walked up to the front door of the Amore offices. I dodged behind a tree and someone grabbed me from behind.

CHAPTER TWENTY-NINE

Dear Natasha,

My sister's mother-in-law (note that I am *not* the one who married into this family) made a huge fuss about someone confusing chocolate liqueur with chocolate liquor. What's the difference? I don't want to be caught in her web of derision.

—Thankful I'm Not in That Family in Bliss, Idaho

Dear Thankful,

Chocolate liquor is what you get when you grind cocoa beans. In its hardened state, it's called unsweetened chocolate. It's the basis of all chocolate. Chocolate liqueur (note the e and extra *u*) is chocolate-flavored alcohol.

—Sophie

A large hand muffled my scream. I kicked backward but that didn't work well at all. I made contact with my assailant's legs, but I didn't think I was hurting him. One arm had a solid grip around my abdomen and right arm. I jabbed my left elbow into him over and over again. Why didn't I wear pointy five-inch heels like Natasha?

I hardly had time to fight him. In a matter of seconds, he lifted me and carried me a few feet. I heard a car door open.

I was going to die.

I had no control over anything. I saw the van door and did the only thing I could. I bit down hard on the hand that covered my mouth.

My assailant grunted but didn't let go. He swung me into the van and the door closed.

"Quiet, you two!"

My eyes adjusted to the darkness far too slowly. I sought to make out the person who spoke.

A familiar voice whispered calmly into my ear. "Thanks for biting me. I hope you had your rabies shot. I can let you go if you promise not to scream. Everything's going to be okay, Sophie. You just had the bad luck to be in the wrong place at the wrong time."

Wolf! What the blazes was Wolf doing grabbing me off the street like that?

He loosened his grip tentatively as though he was testing me. When he dropped his hand, I turned my head to be sure it was Wolf.

"You drew blood!" he hissed.

Deeper in the van, I could make out two men with earphones and what appeared to be recording devices.

Wolf leaned over and whispered, "It's a sting. You nearly gave us away."

My heart still thundered. "You could give a person a heart attack!"

"Sorry. We had to move fast. I couldn't risk an argument on the street."

"I wouldn't have done that."

"Not much, you wouldn't."

Okay. Wolf was right. I would have demanded information about what was going on.

"Who are you after?"

"Mitch."

"I knew it!" I hissed the words loud enough for the guys with earphones to turn and shush me. "I never trusted that man. He murdered Arnaud?"

Wolf shifted closer to me and whispered so close to my ear that I could feel the heat of his breath. "He's been pulling some stunts at Amore."

Mitch's voice came through a speaker. A little crackly but understandable.

"I need you to locate Marla and bring her back. My best guess is that she's at her mother's house in Philly or at their family cabin in the Poconos. Here are the addresses. Take this along with you as a little gift to let her know there are no hard feelings, and we'd like her to come back."

"How do you know she's not dead?" Vince's lisp left no doubt that he was the other speaker.

"I went to her apartment. She took her cat with her. If someone killed her, I don't think he would have bothered with the stinkin' cat."

"You broke in?"

"I have a key."

"What if she doesn't want to come?"

"Then tell her I know who killed Randy."

"You?"

"Don't be stupid. I never killed anyone in my life."

"What about the old man?"

"Joe? Don't you be worrying about him. He won't be back. I'm in charge now." He chuckled. "Have been for years."

"But your wife—"

"Let me give you two pieces of advice. One, don't ask so many questions. Just do as you're told, and we'll get along fine. And two, nothing better happen to my wife. We need

Coco. Too many bad things happening in this company. It's
time to put our best face forward again, and that's Coco. But
don't tell Marla I said that."

I felt Wolf's entire frame sag with disappointment behind
me. Not only had Mitch not admitted to anything, he'd out-
right denied being responsible for the murders.

They didn't let me out of the van until they had driven
away. Five blocks from my house, they pulled into an alley
and opened the back door. Wolf had warned me it would be
quick. It was. A moment later, I stood by myself, pondering
the things Mitch had said. If he knew what had happened
to Joe and who had killed Randy, then why wouldn't the
police take him in for questioning? For all I knew, maybe
they had.

But if that were the case, the police would know the
identity of Randy's killer. Clearly they didn't, or they would
have made an arrest.

I rounded the corner of the alley and walked up the street.
I would have to ask Alex. In a discreet way, so he wouldn't
know what I had heard. I bet it had something to do with
evidence. Maybe they just didn't have the evidence to support a murder charge. Certainly not against Mitch. It
sounded like his hands were clean as white lilies.

So Vince had been a police plant all along. Who'd have
thought that? The long ponytail, the lisp when he spoke, the
baseball cap—I never would have pegged him as a cop.

I heard brakes squeal before I realized what was happening. A cat scampered across the street in the nick of time.
The driver shook his head, rolled down his window and
yelled, "Hey, lady! You better get your cat inside." He drove
off too fast for Old Town's streets.

The cat ran along the sidewalk at a good clip. "Here,
kitty, kitty," I called. He ignored me and kept going. Right
back to the stoop where I'd seen him before.

I caught up to him and picked him up, ready to grab the
scruff of his neck if he should turn on me. He purred.

I wasn't in the habit of snatching cats, but I truly thought he was the Merano's missing cat, Bacio. I checked for a collar but he wasn't wearing one.

Just to be on the safe side, I knocked on the door. No one answered. I tried again. Still no response.

It was worth a try taking him home. If he wasn't Bacio, the Meranos would tell me, and I could bring him right back. Still, I felt a little bit guilty for grabbing him off the stoop and carrying him away.

I headed for Joe's house and hoped Coco wouldn't be there.

Bacio weighed a lot more than I expected. I paused a couple of times to catch my breath but didn't dare put him down on the sidewalk.

It seemed an eternity, but we finally made it to Joe's front door. I rang the bell. It was far too late for visiting but these were exceptional circumstances, and I hoped they would understand.

Nonni opened the door, clapped her hands against the sides of her face, and cooed, "Bacio! My Bacio!"

I stepped inside the house and shut the door before placing him on the floor. He wound around Nonni's ankles, marking her as his.

"Where you find him?"

"A few blocks away. He was almost hit by a car, Nonni."

"Bacio, you bad boy!" she scolded. "What you doing in the streets?" But she bent to stroke his head, and he obviously wanted more.

"He stay in house from now on. He never leave the garden before. Bacio, where is your collar?"

"Who is it, Nonni?" called a male voice.

Dan sauntered toward us. "Bacio!" Dan swung him up in his arms. "We've missed you around here, old pal."

But his tone grew cold. "Did *you* bring him home?"

Something was definitely wrong. "Yes. I thought I recognized him."

His mouth twitched to the side. "Thank you." He swung the door open and waited, the implicit meaning that I was to leave.

"Dan! You don't be rude to our guest. Come, Sofia, have something to eat."

"No, Nonni!" Dan protested.

"Is Coco here? I'm sorry, I didn't mean to upset anyone."

"It's too late for that. Nonni told us that she asked you to look into who murdered Arnaud." Dan still held the giant cat, but his glare was anything but friendly. "How dare you tell the cops that Stella killed him? Where do you get off doing that?"

"Danny! Stop now!" said Nonni.

"Leave her alone, Dan." Stella emerged from the kitchen. She spoke softly. "Somebody was bound to figure it out sooner or later."

CHAPTER THIRTY

Dear Natasha,

I'm so embarrassed. I just can't warm up to dark chocolate. I know it's better for me. I know I should love it, but give me sweet, soft, melt-in-my-mouth milk chocolate any day and forget the dark stuff. Is it just me?

—Milk Chocolate for Me in Milk Springs, Alabama

Dear Milk Chocolate,

Dark chocolate does contain more chocolate, and generally speaking, less sugar. It's really a matter of developing a more refined palate so you will enjoy that dark chocolate.

—Natasha

Dan nearly dropped poor Bacio. He set the cat on the floor. "What are you doing, Stella?" He rushed over to her, holding his palms up as if to stop her. "Don't say anything more.

Okay? Not another word. I'll get you Alex German, the new guy. They say he's the best criminal lawyer in town."

"I have to get it off my chest. I've been living a lie for far too long."

"Honey, as soon as you have a lawyer, you can spill your guts. But not now!" Dan wasn't nearly as calm as Stella.

"We sit down and listen to Stella. Come, Sofia." It was a direct order from Nonni.

Truth be told, I was glad she had included me. I wanted to hear what Stella had to say.

We settled at their kitchen table. Dan appeared queasy. Nonni poured espresso for everyone and placed chocolate macaroons on the table.

Stella cleared her throat. "You know that I lost my parents when I was very young."

"Stella, honey, not that again." Dan reached for her hand. "Tell us what happened with Arnaud."

"I *am* telling you. My father broke off his relationship with my mother before I was born. They never married. When I was three months old, she took me to see him. I guess it was something of a shock when she showed up at his door with a baby. My grandmother said my mom was certain he would have a change of heart when he saw me. It didn't quite work out that way."

Stella paused and swallowed hard a few times before continuing. "The story goes that he left, and she followed him. They argued on the street, and when he pushed her away, she fell in front of an oncoming car. She was holding me at the time, and I flew through the air. They say he turned to look but didn't stop to help or to see if we were all right. He just kept going. We were both taken to the hospital, but my mother didn't survive. My grandmother came to collect me. She went to visit my father, but he had already fled— moved out and disappeared."

"My poor Stella." Nonni placed her hand over Stella's.

Dan looked at her with pity in his eyes. "Why did you tell me they both died?"

"Because I can't stand it when people look at me the way you are right now. Grade school was the worst. I made up all kinds of stories about my parents just so I wouldn't have to admit that my mother was dead, and my father didn't want me. Nobody wants to play with *that* kid. Family is all that little kids know. It makes them uncomfortable to think that one of their friends doesn't have the normal family setup with parents. My grandmother was very patient. She made both my parents sound wonderful. I imagined that my father was a handsome prince who would arrive one day, all kisses and love. But the years passed, and he was a no-show. No kisses, no love, no letters, nothing. Eventually, my grandmother told me the truth. As I got older, it was just easier for me to tell people they were both dead."

She cupped her hands and held her forehead. "The real truth is that my grandmother, bless her, was relentless in her search for him. When I was six, she spotted him in a magazine, using a new name. She was certain the young, upcoming chocolatier was Arnie. She hired a lawyer and went after child support. That's why he didn't open a store in the United States sooner. The authorities were after him for my support. I guess he figured enough years had expired for it to be safe now. Even knowing all that, when I heard he was coming to town, I held out hope that he wasn't as bad as I feared. That maybe he hadn't run away while my mother lay dying. Or that he regretted his previous callous behavior. That he had changed and become a different man."

Nonni frowned. "Arnaud is your daddy?"

"I knew it would come out sooner or later. I'm sorry. I'm so sorry that I've made such a mess of everything."

Dan sat back in his chair. "Wow. I didn't see this coming. I don't get it. Did you really send him an invitation to the tasting? Why? So you could meet him?"

"I stalked him a little bit first. Not in a sick way," she hastened to say. "I just wanted to see what he was like, you know? My grandmother always said that even the most disagreeable person must have some redeeming qualities. I couldn't find any. He was a heartless, vulgar, sloppy-drunk, egocentric jerk. I honestly believe that he killed my mother by shoving her in front of a car. I sent the invitation so I could murder him."

Nonni and I gasped. Dan turned whiter than the sugar on the table.

"I stole pills from Dan's mother. I knew that Arnie drank like a sailor. A few of those pills, and he would have been fried. It was actually too kind a death for him."

"But the pills were in the champagne glass," I said. "You decided not to kill him after all? Did you find something redeeming in him?"

"No. I found something lacking in me. I didn't have it in me. I didn't have the strength or the courage." She closed her eyes for a moment and lifted a trembling hand to her head. She snorted a sad laugh. "I think I must have inherited it from him. Most of the horrible things he did were acts of cowardice or sloth. He ran from everything in his life. He ran out on my mother, and on Coco and Kara, and who knows what other women. He ran out on me. He was a slug. Apparently, I share his lack of courage. I dumped the pills in a discarded champagne glass and walked away, just like him. He never took responsibility for anything or anyone. He just walked away and let them perish. And I did the same thing, except I thought he would live."

We sat in silent disbelief, until Dan said, "He deserved what he got."

"Dan," Stella said gently, "I will probably be tried for Arnaud's murder. But I want you to know that I didn't do it."

I figured it was time for me to take off and leave Stella and Dan to work things out.

Nonni walked me to the door and gave me a big hug. "We

will help our Stella and stand behind her. We will be her family."

I walked into the night thinking of all the lives Arnie had savaged. He had turned entire families upside down. And Stella was right. It seemed his method of coping with the mayhem he caused was to run away. But this time, he hadn't managed to make a clean getaway from someone.

⌁⌁

I couldn't sleep that night. My twisting and turning irritated Mochie, who tried to settle on my bed but was constantly disturbed. He finally nestled near my neck, which made it impossible for me to turn. "Would you look for me if I didn't come home?" He purred, which I took to mean *yes*.

I hoped Bacio would stay home and wouldn't sneak out again. And then I annoyed Mochie by sitting up. How stupid could I be? There had to be a reason Bacio kept sitting on that stoop, and I didn't think it was Vince. Could Joe be alive? We didn't have any reason to think he was dead. We'd all assumed the worst—that he'd been murdered.

Something in that house drew Bacio to it. Cats were funny creatures. Was it Nonni or Coco who told me that Bacio had never left their garden before? I walked along that street all the time and had never noticed Bacio on that stoop until recently. What had changed? Joe had disappeared. I kept coming back to Joe.

Could Joe be hiding out there? But why? Had he been in the house the whole time?

Vince had walked out of the house and locked it behind him. He was cooperating with the police. Could he be helping Joe? Bringing him food or groceries, maybe?

The only one who could be trusted was Bacio. That cat knew something we didn't—and I suspected he had discovered where his beloved Joe had gone. The more I thought about it, the more convinced I was that Joe was living in that house. It was time we knew the truth.

I threw on a sleeveless shirt and a pair of cotton pants that were entirely too tight. A few deep knee bends loosened them up, but not as much as I would have liked. I wasn't in the mood to try on clothes, though. I pulled on my Keds for a quick walk. Leaving Mochie on my bed, I hurried downstairs as quietly as I could. Mars was snoring. Luckily, I hadn't wakened him. I snapped a leash on Daisy, and we were out the door.

At two in the morning, the streets of Old Town were blissfully empty. No cars traveled the streets, and few people were out and about. If I hadn't been so excited and full of anticipation, I would have enjoyed the peacefulness. In a matter of minutes, we reached the stoop where Bacio liked to sit. It was a huge relief that he wasn't there.

Sucking in the warm night air to bolster my courage, I knocked on the door. I clutched my phone in one hand, ready to call 911, if necessary. When no one answered, I pounded on the door.

In the quiet of the night, there was no mistaking the creaking sounds of someone sneaking down the stairs inside the house. But he didn't answer the door.

I knocked again, more softly. "Joe, if you don't let me in, I'm going to tell Coco where you are."

The door opened swiftly. "Hurry."

Daisy and I were inside in less than two seconds. He hadn't turned on any lights but my eyes had adjusted to the darkness during our walk, and the streetlight shone in just enough for me to know that I had been right.

Joe beckoned me into the living room and drew the curtains closed before turning on a small lamp. "It pains me to sound so very impolite, but what are you doing here?"

"I believe the real question is *what are you doing here?*"

"Wolf is going to be madder than a wet hen. He told me how you nearly blew our cover earlier."

Our cover? So Joe was in on the sting.

"Joe! Don't you realize what you're doing to your family? I don't understand. Why are you hiding out here?"

Joe sighed like I was a huge annoyance. "Have you ever seen the TV show where a CEO goes undercover in his own company?"

"Yes, I think I have." Daisy sat quietly beside me.

"There were some things going on at Amore that I didn't like—"

"The inferior chocolate used in the boxed chocolates?"

"You see? Customers have noticed. But when I went through the paperwork, everything seemed to be in order. I wanted to go undercover to find out exactly what was going on in the company but without the TV show. Just on my own."

I couldn't believe what I was hearing. He'd been among us all along. But it wasn't until I noticed an Amore baseball cap laying on a chair that things began to gel for me. A long gray ponytail was attached to it. "You're Vince?"

"Right."

"But the lisp?"

"They gave me something to put in my mouth. Otherwise everyone would have recognized my voice. I wore the ponytail and glasses. Mostly I kept to myself, which worked out well because it gave me a chance to snoop around. It wasn't easy staying away from Coco, Mitch, and Dan. I lived in fear that one of them would recognize me."

"Couldn't you have accomplished everything in a day or two? Why are you dragging this out?"

"Because someone wants to kill me."

CHAPTER THIRTY-ONE

Dear Sophie,

My stoopid sister thinks she can use hot chocolate mix instead of cocoa powder in recipes. I think that's why her desserts taste so lousy. Please tell her she has to use real cocoa powder! She won't listen to me.

—The Smart Sister in Mix, Louisiana

Dear The Smart Sister,

I don't think your sister will like hearing this from me, either. Chocolate milk drink mixes usually contain other ingredients, and very often sugar, which will throw the recipe off. For baking, one really ought to stick to unsweetened cocoa powder or baking chocolate.

—Sophie

My knees went weak. I leaned against the arm of the sofa to steady myself. "What? Who? How do you know that?"

"One of my most loyal employees told me that he had been solicited to do the deed."

"He? Then it wasn't Marla."

"Randy."

"Who wanted to kill you?" I smacked my forehead. "Of course. Mitch. That's what you were doing there tonight. The police hoped he would try to hire Vince now that Randy's gone?"

"That's about the size of it."

"So Mitch tried to hire Randy to kill you and Randy warned you."

"He told me on the night of the welcome dinner. I had planned to go underground, so to speak, so everything was set up. But when I learned about this, the cops thought I should stay missing for a while for my own safety."

"That makes sense." I winced as I grasped the problem. "But now you have no evidence because Randy is dead."

"Yes." It was a simple, small word. He barely muttered it.

Maybe Mitch didn't know how close Randy was to the other members of the Merano clan. "No one else knew about it? Mitch didn't approach anyone else?"

"He may have. I don't know. Randy was in on my little undercover act in the company. He was helping me."

"The police have known about this all along?"

"Apparently we should have let *you* in on it."

I got his message. I was interfering. Oh boy, had I stepped into a pile of poop this time. "So, after Randy's death, you thought Mitch would hire you, as Vince, to do his dirty work?"

"Right. Randy played coy and didn't tell Mitch when he asked about the location of my dead body. Mitch thinks that Randy already killed me and hid my body."

"But wouldn't Mitch have required some proof that you were dead?"

Joe snorted. "Randy brought him my wedding band."

I was flabbergasted. "Wait a minute. You were very good to Randy. Why would Mitch think Randy would turn on you and do something so heinous?"

Joe inhaled deeply. "The oldest reason on earth. Money. I'm sick about the whole thing. If I had known what would happen, I would rather have been murdered by Mitch than see Randy die."

I hated to spill Coco's secret but maybe she would approve. After all, this was her father. She wouldn't want him living with guilt. "If Mitch killed Randy, it might have been out of jealousy."

"Why would a guy like Mitch be jealous of Randy?"

"Because Coco was in love with him."

"What?" Joe shook his head at first, but I could almost see him coming to terms with it. "I can't believe I didn't realize it. It makes so much sense in retrospect." He shook his head. "No. If Mitch murdered Randy, it was probably because of me. They tell me you were the last one to see Marla before she took off. Was she okay?"

"I think so. She was scared, though."

"She probably thinks she's next."

"If the police know that Mitch killed Randy, then why don't they arrest him?"

"Because we don't know that. Mitch has alibis for every second of every day, and he's at home with Coco at night. His fingerprints aren't in Randy's house. They're not on the box of chocolates. There isn't one shred of evidence connecting him to Randy's murder."

"So it could have been someone else after all. Do you know who killed Arnaud?"

"Not the first clue." He looked away from me.

"You're afraid it was one of your children." It was a statement, not a question.

"We lost so much because of that man."

"There's one other thing I don't understand. Why didn't

you tell your family about this undercover business? They're worried sick about you."

"For starters, Coco can't keep a secret for anything."

Maybe Joe didn't know his daughter as well as he thought he did. He hadn't known about her affair with Randy. She had kept that quiet.

"She would have blabbed to Mitch and everyone else." He exhaled. "And I had an ulterior reason. I hoped that my mysterious absence would bring my children together again. People unite in times of disaster. I desperately wanted my daughter Kara to come home."

"She's here."

"She's back?"

"I don't know how long she'll stay, but she's seen Coco and Nonni."

Joe hugged me close, like I imagined he wanted to hug Kara. "Then we have to resolve this mess, so I can see my Kara Mel again."

"Caramel? You named her Caramel?"

"Two names. It's cute. Kara with a *K* and Mel as a middle name."

I was willing to bet a small fortune that Kara Mel didn't think it was so cute.

"Would you mind leaving by the back gate?" he asked. "Wolf's going to chew us both out tomorrow as it is."

"They're watching the house? Who does it belong to?"

"It's a rental. Anyone can rent it by the day or the week for the Old Town experience. I booked it in advance, before I knew Mitch wanted to do me in. The police thought it safest for me to continue staying here until everything was resolved."

My head spinning as I tried to make sense of everything, I stepped out into the night with Daisy. We crossed the small fenced garden in back. I opened the latch to the wooden gate, and we entered the alley.

Daisy's tail wagged so hard that it hit my legs while I closed the gate behind us, making sure it was latched securely and wouldn't swing open.

Behind me, a man's voice said, "Thank you for—"

I stifled a scream.

CHAPTER THIRTY-TWO

Dear Natasha,

Is it true that chocolate will keep you up at night? My father-in-law refuses to eat chocolate desserts at dinner because he thinks he won't sleep.

—Daughter-in-Law in Sleepy Eye, Minnesota

Dear Daughter-in-Law,

Tell him the dessert is made with carob. What he doesn't know won't keep him awake.

—Natasha

My heart pounding, I realized it was Wolf.

"Thanks for getting me out of bed in the middle of the night."

"I'm sorry they called you."

"You're *lucky* they called me. Sophie, honestly, I don't know what to do with you. How did you figure it out?"

"Joe's cat followed him and kept sitting out on the stoop, waiting for him."

I could hear Wolf trying to keep from laughing. "Foiled by a feline."

We started walking toward the street. At the end of the alley, just as we stepped onto the sidewalk, Daisy barked at a dark, shadowy figure approaching us.

"Uh-oh. We're going to give away Joe's location," Wolf muttered.

"Should we run the other way?"

"No time. Play along." Wolf pulled me into his arms, swung us around so his back was to the street.

"What—" I began.

He silenced me with a kiss on the lips.

My heart beat even faster. But I knew it was all an act.

He released me abruptly, and we watched the dark form of the person scuttle away into the night. "That was close."

"Are we going to do that every time we see someone on the street?" I teased.

Wolf swallowed hard. "I'm sorry. I apologize. I never should have done that. We were still too near to Joe. If the wrong person saw us, it might have given away his location."

"Of course," I said, as if I kissed men every day to prevent giving away someone's hideout.

Wolf breathed raggedly, as did I.

"I'm so sorry, Sophie. It was instinct. At least if anyone saw us it will have looked as though we were having a fling instead of providing a clue to Joe's whereabouts."

We resumed walking.

I kept an eye out for anyone who might be prowling the streets in search of Joe. Being hyperalert was *almost* enough to distract me from that kiss. I knew it didn't mean anything. I understood what had happened. Still, I had dated Wolf for a long time, and that one moment brought back a rush of feelings that I had tucked away. I had to act nonchalant. Let him know that I got it. There wasn't anything romantic about it. We had kissed to protect Joe—nothing else.

"Look," said Wolf, "I don't know who that was or what he saw. It's possible that a rumor will get around. If you have a difficult time with Alex or Mars about it, let me know, and I'll explain to them. Okay?"

"Same here—if your wife hears something."

Wolf snorted. "Yeah. A phone call gets me out of bed in the middle of the night, I went to be with you, and someone saw us kissing? There's something she would never understand. But better that than being the cause of Joe's death."

He was right, of course. But now I felt worse. Why would any wife understand? I stopped walking and grabbed Wolf's arm. "You can tell her that if there's one thing I know about myself, it's that I don't ever want to be the other woman. Aside from the impropriety, it's entirely too nerve-racking. I would never do that. *Never!* But I understand the need to conceal Joe's hiding place at almost any expense. If that's what we had to do, then at least we kept him safe."

"Promise me you'll stay out of this matter now and let us handle it."

"Of course I will. I had no idea that I was interfering with anything. I would never have intentionally put Joe in danger or impeded your investigation. I'm sorry if I've put you in a bad spot with your wife."

We walked silently after that until we reached my gate.

"I'll wait here to be sure you make it inside safely."

"Thanks, Wolf."

He held up one finger as a warning. "Remember, you promised."

"Yeah, yeah, yeah." He would never let me live this down. I unlocked the kitchen door and unlatched Daisy's leash.

I didn't hear any sounds coming from the family room. I hoped we hadn't awakened Mars. I headed straight upstairs, eager to shed my tight pants. The ancient steps creaked under my weight just as the stairs in Joe's rental had squeaked under him. I changed into an oversized nightshirt and stared at my bed. There was no way I could sleep. I was far too agitated. I wasn't a big drinker, but if ever anyone deserved a drink, it was on a night like this.

Daisy and Mochie followed me down the stairs. A Chocolate Kiss would do the trick. Warm milk helped everyone fall asleep. I spooned unsweetened powdered chocolate and sugar into a couple of tablespoons of water to make a little slurry before I added milk to my mug. I popped it into the microwave to warm it.

The *thunk*, *thunk* of Mars's crutches caught my attention. He flicked on a light. "Can't sleep?"

"I thought I'd have a Chocolate Kiss. Want one?"

"Sure. It's chilly tonight."

"Is it? I hadn't noticed." I fixed another mug for Mars. To both mugs, I added coffee liqueur, peppermint schnapps, and leftover whipped cream that I had in the fridge.

We settled in the dark sunroom, with only the twinkle of fairy lights glowing in the glass ceiling. Daisy nestled at my feet, and Mochie curled up next to me.

I wished Mars were Nina, so I could talk to him about what had just happened with Wolf. But if I mentioned it to Mars, it would surely bring up the subject of the night something very similar had happened between Mars and me. It seemed these unexpected kisses always happened in the middle of the night out on the streets of Old Town. I had to remember not to venture out in the night like that!

Mars and I had never discussed that night. For a while, I had avoided him, but we fell back into our normal pattern of friendship, and it had never happened again.

Wolf's kiss had revived the guilt I felt, though. I just wasn't that woman. I wasn't the kind of person who chased after men who were in relationships. Even if I was once married to Mars or had dated Wolf. But this had been different, anyway. It had been an act intended to deceive. I felt just a little like an undercover agent engaged in espionage.

"What's wrong, Soph?" asked Mars.

I sipped my warm drink, feeling the heat as it went down. What could I say? I couldn't breathe a word about Joe. Instead I told him about Stella. About Arnie being her father and, for all practical purposes, killing her mother.

Even in the darkened room, I could sense Mars's shock. "It's amazing she turned out as well as she did. Wow. Some people go through unimaginable misery. You know, a father who rejects you like that can do a lot of damage to the psyche. I'm convinced that Natasha's dad running out on her and her mother has a lot to do with the problems she has as an adult. She's always trying to impress the father who abandoned her. You and I were so lucky to have great parents. You have to feel for a kid like that. Do you think Stella murdered her father?"

"I honestly don't know. She had as much, if not more, reason to hate Arnie."

"It's probably deeper than hate. After all those years of pain, it has to be resentment and loathing and rage. I wonder if a sharp attorney like Alex could make a case for some kind of insanity?"

"I don't know. I'll officially release him as my attorney tomorrow. She'll need his help. They have the invitation and the glass with the medicine that she ditched. It might be hard for a jury to believe that she didn't take the final step and choke him."

"It doesn't look good for her, even if she did change her mind. The only sure way to prove she didn't kill him would be to find the real murderer."

I glanced over at Mars. "Any idea who that might be?" *There. That wasn't so hard. I hadn't given away anything.*

Mars sipped his drink. "Everyone had a motive. Everyone had opportunity." He finished his drink. "My heart breaks for Stella. I never thought I'd say that about a murderer. I hope Alex has some good tricks up his sleeve for her."

❧

We slept late in the morning. While I didn't like being fired, I was glad I didn't have to rise early after my night out. I lingered in the hot shower, resolving not to cause any more problems in the police investigation. The kiss that had induced such guilt in me was business, plain and simple. In fact, it had kept me out of trouble. If that guy in the shadows had been Mitch or someone he hired, Joe would be dead, and it would all be my fault for giving away his location. That should teach me a lesson.

I blew my hair dry, slipped a red cotton dress over my head, zipped it, and headed downstairs barefoot. I could hear Mars up and about in the family room. I put on coffee, let Daisy out, and fed Mochie.

"Eggs Florentine?" I called to Mars.

He hobbled into the kitchen. "Do you have sausage? Nat never makes sausage."

"Sure." I pulled a package from the fridge along with raspberries, blueberries, eggs, butter, spinach, and milk. In minutes the sausage sizzled on the stove, and the scent of sage perfumed the kitchen. I mixed the berries with a little sugar and a squeeze of lemon and set the bowl on the table. It didn't take long to poach the eggs and assemble our breakfast with lovely, decadent hollandaise sauce on top.

We were eating our eggs when Coco showed up at my kitchen door.

"Oh no," I whispered to Mars. This wasn't how I wanted to start the day. I took a deep breath and braced myself.

I opened the door, and Daisy shot inside, wagging her tail.

"Good morning." I said it as cheerfully and graciously as I could.

"Perfect!" said Coco. "I see I'm in time for breakfast." She handed me a white bakery box. "A peace offering."

I opened the box. Beautiful fresh chocolate croissants were nestled inside. I arranged them on a platter. "Would you care to join us for eggs or coffee?"

"Only coffee, please. I want to apologize. I was simply horrible to you. I hope you can understand that I wasn't prepared to see Kara here. After so many years of anger and tears, it would have been a tough reunion under any circumstances, but it wasn't right or fair of me to lash out at you, Sophie. I hope you'll forgive me."

I handed her a mug of coffee. "Of course. I understand." I was dying to ask how things stood between them. Had they put aside the old issues?

"Thank goodness," said Coco, scooting into the banquette and helping herself to a croissant. "Because Cheryl Maiorca and Lori Speer are driving me nuts."

"Oh? What's their problem?"

"They think they're detectives or something. They turn up everywhere. If I didn't know better, I'd think they were spying on me."

I bit my lip to keep from smiling. They probably *were* spying on her.

"What's that?" asked Mars, pointing to a bag she had set beside her. "More peace offerings?"

"It's Randy's goody bag from the chocolate tasting. Do you want it? Randy's son hired someone to clean out his house so he can put it on the market. I stopped by to pick up a few of my things. They were going to throw out the chocolate."

"Sure!" Mars reached for it. "I don't have problems eating chocolate. We had a ball taste-testing them yesterday." He paused for a moment. "You don't suppose these are the chocolates that poisoned him?"

Coco didn't even blink. "They took those away to the lab. Besides, these are all still wrapped in their original wrappers." She gulped coffee. "Mitch and I can't believe we never noticed the change in the quality of the chocolates. Of all people, we should have known. Open one of those boxes, will you, Mars? Let's try them."

"Don't you eat your own chocolate?" asked Mars.

"Of course I do! But I usually pick up the hand-dipped artisanal ones. I'm ashamed to admit that I never take home a whole box unless it's a gift for someone. I've certainly learned my lesson. It's incumbent on all of us at Amore to keep tasting them. They say chocolate is good for you!"

Mars unsealed the box and handed it to Coco.

She selected a rectangular piece of milk chocolate and bit into it.

I held my breath, hoping she wouldn't collapse again.

She ate half of it, savoring it slowly. "We would have noticed the change right away. My goodness. It's still edible but it's not Amore quality. No wonder sales have fallen off. With all the fantastic new small-batch companies out there hand-dipping and using new flavors, we can't afford to slack off."

"Do you know who's responsible yet?" I waited with bated breath. It had to be Mitch, didn't it? Wasn't he next in charge behind Joe?

"Mitch is looking into it."

Oh great. I finished my eggs, wondering if Coco and Joe had put too much faith in Mitch. It wasn't really any of my business, and after last night's fiasco, I thought I'd better keep my opinions to myself, but wasn't that kind of like the fox checking the security of the henhouse?

Daisy perked up her ears and a moment later, Alex knocked on the door and opened it.

"Good morning, all." He leaned down to kiss my cheek. "Mmm, looks good. What was for breakfast?"

"Eggs Florentine. I can make some for you."

He poured himself a mug of coffee and joined us at the table. "No thanks, I've eaten." He checked his watch. "Isn't it a little late for breakfast?"

"We had a late night," said Mars.

I could almost see Alex's amiable mood melting away. "Did you? Just the two of you?"

Under the table, I kicked Mars's good foot and passed Alex the croissants, saying, "Coco brought these. Won't you have one?"

Alex had seen exactly what I did. I really had to start dating men who weren't so clever.

"Thanks." He picked up a croissant.

I passed him a napkin and a plate.

"I just stopped by with great news," he said. "I don't think Wolchik will be bothering you anymore."

CHAPTER THIRTY-THREE

Dear Sophie,

I wanted to bake a layer cake and use frosting only between the layers and on the top. You've seen those cakes, I'm sure. The sides don't have frosting. It's such a cool look. But the flour from greasing and flouring the pan stuck to the sides of my chocolate cake and it wasn't pretty! Is there a way to avoid that?

—Frustrated in Side Lake, Minnesota

Dear Frustrated,

There's a very easy fix. The next time you grease the pan, "flour" it with cocoa powder!

—Sophie

I tried to keep my cool, but on the inside, I was leaping for joy. Maybe the cops had nailed Mitch, and Joe was out of hiding!

His elbows on the table, Alex leaned forward, excited once again. "Yours are not the only fingerprints on that box. They found matches for Arnaud, who probably made the chocolates, and for Randy, who obviously ate some. For some reason, they have your fingerprints on file, so they were able to establish that one more person handled that box."

"So Sophie's off the hook?" asked Mars.

"Not completely, but that's certainly enough to establish reasonable doubt."

The day was looking far better than I expected. "Speaking of which, you can keep the huge retainer I paid you, but I officially decline to be your client anymore. I think Stella Simpson might call you."

Coco's eyes grew wide. "Heavens, yes! Nonni told me all about it this morning. I don't think she would ever have admitted it if you hadn't noticed the fake invitation." Coco proceeded to tell the entire sad saga to Alex.

At the end, I added, "Stella claims she didn't kill Arnie. She wanted to, but she says she didn't do it."

I could see a spark in Alex's eyes. To him, poor Stella's case would be a fascinating challenge—if, as she claimed, she didn't kill Arnie.

Mars rooted through the gift bag. He popped an Amore baseball cap on his head. "Hey, cool! We didn't get one of these in our bag. Or maybe Natasha hid it from me. I hate it when she does that!" He drew a necktie from the bag.

A print of yummy chocolates adorned a cream-colored background. I recognized it immediately. Surely more than one tie had been made from that fabric but one exactly like it had been worn by Arnaud the night he was strangled.

I almost choked. "Put that back in the bag and set it on the table. Stop touching it!"

The three of them gazed at me as though I had lost my mind.

My words came out in a raspy whisper. "That could be Arnaud's tie. It might have been used to murder him."

Mars dropped the tie in his lap like it was a hot potato, but he couldn't jump back because his broken leg was propped up on a stool. "Ack! Soph, give me a hand!"

"Not a chance. They're not finding my fingerprints on that tie. Wolchik would throw me in the slammer."

It wasn't easy, but Mars used a napkin to pinch it between his thumb and forefinger, and dropped it into the bag in short segments, not unlike a snake.

I hopped up, grabbed the phone, and called Wolf's personal cell phone.

I could hear the wariness in Wolf's voice. "I hope you're behaving."

"We might have found the murder weapon—a tie that looks remarkably like the one Arnaud was wearing that night!"

"Sophie," he growled, "you promised!"

"I didn't even leave the house. It came to me. I swear!"

"Like I believe that. I'll be there in a few."

I hung up. "He's on his way. Nobody leave. I need witnesses, and Wolf will want to know where the bag came from."

"Maybe you shouldn't be so quick to release me as your lawyer, Sophie," said Alex. "Where *did* the bag come from?"

Coco looked like she might burst into tears. "It was Randy's. I picked it up at his house this morning."

I voiced what the others were probably thinking. "Could Randy have murdered Arnaud?"

A bad move. I should have been more sensitive. It opened the floodgates. Coco bawled.

I fetched a box of tissues. "Coco, I'm sorry. I know you were close to Randy but—"

She scooted out of the banquette. "Excuse me. I need a moment alone. Where's the powder room?"

I led her to the foyer and pointed down the hallway.

When I returned to the kitchen, Alex was saying, "Brilliant, just brilliant. Everyone got an identical bag. So no one would find it odd that Randy left with one. All he had to do was slide the tie in the bag and walk out. No one would be the wiser."

Mars tilted his head and raised his eyebrows. "Anyone could have tucked it in a random bag. Most of the people in attendance wouldn't have realized what it was when they unpacked it. They would have assumed what I did, that everyone received a tie. After all, there's a cap and a T-shirt."

"True," mused Alex, "but that would have left a lot to chance. How much more clever to walk out with it in his possession. Then all he had to do was wait until the fuss cleared. He could have taken it on vacation and tossed it in the ocean. Or driven out in the country and left it in the woods to deteriorate."

"He had no reason to kill Arnaud." Coco had pulled herself together and spoke from the doorway. "Randy would never have hurt anyone. It wasn't in his nature."

Wolf knocked on the door and walked in with a guy I didn't know. After greeting everyone and shooting me an annoyed look, he asked, "Where's the tie?"

Mars and I pointed to the bag on the table.

Wolf peered inside but didn't touch anything. "Pretty distinctive pattern. I can't say I've ever seen a tie like that before." He turned to Coco. "Have you?"

Coco swallowed hard. "No."

"So this was not the tie Randy wore to the tasting?" Wolf pressed her.

Coco appeared to take a minute to think back. I had to resist the urge to shout that it was the tie Arnaud had worn.

"I think he wore an Amore T-shirt that night, not a shirt and tie," said Coco. "He was helping set up."

"Mars and Alex, you were there," said Wolf. "Did you notice the tie?"

Alex cleared his throat. "I only stayed a few minutes."

Mars turned the color of beets. "I'm not even sure what I wore that night, much less anyone else."

Wolf turned to me. "Are you certain that Arnaud wore this tie?"

"Absolutely. I noticed it because of the chocolate theme. It seemed so appropriate. Who happens to have a tie like that? Probably only someone addicted to chocolate or someone in the business."

Wolf nodded to the other man, who slid the entire goody bag into a large paper bag.

"Hey!" said Mars. "What about the other stuff in there?"

"For pity's sake, Mars. You can have mine." What was he thinking?

The man with the bag departed but Wolf sat down.

"Coffee?" I asked.

"No thanks, I won't be here long. If you didn't leave your house, how did the tie happen to arrive?"

Coco braced herself against the kitchen counter. "I saw it at Randy's house. They're cleaning it out and were going to throw the bag away." She shrugged. "I rescued it. No point in throwing out perfectly good chocolates. I was on my way over here so I just carried it with me."

Wolf stood up. "How did we miss it when we collected evidence from Randy's house? I apologize, Sophie. Thanks for calling me. Coco, would you mind walking over there with me? I'd like to have a word with the people who are cleaning."

"Yes, of course. But you understand that someone must have hidden the tie in a random bag, and Randy just happened to get that bag."

"I appreciate that that's a possibility."

Coco gulped and her brow furrowed. "I, um, I guess I should tell you that you probably missed it because it was behind a hidden panel in his closet. Even if you moved the clothes, you would never have known it was there. Some previous resident must have had something to hide. His son told the movers to check it, in case Randy had stashed anything valuable there. I guess that makes Randy look guilty, doesn't it?"

Wolf was kind. "Let's get going. I'd like to see this."

"Sophie," said Coco, "you'll be at the farewell dinner for the winners tonight, won't you?"

"Sure." She was big enough to have pushed her anger away and apologized. I was back in the saddle.

The two of them walked out, taking the oppressive air of tension with them. Alex, Mars, and I all heaved breaths of relief.

"Why is she so determined to protect Randy?" asked Alex.

"Because they had an affair."

"Mars! That was confidential," I exclaimed.

Alex frowned. "But very interesting. So Stella allegedly invited Arnaud, planned to murder him but didn't, and then Randy strangled him? Is that how it looks to you?"

"That does seem to be how it's shaping up. But why would Randy do that?" I asked. "He didn't have any connection to Arnie that I know of."

Mars poked a finger under his cast to scratch. "What if he knew Arnaud's real identity as Arnie and was afraid he would hurt Coco again?"

"Oh come on. In the first place, lots of years had passed, and in the second place, wouldn't you just talk with him? Give him a verbal warning to stay away from Coco?"

Alex stood up fast. "I'd better go. I'll draw up a release for you to sign, Sophie."

"So formal?"

He ignored my question and eyed Mars, who had slid a knife under his cast. "How much longer do *you* plan on being here?"

Mars didn't seem to pick up on Alex's ire. "As long as"— his eyes widened—"Sophie, hand me the phone! We haven't heard a word from Natasha this morning. There's no telling what she's up to."

Alex waved good-bye and left. I handed Mars the phone and cleaned up the kitchen. As I rinsed the dishes and placed

them in the dishwasher, I wondered if Stella had killed
Randy. Maybe she'd had a change of heart about Arnaud.
What if she saw Randy coming down the stairs? What if she
saw him stuff Arnie's tie into his goody bag? Might she have
taken revenge against the man who killed her father? She
had hated him. She thought he killed her mother, yet he was
her only close living relative. Maybe blood was thicker than
hatred.

Mars was still on the telephone when I left for The
Laughing Hound to check on their preparations for the winners' farewell dinner. Construction noises on the other end
of the street made me turn around to look. Natasha walked
back and forth in front of her house, the phone to her ear.
Someone sawed wood and another guy disappeared into the
house. I hoped the repairs would be finished soon.

I passed Randy's house on the way to The Laughing
Hound. Wolf couldn't yell at me for pausing to look at what
was happening. The front door stood open. Two men carried
a sofa out and loaded it on a truck parked at the curb. His
son probably didn't have the time to clean out the house
himself, and maybe that was just as well. I felt a pang when
I looked in the truck at Randy's belongings, and I'd barely
known the man.

It was past noon when I arrived at the restaurant, but the
place was still packed. I hunted down Bernie. "Got a minute
to go over the details for tonight's dinner for the chocolate
contest winners?"

"I always have time for you, Soph." Bernie led the way
to the outdoor garden. "You're a little early. We won't set
up until after the lunch rush."

He handed me a card printed with the menu. "Chosen by
Coco herself. Shrimp crostini with nasturtiums, crab-stuffed
mushrooms, summer salad with mixed local tomatoes,
choice of grilled spiced swordfish, mushroom galette, or
seared filet mignon. All served with garlic mashed potatoes,
citrus roasted carrots, and asparagus with hollandaise."

"Wow. Remind me not to eat anything during the day. Dessert? As if anyone will have room?"

"Your favorite. The Laughing Hound's chocolate mousse."

"Sounds wonderful!"

"I'm being summoned. See you later, Soph." Bernie hurried off to someone who waited for him.

I walked out of the restaurant and smack into Nina. Truffles sniffed my legs and wagged her little puppy tail.

"Where have you been?" Nina demanded. "I stopped by for breakfast and not a soul was moving in your house, not even Daisy or Mochie."

"Mars and I slept in."

She raised an eyebrow. "Together?"

"Stop that! Of course not. I couldn't sleep, so we talked—"

Nina grinned at me.

"—about the murders. Okay?"

"Aw, too bad. You have him all to yourself right now, and he's furious with Natasha."

"Not as angry as one might expect. Where are you off to?"

"On my way home. We're just coming back from a training class for Truffles. She was a perfect little inattentive, restless, spunky, wild puppy."

Laughing, I bent to pet Truffles. "I'm heading home, too."

We set off together. I filled Nina in on all the developments, except for those involving Joe and Wolf. We approached Randy's house just as I finished telling her about the tie. The big moving truck was gone.

Nina pushed open the gate.

"Noooo."

"C'mon, Soph. Maybe just being there will help us figure out something. Maybe Randy's spirit remains in the garden, and he'll give us a sign."

I snorted at her. "Nina, you're just going to get us into trouble."

"Don't be silly. There's no reason we can't walk into the backyard."

"Oh, that's right. I forgot about the special exception that exempts Nina Reid Norwood from all the trespassing laws."

"Shh. Listen," she whispered.

No question about it. Voices came from the backyard. "All the more reason to move on. It's probably his son."

"Then he'll be glad we were keeping an eye on the place." She tiptoed into the passageway, keeping Truffles on a short leash.

"Nina!" I hissed. *I had to find a new best friend.* I glanced around before I followed her, against my better judgment. I was right beside her when we peered around the corner.

Four women screamed simultaneously.

Lori and Cheryl appeared as aghast as we were. All four of us broke into relieved giggles.

"What are you doing here?" I asked.

"Someone's staying here," said Lori.

"Probably Randy's son," I said. "We'd better get out of his yard."

"We don't think it's family," said Cheryl. "We saw a light inside last night. But not a normal light. It was more like a flashlight. Like someone looking for something."

Panic coursed through me on two levels. "What time last night?" Surely they hadn't seen me with Wolf?

"About midnight," Lori made a vague attempt to smooth her wild hair.

Whew. What if Randy wasn't Arnaud's killer? What if someone had been looking for the tie? "Well, they emptied the house today, so if anyone was in there, he or she is probably long gone."

"Rumor has it that they're going to arrest Stella," said Lori. "Do you know why?"

Nina filled them in about the fake invitation and the discarded medicine. "Turns out she's his daughter!"

"Then she's related to me. A cousin twice removed or something," Cheryl exclaimed.

"Your cousin got me in a heap of hot water by dumping those pills in my champagne glass." Lori scowled at Cheryl. "I'd probably arrest her, too."

"Actually," I said, "some new evidence turned up this morning. I think it may prove Stella's story correct. Randy had Arnaud's tie in his house."

Lori's eyes went wide. "The one used to murder him?"

The sound of someone screaming *no* inside the house forced us to turn.

Someone stood at the window looking out at us.

CHAPTER THIRTY-FOUR

Dear Natasha,

I found a recipe that said to *bloom* the cocoa powder. Isn't the bloom the gray stuff on chocolate? Why would I want to do that and how is it done?

—Confused in Bloomfield, Connecticut

Dear Confused,

That's a different kind of bloom. If a recipe calls for blooming cocoa powder, they mean for you to put it in a hot liquid to bring out the flavor.

—Natasha

All four of us screamed again.

Marla's pale, drawn face gazed out at us. She unlocked the back door. "Is anyone else here?" she whispered.

"No, it's just us. Are you okay?" I asked.

"Randy couldn't, wouldn't have murdered Arnaud. He was kind and good and—" She broke off abruptly.

"What's wrong?"

"I'm . . . I'm just thinking. Oh no. Oh no!" She nearly collapsed but we caught her. "It's my fault. I should have known," she moaned.

"Known what?" asked Cheryl.

Marla gazed around and whispered, "It's not safe outside."

"Can you walk?" asked Nina.

"I think so." Marla locked the door and pulled a hoodie over her head. It was way too warm for the weather. "Let's get out of here."

Without a word, we hustled through the little passageway alongside the house. On the sidewalk, we surrounded her. We walked fast and in a matter of minutes, we were in my kitchen.

Mars hobbled out of the family room. "If I'd known we were having company, I'd have worn my fancy cast."

Truffles and Daisy greeted each other and promptly engaged in puppy games.

Marla removed her hoodie immediately. "Man, those things are hot in the summer."

Luckily, I had leftover chocolate cake. "Could I interest anyone in cake and coffee?" After my late night, I needed some caffeine but I promised myself to have just a bite of cake in anticipation of the fabulous supper.

Everyone was in agreement. With Nina's assistance, plates, napkins, forks, spoons, cream, and sugar were on the table in short order. I sliced the cake at the table, loaded the plates, and passed them around.

Marla ate and drank like she was starving. The rest of us watched her.

"I told you someone was staying in that house," said Lori.

Marla's eyes widened. "How could you tell?"

"We saw your light last night," said Cheryl.

"I thought I was being so careful. It's not easy to hide."

"What were you going to tell us?" asked Lori. "What's your fault?"

Marla held her coffee mug with shaky hands. "Randy was my friend. We dated a couple of times. Nothing came of that but we stayed friends. He was the guy I called if I needed a hand with something. Just a really good, decent man. You know the type? It about killed him that he had to keep his relationship with Coco secret."

Cheryl gasped. "Are you kidding me? I never would have suspected."

"If he hadn't been a close friend, I don't think I would have guessed, either. That's what I should have realized. Randy would have done anything for Coco. Anything! Randy didn't think he was good enough for Coco. He must have perceived Arnaud as a threat. Maybe he was afraid that Coco would dump him for the famous chocolatier who was her first love."

"I can see that," said Mars.

"He was very jealous." She toyed with her fork. "Coco would be out and about with Mitch in their social world, and the next day Randy would see pictures of them. It tore him up inside. So he came up with this wild idea to get Mitch out of the scene. He was going to plant the idea in Joe's head that Mitch had it in for him."

"Wanted to kill him?" I asked, somewhat incredulous. Had Joe been hiding from Mitch for nothing?

"Right. I told him it was a bad idea. He said he just wanted to create a wedge so that Coco would finally divorce Mitch and that would open the door for Randy. Mitch had used his religious beliefs as a reason not to divorce."

"Religion is a big motivating factor for a lot of people," Lori pointed out.

"Not for Mitch. Ask anybody when's the last time he attended mass. It was a bunch of hooey but he had Coco convinced. If it worked, Randy's plan would have opened the door for me to be with Mitch, too."

Mars jerked forward with surprise, nearly knocking his foot off the stool.

"You and Mitch? Wow. Amore was like a little Peyton Place!"

"Wait," said Cheryl. "Wouldn't Coco have just told her father he was being paranoid? Would Joe have believed that his son-in-law wanted him dead?"

"Maybe," I mused. I tried to phrase my thought so I wouldn't give away anything about Joe. "If Joe had noticed the change in the chocolates and thought something fishy was going on inside of Amore, he might have believed Randy and been suspicious of Mitch." I stopped talking before I got myself into trouble. For Randy's plan to work, Joe would have had to convey his concerns about Mitch to Coco. I gathered he hadn't done that. Joe was a prudent man. Maybe he didn't want to upset Coco by saying anything prematurely.

"You haven't told us why you're hiding," said Lori.

"Because Mitch tried to kill me."

CHAPTER THIRTY-FIVE

Dear Sophie,

I keep seeing something called fair trade chocolate. What does that mean?

—Chocolate Lover in Fairview, Indiana

Dear Chocolate Lover,

It's not just about chocolate beans. The ingredients in any product marked *fair trade* came from farmers and laborers who were paid a fair price or wage and were not exploited.

—Sophie

"I had to go somewhere Mitch would never look for me," Marla said. "I left my car at the airport to throw him off my tracks. Then I took the subway back to Old Town. I knew that Randy kept a spare key under a fake rock in the back. It wasn't like anyone was living there, so it seemed like a good choice. I was still anxious, of course, but I felt certain that Mitch would never think to look there."

"Why would Mitch want to murder you?" asked Cheryl.

Marla's shoulders sagged. "I feel like such an idiot. You get to a certain age in life where you think you should be more clever. When you've lived through ups and downs, and been married and divorced, and you feel like you've developed a sense about people. I trusted him. I . . . loved Mitch. How stupid could I have been? We'd been together for two years. His marriage had deteriorated, and I thought he would leave Coco one day. When Joe disappeared, Mitch was out-of-his-mind anxious. Everyone was worried, but Mitch seemed more troubled than everyone else. We waited for ransom calls that never came. No messages. Just nothing. Coco burst into tears if anyone looked at her. It was awful."

"Mitch?" prompted Lori.

Marla sniffled. "I heard Randy had been poisoned. It broke my heart. I was hollow inside. You know that feeling when someone dies? I couldn't think straight. I walked around like a mindless zombie just going through the motions. The day that Sophie came by to check out Joe's office, she asked me if we, Amore, used any boxes that weren't in Joe's display. It wasn't until that moment that it occurred to me that Mitch had given me a special box of chocolates. He'd said they were a little gesture to thank me because he knew how difficult things were without Joe around. It was a little red box, unmarked, with six gorgeous chocolates inside. I thanked him, but let's face it—I work for a chocolate company. I'm kind of sick of chocolates. They're not anything special to me anymore. The box was laying on my desk when Randy came through and asked if he could try one."

Marla gazed at us with teary eyes. "If I had only said *no*. Instead, I told him he could have the entire box."

"The poisoned chocolates that killed him." Icy shivers rippled down my back. "Mitch meant them for you! I'll call Wolf." I jumped up to fetch the phone.

Marla shrieked, "No! Please don't involve the cops, Sophie. All due respect to you, Lori, but if I tell the police,

Mitch will be out on bond in a split second and then where will I be? No, I have to outsmart him."

There was probably some truth to what she said. If the police didn't have enough information to prosecute, they might not even bring charges. "What about the fingerprints inside the box? Wolf told me they found an unidentified set."

"They must be mine. I would be very surprised if Mitch was that sloppy. I'm sure he wore gloves when he poisoned them."

"Surely he wasn't wearing gloves when he handed them to you."

Marla frowned at her. "The box was in one of those cellophane wrappers—the kind that's like a bag and ties at the top. I remember thinking Mitch was being very tidy to whisk it away when I opened it. He's not a dummy. That's where you come in, Sophie," said Marla. "I have a plan."

Nina had been quiet through the entire revelation. *Now* she came to life. "Let's hear it!"

"No." I said it as calmly and quietly as I could. Not that it was easy. "I'm in so much trouble with the police right now. You can't even imagine."

"Really?" Nina sounded suspicious. "Why don't I know about this?"

I kept my explanation brief. "They feel like I've been interfering with their investigation. That's all."

"This won't get you into trouble," Marla argued. "It's not illegal or anything."

"Hear her out," said Lori.

Marla leaned forward in her eagerness. "I know you're good friends with Bernie. I need you to call in a favor if you can."

Mars laughed. "No problem. Bernie would do anything for Sophie."

And then, just as I was about to say *no*, Marla said, "You know, it's very weird being on the lam. It's amazing what you see out on the streets around, say, three in the morning." She gazed straight at me.

I knew exactly what she had seen. She was blackmailing me! I sat down again and listened. If not for me, then for Wolf's sake. Even if I took the heat for her plan.

~~~

At five o'clock that afternoon, a full hour before the guests were to arrive, Nina drove Mars to The Laughing Hound, while I escorted the hoodie-clad Marla up the alley behind the restaurant and in through the service entrance.

Bernie waited for us. He handed Marla a waitress uniform that consisted of a long-sleeved white shirt, a black vest, and a black skirt.

When she left to change clothes, Bernie whispered, "Are you okay?"

"What a funny thing to ask, Bernie. I'd think you'd be more concerned about us causing a scene."

"Should I call Wolf?"

I squared my shoulders. "I think I'd better do that. Keep Marla here, okay? I'll be back."

"Where are you going?"

"To see a friend."

~~~

One of the many things I loved about Old Town was the ability to walk almost everywhere. It came in handy, especially when someone was in hiding and not answering his telephone. I let myself in the back gate to the rental house where Joe was staying. The police were probably notifying Wolf of my presence right that minute.

I knocked on the living room door. No one answered.

I knocked again and heard a male voice hiss, "Go away!"

"It's okay, Joe. It was all a lie. Randy just wanted you to *think* Mitch was after you."

The curtain over the glass door edged over a hair. Joe opened the door and let me in. "A lie?"

"Marla told us. Randy hoped to drive a wedge between

you and Mitch so he would leave Amore, and Randy could have Coco all to himself."

Joe stared at me, clearly confused.

"Randy wanted to discredit Mitch so you would toss him out, and Coco would finally divorce him."

Joe staggered backward and reached for the sofa to steady himself. "Are you telling me that I've been hiding out here because Randy made up that story about Mitch hiring him to kill me?"

"That's about right."

His eyes narrowed. "Have you informed the police?"

"It's kind of a long story but Marla fears Mitch and thinks if she goes to the police, they won't arrest him and then it will be worse for her. So, she's going to play a little trick on him at the dinner tonight. I thought you might want to come and celebrate with your family. They will be so thrilled to know that you're alive and well."

Joe smiled. "I'm not prone to big displays, but this one time, I think it might be fun. I'll be there."

I turned to go and had opened the door when Joe said, "And we'll tell Wolf this was my idea. Okay?"

"Thanks, Joe." I left the premises in a hurry, but Wolf weighed heavily on my mind. I pulled out my cell phone and called him.

"I'd like to invite you to join us at The Laughing Hound for dinner tonight."

"I thought you understood. I can't, Soph. We can't social-ize. And what are you doing at Joe's? You promised me."

Good grief. "It's business, you dufus. I thought you might want to be there."

He didn't say anything for a long moment. I imagined I could feel his embarrassment.

"Okay. On my way."

I heaved a huge sigh of relief. Now, if Marla could just pull this off without Mitch jumping up and stabbing her with a steak knife.

CHAPTER THIRTY-SIX

Dear Sophie,

I've told my daughter-in-law that I can't sleep if I eat chocolate at dinnertime. Now she's trying to trick me by saying she used carob. Hah! I know the difference because I'm the one who is up all night. My family makes fun of me when I won't eat her desserts. Help!

—Who Did My Son Marry in Sleepy Eye, Minnesota

Dear Who Did My Son Marry,

Show this to your son. Chocolate contains caffeine. Dark chocolate has more caffeine than milk chocolate. In addition, the theobromine in chocolate is a stimulant. Tell your daughter-in-law that white chocolate is your favorite. There's no theobromine and very little caffeine in it.

—Sophie

I walked into The Laughing Hound through the front door and hurried to the outdoor garden. Never in my life had I been so late checking to be sure everything was set up.

I burst through the doors, alarming a few early bird guests who already milled around with drinks in hand. The tables were set with white cloths, light green napkins, and centerpieces of dahlias in shades of red and gold. Lights hung on long strands overhead, to be turned on as the sun fell. Passersby peered over the brick and wrought iron fence. I wasn't surprised. The outdoor dining patio was charming.

I greeted the guests, but as soon as I could without drawing attention to myself, I fled for Bernie's office. Nina and Mars had made themselves comfortable. Marla, wearing her waitress outfit, paced the floor.

"Everything set?" I asked.

"You bet," said Mars. "You just have to keep your cool."

"Me? No one will even notice me. It's all up to Marla now. I'm going out to mingle. If you need me, send Nina."

I hoped Mars and Nina would keep Marla calm. When I returned to the dining patio, I spotted Nonni, as adorable as always. She toddled over to me.

"You find killer of Arnie yet?"

"Nonni, it looks like it was Randy."

"Randy?" Her hand flew to cover her mouth. "To protect his Coco."

"You knew about that?"

"You think Nonni is blind?" She shook a gnarled forefinger. "It was wrong but Mitch is such a . . ."

"Rooster?"

Nonni laughed aloud. "Look," she said, pointing. "Dan has accepted Kara. They put old problems behind them."

Indeed, Dan appeared to be introducing Kara to some of the winners. Stella was with them, but she seemed a little bit unsure of herself.

Relief flooded her face when she saw me. She hurried

toward us. "Nonni, you wouldn't believe what a nice boy-friend Sophie has, and handsome, too."

"I gather Alex is representing you?"

"Now that Arnaud's tie has been found, we're not sure that he'll need to. So far I haven't been charged with anything."

Nonni wrapped an arm around Stella's waist. "Stella is good girl."

Cheryl swooped in on our conversation. "Did you hear, Stella? We're cousins!"

"What? I don't have any relatives."

"Oh baby, you do now. A whole huge bunch of them who all want to meet you!" Cheryl beamed at her.

I wandered away as they tried to figure out exactly how they were connected.

Coco and Mitch had arrived. I felt a pang of guilt. After tonight, their lives would change in ways they hadn't anticipated.

In due course everyone sat down to eat. My heart thundered in my chest so hard that I was afraid everyone could hear it.

Wolf slid into a chair at the table where Mars and Nina were seated.

The appetizers arrived. No sign of Marla.

The pressure of waiting was terrible. Not even the sight of pink and orange blossoms on the shrimp crostini distracted me. Who could eat at a time like this?

I tried not to watch Mitch but it was hard. He looked so comfortable that it disturbed me. If Marla had eaten those chocolates, no one would have known that Mitch had poisoned her. Or if she had run away and kept her mouth shut about it all, he would have continued living the high life. He nearly got away with murdering Randy.

The waitstaff picked up the appetizer plates and started serving the entrees.

Marla carried in Mitch's steak and set it down in front of him. He didn't even notice her. She leaned over very slightly. Even from a short distance I could hear her ask, "Could I get you another Scotch, sir?"

Mitch froze for a second. He turned slightly to look up at Marla, his shoulders twinging with the slightest jerk. She just stared at him.

"No, thank you."

She took a step back but continued to watch him.

Mitch leaned toward Dan, at the next table. "Hey, I think I got your steak, buddy. Mine is overcooked."

Dan acted like Mitch was confused. "Sorry, I've got the correct dinner. I'm having the swordfish."

"What's wrong, Mitch?" asked Coco.

"Overcooked. The steak. It's overcooked."

"Just send it back." Coco turned and lifted her hand. "Marla! What are you doing here?"

"Moonlighting."

Coco studied Marla for a moment, obviously confused. She nudged Mitch. "Did you see Marla?"

"I did."

"Marla, could you bring Mitch another steak, please?"

"Of course. It would be my pleasure."

Everyone else started eating, except for me. I was entirely too nervous.

Marla took her sweet time returning with Mitch's steak. "How's this, sir?"

"Thank you."

"Perhaps you'd try a piece so we can be sure?"

Coco frowned at him. "What's going on? You don't like this one, either? For heaven's sake!" She reached over and cut a slice of the filet. "It looks wonderful."

Mitch hastily knocked her fork out of her hand and tipped the plate so his food slid off it.

"Mitch!" cried Coco. "What's with you tonight? I'm so sorry," she said to the waitstaff who rushed to clean it up.

Wolf, seated next to Mars, leaned over to confer with him.

Marla waited until the mess had been cleaned up before she brought Mitch another plate. "I hear the mashed potatoes are to die for." She took two steps back and waited.

Mitch reached for his glass and drank the last little droplet. Anyone else would surely have requested a refill. He eyed his water but reached for Coco's and drained it.

Most people were finishing their entrees by that time. While Mitch's behavior seemed logical for someone who feared Marla might poison his food, I doubted that it was enough evidence to make a case against him.

He fidgeted like a kid. If he paid any attention to the people around him, I couldn't tell. He appeared to be deep in thought.

I was about to blow a gasket. He must have worn gloves when he broke into my house and stole the chocolates. None of the other mystery chocolates had been poisoned. Mitch must have inserted the poison. That would to be easy to do with a syringe. Who would notice the tiny hole it left? Just thinking about it made me glad he was squirming now.

I noted that Mitch grabbed a dessert plate from a tray and sat down with it. No sooner had he done so than Marla whisked it away and repositioned a new dessert plate before him.

Mitch excused himself and stood. He walked to another waiter. I couldn't hear him, but the waiter nodded.

Mitch returned to his seat, looking pleased with himself.

But it was Marla who delivered the drink and dessert to Mitch. He closed his eyes momentarily, and his jaw tightened. He rose again, grabbed Marla's sleeve and propelled her inside the restaurant.

Wolf and I were right behind them. Wolf held out his arm to stop me. We could hear Mitch whispering on the other side of a partition.

"What do you think you're doing?"

"What's the problem, Mitch? You haven't eaten a bite."

Mitch let out an ugly chuckle. "I was going to say that you would live to regret this, but you won't. There's no place you can go that I won't track you down. Do you understand me?" he hissed.

Coco joined us. I held up a finger across my lips in a signal to be quiet.

Mitch continued his tirade in a low voice. "You thought you were so smart coming here tonight with all these people to protect you. Well, you know what? They're going home. And then you will be all alone. And when you least expect it—"

"What? You'll send me more poisoned chocolates? Don't you feel *any* remorse for killing Randy?"

"I didn't poison him, you did. You're the one who gave him the chocolates, you idiot. Besides, you did me a favor."

"A favor?"

"Sure. Randy knocked off the old man for me. When you murdered Randy with those chocolates, you took care of the only person who could link me to Joe's death."

Coco gasped and covered her mouth with her hand.

Uh-oh! I was going to be in huge trouble with Wolf! Mitch really had wanted to kill Joe!

Mitch's tone changed. It was sickeningly sweet. "We're halfway there, baby. I'm in charge of the company now. We just have to wait awhile, let things settle down."

"Baby? You must think I'm really stupid. You tried to kill me! That could have been me instead of Randy. What did I do to you?"

"It wasn't about you. Don't you get it? With Randy gone, you were the loose link. You were the only one who could ruin things for me with Coco. I'm nothing without her. I can't lose Coco. Without her I don't have Amore. Without Coco, I cease to exist—no company, no house, nothing. Everything has to happen in logical order. Just bear with me, baby. Eventually, Coco will have an accident, I'll be in charge, and then we can be together. But I need you to keep quiet, darlin'.'"

Coco pushed past Wolf and me. "Marla," she cooed. "I'm so glad to see that you're all right. With Daddy missing, I was afraid something awful might have happened to you, too. And by the way, I'm putting you in for a substantial raise. You deserve it."

And then we heard a painful crack and a groan.

Wolf and I pressed to the other side in time to see Mitch bend over in pain. "My dose! You broke my dose!"

Coco massaged her knuckles. "Man, that hurt. But it was worth it. That was for my father!"

Wolf, after grumbling something about dealing with me later, handcuffed Mitch and escorted him from the restaurant.

Coco bowed her head and sniffled. "I can't believe he killed Dad. It's my fault. I brought him into our family."

I had to coax her to return to her guests. She cleaned up her tears, and we went to our seats as though nothing had happened, except Coco invited Marla to sit next to her where Mitch had been.

Coco clinked on her glass and stood up. "I apologize for the absence of my father. I know he would have loved to be here with us tonight."

Her voice stayed firm and didn't break. I was so proud of her.

Vince rose from his seat. He pulled off the glasses and ponytail wig, and peeled off his fake nose.

Coco stared at him in horror, which quickly changed to joy. "Dad?"

Kara jumped to her feet. In no time at all, Joe's family surrounded him, and the rest of us applauded.

Joe took the floor. "I would like to apologize to all of you, and especially to my wonderful family. My little disappearance was for an undercover examination of Amore Chocolates. I was stunned and deeply pleased to find such fabulous and dedicated people working for us. We will be making a few changes but they will strengthen Amore, and it will be better than ever. I'm sorry for putting my family through such anguish, and I hope they'll forgive me."

He raised his glass in a toast. "Here's to all of our contest winners. Thank you for making our sixtieth anniversary so very special. May you never run out of chocolate!"

CHAPTER THIRTY-SEVEN

Dear Sophie,

My wife refuses to bake chocolate cakes because she says they're too much for just the two of us. I think she should freeze half, and we'll eat the other half, but she maintains that you can't freeze chocolate cake. Is she pulling my leg?

—Hungry in Freeze Fork, West Virginia

Dear Hungry,

Most chocolate cakes and brownies freeze very well. Don't bake them again, just let them come to room temperature. Don't tell your wife, but some brownies are even better semi-frozen. They make excellent midnight snacks!

—Sophie

Coco ordered champagne, which probably made Bernie very happy. Guests lingered at their tables over coffee, champagne, and dessert. Coco visited every single table and took the time to sit down and talk with her guests.

I moseyed over to Nonni. "Do you feel better now that you know Joe is safe?"

She screwed up her face and clutched her hands together under her chin. "I am so worried about Joe." Then she laughed so hard her frail shoulders shook. "I know all the time," she admitted. "I make a pretty good actress, yes?"

I assured her that she did.

"Two days from now, you come to Joe's house, and I teach you to make real tiramisu, Nonni's way."

"It's a date, Nonni. How is Bacio? Is he staying home?"

"He is so happy to be on the lap of Joe's wife again. Bacio brings her comfort. She feels much better now that he is back."

I lifted my forefinger and pinky in the air as she had a few days ago. "How about the curse?"

Nonni hugged me. "No more curse for the Meranos! Now that we have our Kara back, the curse is gone."

Joe walked over to hug his mom.

"There's one thing I don't quite understand, Joe. Why now? Why did you plan this during the big anniversary celebration?"

He placed an arm around his mother's shoulders. "Two reasons, really. I wanted to see how my family would react. Who would show leadership? And the second but probably most important reason was I hoped my absence would make the news and bring Kara home. It was a long shot, but all I really wanted in the world was to have my daughter back."

I watched Kara laughing with Lori across the room and wondered if Kara would stick around. After all, she had made another life for herself in Colorado.

As if reading my thoughts, Joe said, "We have made room for Kara in our hearts again, and she will take her

rightful place at Amore—if she wants it. I learned things
about my family that I never would have known if I hadn't
gone undercover. I thought Dan didn't have it in him to run
a business. I knew he was talented. And I appreciated his
amazing artistic abilities but somehow, I thought that meant
he wasn't interested in running Amore Chocolates. But he
rose to the occasion. He's just like my father. Strong, honest,
and kind. During my absence, he handled Amore and his
sister Coco with a natural skill that I never knew he had.
And he took care of Nonni."

Coco joined us just in time to hear her father say, "My
sweet Coco. I was so mistaken about you. No one could ask
for a more dedicated daughter. When you thought I was
missing, you moved heaven and earth to find me, but you
never dropped the ball at Amore. You kept everything going.
The interviews and cooking demonstrations never stopped
for a moment. I think you may have been surprised by your
own resilience and strength. You will follow me as the next
CEO of Amore Chocolates."

"Who was responsible for the inferior chocolates?" I
asked.

"Mitch. In a way I think he meant well. He changed to a
lower-cost chocolate supplier and added some cheap ingredients. It made our bottom line look good, but we would
have lost our reputation. Fortunately, it didn't go on very
long. First thing tomorrow morning, we'll be pulling the
boxed chocolates and changing the formula back."

Stella, Dan, and Kara joined the conversation.

"The only thing that bothers me is we'll probably never
know why Randy killed Arnaud," said Dan.

"For love!" said Nonni. "Because he loved Coco and was
afraid to lose her."

Stella sucked in a deep breath. "Nonni's right. I was talking with Randy at the tasting when Arnaud joined us. I'm
sorry, Coco, but he asked where Kara was. No one ever
mentions her, so he caught our attention. And then he

boasted, 'I slept with both sisters . . . back before they looked like old cows.' He was laughing about it and said something about seducing you both again. I think Randy was as sickened by him as I was. We were kind of alike, Randy and me. We were outsiders who were embraced by your family. Not just at Amore but in our personal lives. Both of us would have done anything to protect you. He wasn't going to let the man who ruined your lives come back into them again. He didn't want to lose you to that worm."

I managed to pull Kara aside for a moment. I didn't want to embarrass her or cause problems in front of her family but there was one thing that still bugged me. "Kara, I saw you at the Honeysuckle B and B the night that Joe went missing."

She looked horrified.

"You were in town before Marla ever called you. Your dad's disappearance wasn't the real reason you came to Old Town, was it?"

Kara glanced around as if checking to see if anyone would overhear. "I'm just getting my family back, Sophie. I would appreciate it if you didn't share what I'm about to tell you. I'll probably confess to them in my own good time but it might throw a big kink into the reunion if they knew the truth."

She studied the floor. "I figured out that Arnie had become Arnaud and read about his new store opening here in Old Town. He was the worst thing that ever happened to me. Because of him, my entire life turned upside down."

Kara raised her eyes to meet mine. "I'm not saying I didn't cause some of my own problems. I can't go back and undo anything. I have to live with that guilt for the rest of my life. I came to Old Town to confront him face-to-face. I wanted to look into his eyes and let him know what evil he did to me and my family. Arnie always got away with everything. He was like a tornado, moving on and leaving devastation behind." Kara chuckled. "I liked to imagine that I would punch him in the nose. I knew that I wouldn't, but I liked to dream about it. I came here to face my past."

⚜

A lot of people slept better that night with the knowledge that Mitch was safely in police custody. Marla collected her cat from a friend and went back home to her own place. Nina drove Mars back to my house, and I stayed until the bitter end, when the very last guests had gone back to the hotel.

In the morning, I forced myself out of bed at eight o'clock anyway. After a quick shower, I stepped into a cool blue sheath dress, and zipped it up. Sandals, earrings, and I was ready to wrap up the Amore anniversary events. I paused in the kitchen, where Mars made coffee without the aid of his crutches.

I was about to ask him to feed Mochie, but my sweet kitty was already chowing down on something. "Back soon," I assured him as I fled out the door.

I heard him yell, "Bring breakfast!"

Old Town puttered to life. Cars crowded the streets, and people hurried to work. Taxis and limos idled in the hotel driveway, ready to whisk people to the airports and train station.

The entire Merano family had made the trip to the hotel to say good-bye to their guests. Even Nonni and Kara walked around the lobby, thanking everyone.

Joe pecked me on the cheek. "Thank you for all your help, Sophie. I'm afraid I put you through the wringer."

"I'm just glad the anniversary was a success and that you're alive!"

"It was a huge success. Frankly, I know people who paid more for one wedding than we paid to host all these folks. And it was worth every penny. We can already see an increase in sales of our baking chocolates as a result of the TV appearances and demonstrations that Coco arranged." He paused. "And I would have paid *anything* to have my Kara back."

"She seems happy."

"I suspect we'll have some rough patches ahead, but that's all part of being a family. We're Meranos. We'll make our way through it, come what may."

Lori Speer and Cheryl Maiorca were a bit tearful at having to part. "This was the best vacation ever!" said Lori. "Well, except for the deaths, of course. I wouldn't wish that on anyone. Cheryl and I are making plans to get together again."

"Maybe on a cruise," said Cheryl. "You should come!"

"I think it would have to be a mystery cruise to keep the two of you entertained."

"Hey, did you hear about Stella? Dan, come over here," called Lori.

Oh no. Dan strolled over.

"Was she arrested?" I asked.

"Only Mitch was arrested," said Dan. "You won't believe this. Stella got a call at five in the morning from the lawyers who handle Célébration de Chocolat's legal matters in Belgium. It seems they insisted that Arnie write a will. He has only one heir, Stella Simpson."

"He wouldn't pay her support. Didn't even bother to meet her, and yet he left her everything?" I asked.

"I guess he didn't have anyone else. He alienated everyone he ever met."

"My new cousin is loaded," laughed Cheryl. "Can you believe it?"

Over the next hour, the Amore contest winners departed. The Meranos took off, but not before Nonni reminded me to come by to learn to make tiramisu.

On the way home, I picked up more food than we could possibly eat. Savory pesto and ham tarts, a spinach salad with bacon and onions, strawberry cinnamon buns with a sugary drizzle that made my mouth water.

But when I reached my house, Alex and Wolf were helping Mars out the front door. "What's going on here?"

"Natasha has something to show me," grumbled Mars.

I left the food in the kitchen, attached Daisy's leash, and followed the guys to Natasha and Mars's house, expecting to see a couple of very modern bathrooms.

Natasha waited for us, her makeup and hair perfect. She wore impossibly slender gray trousers with a matching silk blouse that made me feel positively frumpy.

Mars lurched around the side of the house to the back. Natasha had torn out the small windows on the basement level, dug down to create a patio, and installed glass doors. She opened them wide.

Inside was the ultimate man cave. A huge TV occupied one wall. Seating that looked too cushy to ever leave faced the TV. New shelving and a fabulous desk in the corner marked Mars's home office. Lights shone down on a highly polished bar with brass fittings. Nearby, a game table with a felt top awaited players.

Natasha floated to the game table. "It has a dual function. There's a wood top that turns it into a conference table."

The three men gazed around the room.

"Well?" asked Natasha.

"I would never go upstairs," said Alex.

"Why would you need to?" asked Wolf.

"Mars! Say something!" Natasha wove her fingers together anxiously.

"It's incredible. It almost makes up for breaking my leg."

"Almost?" Alex turned to Natasha. "Feel free to break *my* leg anytime."

"Why, Alex!" Natasha giggled as though he had made a pass at her.

"It's amazing, Natasha," I assured her. "Who wouldn't love this? You outdid yourself."

Mars reached out to hug Natasha.

It was a grand gesture on her part. Mars always complained about everything in the house being for Natasha, decorated in her style, with her preferences. She had given over almost the entire basement to him.

"Will you come back home now, Mars?"

"Is there running water?"

"I go to all this trouble, and that's what you ask?"

"Is there?"

"Soon. I promise. Probably this afternoon."

"Okay. I love my man cave. It's better than anything I could have imagined."

"There is some bad news, though."

Uh-oh. I could see Mars tensing up.

"I didn't get the chocolate shop."

I had to bite my upper lip not to laugh. It was all a matter of perspective. Mars was probably trying not to show his glee, as well.

"Célébration de Chocolat?" asked Alex.

"Yes. I understand they're planning to open the store after all."

"Stella's already busy," I said.

Wolf frowned at Alex. "She inherited it? What about the slayer laws?"

"That sounds horrible." Natasha wrinkled her nose.

"It just means you can't inherit from someone you murder," said Alex. "But Stella didn't kill Arnie. If they find Randy's fingerprints or DNA on that tie, and I believe they will, then I think she's home free."

"Sophie, did you bring food home? I'm starving!" said Mars.

We trooped back to my house, picking up Nina and Truffles on the way.

But when Mars disappeared through the front door, Wolf tapped my shoulder.

"I'm not coming in, but I wanted to have a word in private."

I knew it would happen. It had to be said. I closed the door and waited for him to chew me out.

Wolf looked down at his shoes. "I've been pretty lucky in my relationships."

No! I didn't want to hear this!

"I think—"

I seized his hand. "Let's not go there." I dropped his hand quickly lest I give the wrong impression. "What's the point? We did what we had to do—to protect Joe. Nothing more. I'm really sorry for interfering with your investigation. Truly, I am. I understand fully that I could have put Joe in jeopardy. I don't even want to think about what could have happened. I've learned a big lesson."

Wolf grinned at me. "I guess we both have. Thanks for understanding—about both things."

"One last thing, Wolf. If Mitch hired Randy to kill Joe, then why did he ask me to find Joe?"

"Apparently he didn't trust Randy. He wanted to see Joe's body but Randy wouldn't, couldn't, tell him where it was. I gather Mitch was afraid to hire a professional because of his own involvement and thought you would lead him to Joe without involving the police. Woe to the killer who underestimates you, Sophie Winston!"

Wolf laughed and walked away, but I was okay. I took a couple of deep breaths, and opened the door, only to find Alex glaring at me.

Men!

I ignored his sour expression and hurried to the kitchen. "Coffee! I need coffee! Anyone else?"

Over lunch, I told my friends how close I had come to messing up the police investigation, omitting the part about the kiss, of course.

Natasha shook her head. "I'm shocked that no one murdered that Arnaud before. The man was nothing but a cheat and a thief."

"A thief?" asked Nina. "Oh, you mean stealing from Cheryl and her family?"

"Cheryl? No, he cheated me. I met with him when he came to town because I was thinking about going into the chocolate business. I ordered special artisanal hand-dipped chocolates from him. I paid him and everything, but they were never delivered." She held up four fingers to emphasize her point. "Four times I had to call him and ask for them. I never did get them, and now he's dead."

Nina's eyes met mine. "Your chocolates!" she exclaimed.

"The mystery chocolates in the unmarked boxes. They were delivered every day for five days." I heaved a sigh of relief. "They were supposed to be delivered to your house?"

"*You* got them?" Natasha's eyes flicked from Mars to me and back. "You two didn't *eat* them, did you?"

"Why? What was in them?" I asked.

Natasha's mouth twitched to the side. "Did you eat any?"

"No."

"Oh, thank goodness," she sagged with relief. "They were his aphrodisiac specialties. One or two of those chocolates, and he guaranteed a hot night. He has them delivered in unmarked boxes so no one will be the wiser."

"You were going to feed me aphrodisiacs?" Mars sounded peeved.

"Don't be silly." Natasha flicked her hand at him but muttered to me, "Wouldn't have been the first time. Where are they?"

"Most of them went to the lab to be analyzed, and the final box was stolen by Mitch, poisoned, then eaten by Randy, who died. The remaining one is in the possession of the police."

"My chocolates? Now I'll never get to try them!"

"As amusing and fascinating as this has been, I'd better get back to my office." Alex scooted out of the banquette. "Could I have a quick word with you, Sophie?"

I cringed inside. Wolf wasn't enough? Now I had to have the awkward conversation with Alex, too? Ugh.

I walked outside with him.

"I honestly don't know what to do with you. I hate that you have Mars and Wolf in your life."

We'd been through that before. I could see what was coming. The official dumping.

"Even worse, I cannot believe that you were whisked into the police van and then went to a safe house at two in the morning."

Aargh. Even Wolf hadn't chewed me out for that again.

"Yet, oddly enough, while part of me is completely appalled, another part of me finds you utterly fascinating. Which makes me worry about myself. There are so many women around who aren't up to their necks in murder investigations. If I were smarter, I would date one of them. But it looks like I'm stuck on you, Sophie Winston. I'd like to think you feel the same way about me?"

Nina ran out of the house with Truffles, interrupting us. "I just got a call," she wailed. "Someone is adopting Truffles. They're on their way! I hardly had any time with her."

At that moment, Kara ran up the street toward us. She knelt on the sidewalk and held out her arms. Truffles ran straight to her, wriggling with joy.

"I should have known," said Nina. "A chocolate Lab for a chocolate family. What do you bet Truffles shows up on the Amore logo sometime?"

Alex slid his hand into mine. "I'm a sucker for a happy ending," he said. "What do you say? Tonight, a picnic in the park? Just the three of us?"

"Three?"

"Don't you want to bring Daisy?"

I gave him a little kiss, smack on the lips. And it wasn't fake. It wasn't a cover for anything. "Sounds wonderful. Daisy and I would love it. Just one thing—I think I've had enough chocolate for a while."

He kissed me back.

RECIPES

Desserts

Nonni's Tiramisu

1¼ cups strong espresso or coffee (3 tablespoons
instant to 1¼ cup boiling water)
¼ cup Kahlúa (coffee liqueur)
4 egg yolks
½ cup sugar
½ cup Marsala wine
2 (8-ounce) containers mascarpone cheese
1½ cups heavy cream
2–3 packages of crisp ladyfingers (savoiardi)
1 square semisweet baking chocolate

1. Mix the coffee with the Kahlúa and set aside. Take the mascarpone out of the fridge and let it come to room temperature.

2. Find a bowl that fits on top of a pot. A double boiler would work, or just a bowl over a pot. Bring the water to a simmer. Beat the eggs over the simmering water about five minutes, until they are fluffy. Add the sugar and the Marsala wine and whisk over the simmering water for about 8 minutes. It will almost double in size and be quite thick.

3. In another large bowl, use a spoon to mash the mascarpone cheese against the sides to soften it. Don't skimp on this step. Mash and stir until it's creamy. Pour the egg mixture into it and combine until smooth.

4. Whip the cream and fold it into the egg and mascarpone mixture.

5. Briefly dip each ladyfinger into the coffee mixture and place in the pan, lining them up so that the pan is covered. Pour half the creamy mixture over them and spread. Repeat with a second layer.

6. Use a grater or vegetable peeler to shave the semisweet chocolate over the top as decoration. Refrigerate several hours, preferably overnight.

Devil's Food Cake with Vanilla Buttercream Frosting

1½ cups flour
3 tablespoons cocoa powder
1 teaspoon baking powder
1 teaspoon baking soda
½ teaspoon salt
2 tablespoons unsalted butter
3 ounces unsweetened chocolate
2 teaspoons instant coffee
1 cup hot water
2 eggs
1 cup dark brown sugar

½ cup vegetable oil
2 teaspoons vanilla

Preheat oven to 350 degrees. Grease and flour two 9-inch baking pans. Mix together the flour, cocoa powder, baking powder, baking soda, and salt. Set aside. Melt the butter with the unsweetened chocolate in the microwave on short bursts. Dissolve the coffee in the hot water. Beat the eggs with the dark brown sugar and oil. Alternate adding flour and water. Beat in the melted chocolate and butter. Divide evenly between the prepared pans. Bake 20 minutes or until the edge begins to pull away and a cake tester comes out clean.

VANILLA BUTTERCREAM FROSTING
½ cup softened butter
3 cups powdered sugar
Vanilla extract to taste
Heavy cream

Cream the butter and sugar together. Add vanilla. Add cream by the tablespoon until desired consistency is achieved.

Chocolate Walnut Zucchini Cake

1½ cups flour
½ cup cocoa powder
1 teaspoon baking powder
½ teaspoon baking soda
½ teaspoon salt
1 cup walnuts
2 cups shredded zucchini (about 1–2 zucchini)
1 teaspoon instant coffee or espresso
2 teaspoons warm water

½ cup (8 ounces) unsalted butter plus extra for
*   greasing pan*
1 cup dark brown sugar
½ cup sugar
3 eggs
1 teaspoon vanilla
½ cup semisweet or bittersweet chocolate chips
Powdered sugar for dusting

Preheat oven to 350 degrees. Grease a 10-inch springform pan with butter. In a food processor, combine flour, cocoa powder, baking powder, baking soda, salt, and walnuts. Pulse until the walnuts have disappeared. Pour out into a bowl and set aside. Use the shredding disk in the food processor to shred the zucchini. Set aside.

Dissolve the coffee in the water. Cream the butter with the sugars, and beat in the eggs, one at a time. Add the coffee and the vanilla, and beat. Slowly add the flour mixture. The batter will be thick. Mix in the zucchini and stir in the chocolate chips. Pour into the prepared pan and bake for 45–50 minutes. Cool on a baking rack. When cool, dust with powdered sugar.

Chocolate Cake

2 cups flour
½ cup cocoa powder
2 teaspoons baking powder
2 teaspoons baking soda
1 teaspoon salt
2 cups sugar
1 teaspoon instant coffee or espresso
2 cups boiling water
1 stick (8 ounces) unsalted butter
4 ounces unsweetened baking chocolate

3 eggs
2 teaspoons vanilla

Preheat oven to 350 degrees. Grease and flour two 9-inch baking pans.

Combine the flour, cocoa powder, baking powder, baking soda, and salt in a bowl, stir to mix well, and set aside.

Pour the boiling water over the sugar and coffee. Stir until the sugar is completely dissolved. Place the butter and baking chocolate in a bowl and pour the hot liquid over them. Stir until dissolved and set aside.

Lightly beat the three eggs. Add the vanilla and beat briefly. Alternate adding chocolate mixture and the flour mixture until combined. Pour into prepared pans. Bake 30 minutes, or until a cake tester comes out clean.

Double Chocolate Bourbon Bread Pudding

9×13-inch baking dish
Butter for greasing
1 loaf challah
½ cup unsweetened cocoa powder
1 cup sugar
¼ teaspoon salt
½ cup heavy cream
3½ cups milk (can use nonfat)
4 large eggs
4 tablespoons bourbon (1 airline-sized bottle)
½ cup semisweet chocolate chips

1. Tear the challah into pieces and place in a large bowl.

2. Combine the cocoa powder, sugar, and salt, and whisk together. Stir in the heavy cream and the milk. In another

bowl, lightly whisk the eggs. Whisk them into the cocoa mixture. Add the bourbon, give a final stir with the whisk, and pour half of it over the bread. Turn the bread until it is all coated. Set aside for 30 minutes.

3. Preheat the oven to 350 degrees and grease the pan. Pour the bread into the pan along with any liquid at the bottom. Spread the bread in the pan. Scatter the chocolate chips over the bread. Pour the remaining chocolate mixture over top and bake for 20 minutes.

4. Turn the heat down to 275 degrees and bake another 10 minutes or until the middle is firm and a cake tester comes out clean.

Serve with a traditional vanilla sauce or whipped cream. Or enjoy plain.

Chocolate Chip Cookies

> 2 sticks butter (melted)
> 2 cups flour
> ¾ teaspoon kosher salt
> 1 teaspoon baking soda
> ¼ cups sugar
> 1¼ cup dark brown sugar
> 1 whole egg
> 1 egg yolk
> 1½ teaspoons vanilla
> 2 cups chocolate chips

Preheat oven to 350 degrees.

Melt the butter in the microwave at half power in short bursts.

Mix the flour, salt, and baking soda in a bowl.

Beat the egg and egg yolk with the sugars. Add the cooled melted butter, alternating with the flour mixture. Add the vanilla. Stir in the chocolate chips.

I prefer to use parchment paper, but a lightly greased baking sheet works just as well. Drop the raw dough on the sheet in generous spoonfuls a couple of inches apart. Bake at 350 degrees for 10–12 minutes. Remove to a cooling rack when done.

If you don't want to bake them all right away, roll the remaining dough in waxed paper and slide into a freezer bag. When ready to bake, slice in inch thick rounds and cut each round in half. Bake at 350 degrees for 10–12 minutes.

Brownies

¾ cup flour
1 teaspoon baking powder
¼ teaspoon salt
2 tablespoons hot water
¼ teaspoon instant coffee
½ cup (1 stick) butter, softened
3 ounces unsweetened baking chocolate
1 cup sugar
2 eggs
1 teaspoon vanilla

In the microwave, melt the chocolate in short bursts (about 30–40 seconds), stirring in between until melted and smooth. Set aside.

Line an 8x8-inch baking pan with parchment paper or grease thoroughly. Preheat the oven to 350 degrees.

Mix the flour, baking powder, and salt in a bowl and set aside. Dissolve the coffee in the hot water.

Cream the butter with the sugar. Beat in one egg at a time. Slowly beat in the flour mixture and add the vanilla. Beat in the cooled chocolate and the coffee. Bake 25 minutes or until the middle is just set and doesn't jiggle.

CHOCOLATE SOUR CREAM FROSTING

Note: This frosting works well on brownies as well as cakes. For an 8×8 pan, you may wish to make half the recipe.

1 cup semisweet chocolate chips
¼ cup butter plus 1 tablespoon butter, softened
¾ cup sour cream
1 teaspoon vanilla
2–3 cups powdered sugar

Melt the chocolate chips with ¼ cup butter in the microwave in short bursts, stirring in between. When smooth, set aside to cool. Beat in the sour cream, 1 tablespoon of butter, and vanilla until smooth, and add powdered sugar to desired consistency.

Homemade Truffles

Please note: The flavor of truffles depends heavily on the quality of the chocolate. I recommend using a bittersweet or semisweet Belgian chocolate.

8 ounces bittersweet or semisweet chocolate
½ cup heavy cream
3 tablespoons liqueur, optional (Kahlúa, Grand Marnier, or Chambord)
Unsweetened powdered cocoa (or finely chopped nuts)

Chop the chocolate into small pieces. Heat the cream until almost boiling. Pour over the chocolate and stir until smooth. Refrigerate. If using liqueur, stir in after the chocolate cools but before it begins to set.

After two hours, set out a tray or large plate with cocoa powder or finely chopped nuts. Take a small scoop of the chocolate mixture and roll it into a ball. Roll around in the cocoa or nuts until covered. Place on a tray. Repeat until all the truffles have been made. Chill until set.

Drinks

Peach Sangria

½ cup sugar
½ cup water
1 bottle white wine, sparking wine, or rosé
1 cup peach schnapps
1 bag frozen peaches
1 fresh peach
Sliced fresh strawberries (optional)

In a small pot, dissolve the sugar in the water. When cool, pour into a large pitcher. Add the white wine, peach schnapps, and frozen peaches. Refrigerate.

Before serving, slice the fresh peach and add to the pitcher with the strawberry slices.

Chocolate Kiss

1½ ounces peppermint schnapps
½ ounce coffee liqueur
1 mug hot chocolate
Whipped cream

Pour the schnapps and the liqueur into the hot chocolate and stir. Top with whipped cream.

Moo Cow

2 ounces chocolate vodka
2 ounces Baileys Irish Cream

Pour in a small glass and stir. Makes one drink.

Chocolate Covered Berries

1 ounce chocolate liqueur (like Godiva)
1 ounce Chambord
1 ounce Irish cream

Pour the liqueurs into a small glass. Swirl and enjoy!

Chocolate Martini

2 ounces chocolate liqueur
2 ounces vanilla vodka

Pour into small martini glass and stir. Makes one drink.

*You ask of my companions. Hills, sir, and the
sundown, and a dog as large as myself that my
father bought me. They are better than human
beings, because they know but do not tell.*

—EMILY DICKINSON

"These are the murder weapons." Val Kowalchuk reached
into the chestnut leather tote she had brought with her and
pulled out a pearl-handled pistol.

The new owner of the popular Wagtail pub, Hair of the
Dog, Val was brimming with clever ideas to bring tourists
to Wagtail. Enthusiastic and hardworking, Val was quickly
becoming a good friend. She wore her dark brown hair
short. No surprise there since the hours she worked at her
pub left little time for primping.

We were on our way to Café Chat for brunch to finalize
some details about Murder Most Howl, Wagtail's murder
mystery weekend. I stopped dead. "That looks real!"

Val twirled it on her forefinger with alarming ease.
"Amazing, isn't it?"

We walked on. "Frightening. Someone could mistake it
for a real gun."

Val snorted. "Wouldn't do them much good. It's made of
wood."

We reached the entrance to Café Chat but when we
turned to enter, Trixie, my Jack Russell terrier, took off. I

no longer used a leash to walk around town with her. We had been practicing coming when called and most of the time she listened to me, but she still had a mind of her own and sometimes followed her nose elsewhere. I knew where she was headed this time, though, straight to the doggy play area. "I'll meet you inside," I said to Val.

Trixie sped across the green, the park in the middle of Wagtail's pedestrian zone. When I caught up to her, she was politely sniffing a corgi.

An attractive blonde woman bundled in a puffy purple jacket and faux fur boots talked on the phone. Although I didn't know who she was, I'd seen her around town before and thought the corgi belonged to her.

I looked up at the silvery gray sky. Even though it was ten in the morning, and other people walked dogs, there was a silence in the air. A peaceful stillness that meant snow was on the way.

The woman on the phone whispered, but it was so quiet that she might as well have come right up to me and spoken aloud. *"Blanche is in town."* She paused. *"That's what I thought, too."* She sucked in a deep breath of the cold air. *"I'm finally going to do it. I can't go on like this."*

I gave Trixie a few minutes to play with the corgi. She would behave better at Café Chat if she burned off some energy. I felt a little bit guilty about listening to the woman's phone call, but good grief, if she was going to have a private conversation in public, what did she expect?

"Of course I'm nervous! Why do you think I've put it off for so long?" She smiled at me in spite of eyes rimmed in red from crying.

I dug in my pocket for a treat, held it out, and called to Trixie. She gave the corgi one last look and evidently decided that a cookie was more enticing. As Trixie and I walked away, I heard the woman say, *"This weekend. The sooner the better."*

Trixie scampered into Café Chat, probably as relieved

as I was to be out of the cold. I helped her out of her plush pink coat and hung it on the rack with my own boring winter white jacket.

Zelda York and Shelley Dixon spied me, and waved their hands in the air. Zelda and Shelley worked with me at the Sugar Maple Inn. In her spare time, Zelda was building a pet psychic business. I wasn't sure that she could really read the minds of dogs and cats, but so far, she'd been fairly accurate.

Wagging her tail, Trixie greeted a half dozen dogs on the way to our table. My little girl with the black ears and spot on her rump had the good sense to approach Zelda's cat, Leo, cautiously. She stopped short of him and gently extended her nose toward his.

An extraordinarily confident cat, Leo stretched his white paws forward, showing off the blaze on his chest and demonstrating his total lack of concern about Trixie's presence. Everyone in town knew the large tiger-striped tabby with the characteristic M on his forehead.

I slid into the chair next to Val.

Zelda, as full-figured as she was full of life, held a gold candlestick, turning it in her hands. She had braided strands of her long blonde hair on both sides and pulled back the braids. They hung like beautiful garlands on the sides of her head, reminding me of a Norse princess. "This is so cool. But I don't get it. Why only four weapons? Doesn't everyone get a weapon?"

I guessed the wicked meat cleaver Shelley held was also a weapon. Shelley had cut her light brown hair and streaked it blonde to lighten it. It was a layered bob of large waves that I envied. My own straight brown hair would never cooperate in that kind of cut.

She wore Wagtail chic, a fisherman style knit sweater in cream. Her bulky olive-colored jacket hung over the back of her chair. "You want me to hide this in"—Shelley tilted her head to read a note on the cleaver—"oh my word, it's a little rhyme!"

The waitress interrupted to take my order. I was so

spoiled by the terrific breakfasts at the Sugar Maple Inn that
I found it difficult to eat breakfast out. "Coffee, two eggs
sunny-side up with roasted potatoes, and the same for Trixie,
please, without the coffee."

Zelda looked at Val with an apologetic expression. "I'm
sorry I had to miss the last few meetings. I'm lost. This
sounds like a scavenger hunt."

Val placed a gorgeous bottle on the table. About four
inches high, it had been painted in vivid blues and reds, and
on one side, bore a skull and crossbones painted in gold.
"Murder Most Howl is a cross between a scavenger hunt and
a murder mystery game. The participants all play themselves.
But each of them will have a secret from his or her past to
hide. They'll receive their secrets at the initial meeting at
Hair of the Dog Pub tonight. It's up to each one to decide
whether to share the secret with anyone. The goal is to solve
the mystery of who killed the victim. They have to figure out
who the killer is and how he or she murdered the victim."

"Where do the weapons come in?" asked Zelda.

Val passed each of us a couple of bloodred envelopes.
"I'll get to that. These contain clues. There's a yellow sticky
on each one telling you where to hide it. The players will
receive information that will lead them to the clues and the
weapons. Everyone starts with the same basic information
but obviously, not everyone will find the same clues. Three
weapons will be hidden. They're sort of a bonus. If you're
lucky enough to find one, you can use it to force competitors
to share clues with you. Obviously, having a weapon is a big
advantage, so they'll be trying to steal them from each other.
The merchants around town know more clues, and that will
draw people into stores, restaurants, and businesses to chat."

"That's so clever," said Shelley. "A really great way to
get people out and about in Wagtail."

"Each of you will hide one weapon. All the players will
have the same opportunity to discover them—so make them
a little bit difficult to find, okay? The first victim will be

killed by poison, so I'm keeping the bottle." Val handed me the candlestick.

"It's so light! This could actually be used as a candlestick."

Val grinned. "They're hand-carved. That's real gold leaf covering the candlestick."

The waitress delivered our food and set two small dishes on the floor, along with water bowls for Trixie and Leo.

I glanced at Zelda. "I hope Leo is hungry. Trixie might try to eat his food."

Zelda laughed. "Are you kidding? Look how big Leo is. It's Trixie's food that might be in danger."

I kept an eye on Trixie anyway. She had spent time homeless and scrabbling for food before she adopted me. I assumed her insatiable hunger was a result of that terrible time.

Val was drinking coffee when she groaned. "Not Norm Wilson, please," she whispered. "He's been such a pill."

I glanced up to see him heading our way. Norm had a round face and a rounder belly. I imagined that he looked much like he had as a young man, except heavier. The buttons on his blue Oxford cloth shirt strained against the fabric, threatening to reveal all. He wore khaki pants, loafers, and no socks despite the cold weather—a Southern male affectation that I had never quite understood. His fair hair was sparse but a bit of it hung over his forehead.

"Look at this, the four prettiest ladies in all of Wagtail."

I thought Val might spew her coffee.

The rest of us politely murmured greetings.

He spied the pistol. "Who's packin'? Is it legal to have a gun in a restaurant?"

"That one is perfectly legal," said Val, a bit testy.

He took in the clue envelopes and the candlestick. "Oh, I get it. You're meeting about Murder Most Howl. Mind if I pull up a chair? You should have notified everyone if you were going to have a meeting."

Was Val holding her breath?

I smiled at him. "I think Val has everything under control, Norm. But it's kind of you to offer."

"Always happy to pitch in." He thumped the table. "Y'all just give me a call if you run into trouble." He ambled away muttering, but I was pretty certain he said, "And you will."

I leaned toward Val and spoke under my breath. "What was that about?"

She looked around at us, her brown eyes sincere. "I know I'm new to Wagtail, so don't think poorly of me. I detest that man."

Shelley picked up a piece of toast. "What did he ever do to you?"

The corner of Val's mouth twitched. "I don't really want to tell you. You'll think I'm a petty and horrible person." She paused. "You know what? I shouldn't say anything."

Zelda grinned. "Now we'll be thinking the worst. Spill, girl!"

Val heaved a sigh. "I bought the pub at auction, and Norm was such a jerk. He kept bidding it up and up. Honestly, I don't think he wanted it. I truly think he did it just to jerk me around."

Shelley's eyes met mine. "I don't know, Val. That would have been an expensive mess for him if you had stopped bidding."

"Tell me this, then. If he wanted a pub so badly, why didn't he take some of that money and open one across town somewhere?" She shook her head. "Nope. I paid much more than I should have because he was getting a kick out of it."

I figured I shouldn't mention that she could have stopped bidding.

"It was nice of him to offer to help with the mystery weekend," said Shelley.

Val's hands curled into fists on the table. "Are you kidding? I wouldn't be surprised if he sabotaged it. Norm was against this mystery weekend as soon as Hollis Hobbs tried to limit Norm's involvement. Hollis hates him, too. Norm is not the sweet, amiable guy you might think."

Zelda set her coffee cup down. "Everyone I talked to was excited about the mystery weekend."

"Everyone else has been so generous and helpful. The grand prize is a week at the Sugar Maple Inn, thanks to a certain Holly Miller and her grandmother." Val grinned at me. "Plus a host of free meals at restaurants and cafes, and massages, beds, and food for dogs and cats, not to mention gift certificates to spend at some of the stores. Runners-up will win gift certificates for stores and services, like the zip line and pet grooming."

"So they just run around looking for weapons and clues?" asked Zelda.

Val swallowed her last bite of Eggs Benedict. "No. It's quite interactive. People can play by themselves or in teams. Just you wait. They'll tell lies to throw one another off the track of the murderer. I hear people get very competitive in these types of games."

"So who is the killer?" asked Zelda.

"I'm the only one, besides the killer and victim, of course, who knows who they are."

"Aww, c'mon. Let us in on the secret," Zelda begged.

"Okay," said Val, looking altogether too mischievous, "the victim is the Baron von Rottweiler, a resident of Wagtail."

Shelley, Zelda, and I exchanged glances.

"I've never heard of him," said Shelley. "And I've lived here forever."

Val laughed. "Well, you'd better meet him soon because someone is about to do in the poor fellow."

Zelda scowled at Val. "That's not fair. At least tell us who the killer is!" She leaned forward, gleeful.

Val tilted her head at us. "No way. I'm not having you supply additional clues to someone just because you like him or her."

"You don't trust us!" said Shelley.

"Isn't that always the first rule of a murder?" asked Val. "Trust no one."

KRISTA DAVIS

The Diva Wraps It Up

A Domestic Diva Mystery

The holidays are domestic diva Sophie Winston's favorite time of year. But this season, there seem to be more mishaps than mistletoe.

Sophie arrives at the annual holiday cookie swap with high spirits and thirteen dozen chocolate-drizzled gingersnaps. But when an argument erupts and a murder ensues, it becomes clear that the recent string of events is anything but accidental. Now Sophie has to make a list of suspects and check it twice—before the killer strikes again.

"Loaded with atmosphere and charm."

—*Library Journal*

kristadavis.com
facebook.com/KristaDavisAuthor
penguin.com

FROM *NEW YORK TIMES* BESTSELLING AUTHOR
KRISTA DAVIS

The **Diva** Frosts a **Cupcake**

A Domestic Diva Mystery

❧

Sophie Winston and her BFF, Nina Reid Norwood, share a sweet spot for animals. So Sophie is delighted to help when Nina cooks up Cupcakes and Pupcakes—a fund-raising event for animal shelters. All the local bakeries will be selling treats, with the profits going to pups and kitties in need. But Old Town is in for a whole batch of trouble when a cupcake war erupts between two bakeries—and the employee of one of the bakeries is found dead. Now Sophie and Nina have to sift through the clues and disco seem...

"Reader alert: Tasty
spark intense cup

—*The Washi*

kristadav
facebook.com/Kri
penguir